Which Way to Run

Gil Novak and Lili D'Amico Mysteries, Volume 2

Hy Shaw

Published by Hy Shaw, 2024.

Copyright © 2024 by Hy Shaw

All rights reserved.

No part of this book may be reproduced or used in any manner without the prior written permission of the copyright owner, except for the use of brief quotations in reference or in a book review. For permission requests, contact hyshawauthor@gmail.com.

The story, all names, characters, and incidents portrayed in this production are fictitious or used in a fictitious manner. No identification with actual persons (living or dead), places, buildings, and products is intended or should be inferred.

Also by Hy Shaw

Gil Novak and Lili D'Amico Mysteries
The Dim Light of Dawn
Which Way to Run

Watch for more at https://www.hyshaw.com.

This book is dedicated to my sister Sarah. Over the past year, she survived a terrorist attack on her Kibbutz and was displaced from her home for many months. Then she edited my book. She is amazing!

ONE

M*arch 9, 2023, Siesta Key, Florida*

Lili nudged Gil to prevent him from nodding off again. They were sitting on a couch in the Florida condo they had rented for the winter. *Vera*, one of their favorite shows, was playing on the Britbox channel. *CRASH*! *Thump, thump*! The sounds of running footsteps, shouting, and more crashing were coming from the unit above them. "Call 911!" said Lili. "I'm getting my gun. Tell them I'm armed."

Lili was a semi-retired agent with the Massachusetts State Crime Lab, but she still traveled with her service weapon. She went into the bedroom closet and opened the little safe where she kept her pistol. She put on her flip flops and ran out the front door.

Gil heard more sounds of trouble from above while the dispatcher answered. "Sarasota County Emergency Services. What is your emergency?"

"It sounds like there's a violent fight going on in the condo above mine. We need police to come to Unit 26 at Manatee Point, on Siesta Key." Gil walked out to the parking lot, barefoot, while he was talking. A small crowd was gathering on the second-floor walkway.

"And what is your name, sir?"

"I'm Gil Novak. My girlfriend went up to that condo with her gun."

Lili peered through the screen door into Martha's condo. There was broken glass, an overturned side table, and a pistol on the hallway floor. She thought she saw a man on top of Martha at the far end of the living room. She entered quickly and saw a man strangling Martha with an electrical cord. "Police! Let her go, now!" The guy pulled tighter and just smiled at Lili, his gold front tooth shining in the light. Martha was turning blue and her eyes were bugging out.

"What is your girlfriend's name, sir?"

"Her name is Lili D'Amico. She's an agent with the Massachusetts State Police."

"I have police on the way, three minutes out. I've told them about Agent D'Amico."

BOOM! Fear struck Gil. "There was a gunshot! I'm going up there."

"Do *not* go up there, Mr. Novak."

Lili burst out of the front door onto the balcony and yelled, "Get EMTs out here! Get an ambulance!"

"We need EMTs and an ambulance!"

"Sir, can you find out what's happening?"

"Lili, what's going on?"

"Martha was strangled. She's still alive, but just barely. Her attacker is dead. I shot him." Lili went back in to help Martha.

Gil relayed the information to the dispatcher. His hands were shaking. He felt cold.

A Sheriff's car pulled in, blue lights flashing. Two deputies got out and Gil waived them over. He quickly explained what happened and pointed to Unit 26. The deputies ran up the stairs and made their way past the onlookers into Unit 26. Another sheriff's car and the EMTs from the Fire Department pulled in and Gil showed them where to go. A detective pulled up in an unmarked car and Gil pointed to Unit 26.

"Gil, get my badge!" yelled Lili. Gil got her badge and brought it to her at Martha's door. Lili went right back in.

About ten minutes later, the EMTs brought Martha down the stairs on a stretcher. She looked alive to Gil, but she was unconscious. They loaded her into the ambulance and drove off, lights flashing. A few minutes later, Lili came out with the detective. The detective had her gun in an evidence bag.

• • • •

AT SEVEN A.M., GIL pulled into the hospital parking lot to pick up Lili. "You look pretty good, considering," he said.

"Thanks, I think. The doctor thinks Martha's going to survive. She has an injury to her larynx, and the EMTs had to put a tube in her neck so she could breathe. A crike, they called it. Today, assuming she remains stable, the surgeon will operate to fix her up."

"So, you've been here all night?"

"No, I was at the sheriff's office for a couple of hours, givng my statement. They were very nice. They treated me like one of their own. I asked them to use me as a liaison for Martha."

"Are you hungry? Do you want to stop for breakfast?"

"Sure. I'll sleep by the pool, later."

．．．．

GIL SAT ON THE LOUNGE next to Lili, who was still sleeping. Most of the lounges by the pool were occupied and there were half a dozen people in the pool chatting. Most of the people there were from the upper Midwest or Toronto. There were enough puffy clouds going by that he didn't think Lili would get a sunburn. He was reading a science-fiction novel about first contact with aliens.

Lili stretched. "How long was I out?"

"About an hour. How are you feeling?"

"Not bad, but I could use an iced coffee."

When Gil returned with her coffee, he found Lili surrounded by "the girls," being grilled about last night. "Yes, it's the first time I've ever shot anyone, and no, it doesn't bother me. If I didn't shoot him, Martha would have been dead."

"What did he look like?" asked Francine.

"I can't really talk about the case because I'm an officer of the law. When I go over to the hospital later, I'll find out when you can visit her."

Beryl asked, "Was the detective good looking? Can you talk about that?" The girls laughed. Beryl was in her late seventies and she had been a widow for many years.

Ellen said, "Beryl, I think you'd go more for the bad guy, not the cop." More laughing.

Frank wandered over. "Lili, are you going to be in any kind of trouble over the shooting?"

"I'm not worried about that, Frank. The shooting was justified. I really want to know why someone would want to hurt Martha. Any ideas?"

"Maybe she's a drug lord!" offered Francine.

"Or a weapons dealer," said Beryl.

"Maybe a human trafficker," said Ellen.

"Oh brother," said Gil.

Lili picked up her ringing phone, spoke for a few seconds and hung up. "That was another detective. He's out front and wants to talk to me. I better put some clothes on."

· · · ·

"AGENT D'AMICO, I'M Agent Sammy Arias from the Florida Department of Law Enforcement. If it's okay, I'd like to go through the crime scene with you, and review what happened."

"Sure. Please call me Lili."

As they walked up the stairs, Sammy said, "So you're Crime Scene?"

"Yes, for a long time. I just went part-time, semi-retirement."

"Must be nice. Are you a scientist? Why do you carry a service weapon?"

"I started out as a uniform, then I made detective. It was early days for forensics back then, but I had a degree in chemistry and was given the opportunity to lead a forensics team. I stuck with it, but I maintained my weapons qual."

They went into Unit 26. "So talk me through it." Lili talked him through the whole thing, which didn't take very long. He said, "It sounds like, if you weren't here with your gun, Ms. Eames would be dead."

"No question. He was going to finish the job, even though he knew I was going to shoot him. Do you know who he was?"

"We're still working on that. No ID. Ms. Eames is quite a fighter, though. She disarmed her assailant. He resorted to strangling her with the wire from the lamp she hit him with. His gun's a ghost, no numbers. His prints aren't in AFIS. He's got a lot of tats, though. We're looking at that, and his DNA."

"It's amazing she survived. Martha's in her mid-seventies, I think. I don't know if she has any kids."

"The emergency contact in her phone is her neighbor, Barbara LeClerc. Ms. LeClerc didn't know of any relatives. She checked on Ms. Eames's home in New Hampshire and didn't see anything wrong."

"Well, it looks like you've got a good mystery. Let me know if you need anything."

TWO

G il and Frank were fishing at Turtle Beach the next morning. They each had a rod sitting in a sand-spike rod holder. Gil had a thawing baby mullet on his hook, and Frank was using three frozen shrimps on a multi-hook rig.

"Why the hell would someone want to go into Martha's place and kill her?" asked Frank.

"I don't know Martha that well," said Gil. This is my first year coming here. I didn't even know her last name. What do you know about her?"

"I've known her for about six or seven years. I knew her husband George, too. He was a quiet guy. He designed computer chips. He died a few years ago. Stroke, I think. Martha was a teacher. I don't think they had any kids. Whoa." Frank jumped up and ran to his pole which twitched a couple of times. He gave it a yank, but nothing happened. He reeled it in and found that one of his shrimps was missing. He put another shrimp on his hook and cast his rig back out.

"Hey Frank, I don't even know your last name. What is it?"

"It's Sanborn. What's yours?"

"Novak. It's funny here. I've gotten to know a lot of people, but I don't know many last names." Gil's pole suddenly bent way over. His rod holder tipped over and his rod and reel headed into the waves. He jumped up, ran down, splashed in, and lunged into the water. After a few seconds, he stood up, triumphantly holding his rod up. Suddenly, the rod tip bent over and was almost yanked from his hand. ZIZZZZZ! His reel buzzed as the line peeled off.

Frank yelled, "Point your pole closer to the horizon or it'll snap! It's a big one!"

Gil lowered the tip of his pole. The fish was slowing, but then it sped up again and turned to the right. Gil splashed through the shallows to follow it up the beach. His legs got tangled in the next guy's line and he fell to the water. He managed to untangle himself while the line continued to peel off his reel. Other fishing guys were laughing while quickly pulling in their lines to give Gil room to maneuver. After a few minutes, the fish faltered, so Gil started to reel it in. It was very heavy, and he hoped his forty-pound line would hold. Gil's eyes stung from saltwater and sweat. The fish surfaced and its fins breached the surface a little. It was over a hundred yards out. Then it ran again, this time to the left. Gil followed it back down the beach and it faltered again, occasionally allowing him to reel it in, like a tug of war. "I think it's a stingray!" he yelled.

After about fifteen minutes, the fish finally gave up, and Gil slowly reeled it in to the water's edge. Frank and another guy helped slide it onshore and flip it over, carefully avoiding its barb. Another guy asked, "Do you want me to take your hook out?"

"Yes, please. We'll just put it back in the water. It must weigh forty pounds!" Using pliers, the guy deftly twisted the hook out and a couple of other guys slid it back into the waves. The ray recovered and swam away.

Gil threw his rod on the sand and plopped into his chair. "Well, that was something."

"You gave us quite a show. What a crowd! Hey!" Frank hopped up and grabbed his twitching pole. His line ran in a little racetrack pattern, and he reeled it in with a silvery fish on the hook. "A pompano! Fish for dinner tonight."

* * * *

"SIX BAM!" SAID ELLEN, laying down a mahjong tile.

"Two crak," said Lili.

"Flower," said Francine. Beryl was unresponsive. Francine gave her a nudge and said, "Stay with us, Beryl. You want some coffee?"

"No, no. I'll be fine. Um, nine dot."

"I'll take the nine dot," said Lili. Lili took the nine dot tile and revealed her sequence of four dot tiles on her mahjong rack.

"South wind," said Francine. Beryl was zoned out again. Francine gave her another nudge. "We better take a break after this round."

"Uh, flower," said Beryl.

"Six dot!" said Ellen.

"Four bam," said Lili.

"Seven crak," said Francine.

"I'll take that," said Lili. "Mahjong!" Lili revealed her tiles.

Francine said, "For crying out loud, that's three in a row!"

"It's my lucky day," said Lili.

Francine paid Lili fifty cents and the other two players each paid her a quarter. Everyone then dumped their tiles into the middle of the table. The tiles were clickety-clacking as the women turned them all face down and shuffled them around. Francine got up and said, "I have coffee, tea, iced or regular." She quickly made an iced coffee with a lot of cream and sugar and placed it in front of Beryl.

"I'm so glad it's cool enough to play on the lanai," said Ellen.

"Not too many cool days left for this year," said Francine.

"Is it much hotter in April?" asked Lili.

"It'll start to get hotter and muggier. It gets to me once the nights stay hot. It's like you can't get any fresh air," said Francine.

"May gets even hotter. And it starts to storm almost every day for a little while. We used to stay down here through May because Larry would fish for tarpon. He doesn't fish that much anymore," said Ellen.

"Why doesn't Deb play mahjong?" asked Lili.

"She doesn't like the Orientals," said Ellen. "She's kind of a racist."

"Really?"

"Her brother was in a Vietnamese prison during the war. He was never right after that," said Ellen.

Francine said, "That's part of it, maybe, but I think it's mainly because Debbie's a shopaholic. She wouldn't waste an afternoon of potential shopping to play a game. Sometimes she and Larry play Mexican Train in the evening, though."

"What does she shop for?"

"Art. And antiques, too," said Francine. "At an age when most people downsize, Debbie and Frank bought a bigger house so they'd have room for more stuff."

"Who needs to buy antiques?" said Ellen. "All the stuff we bought years ago is antique now."

"So, is that new detective single?" asked Beryl.

Gil pulled the laundry out of the dryer. He brought it to the bedroom and started to fold each article of clothing. He felt that living with Lili had become less awkward over the last couple of months. They'd been together for about five months, and their life together was reaching a rhythm of sorts, but he still had to think carefully about every little thing he did. Sometimes, when he was doing something without thinking, he would catch himself from feeling he was still with his late wife, Cynthia. She had died a year and a half ago from COVID.

Gil became in charge of laundry duty and took out the garbage. Lili did the dusting and arranged social engagements. They both vacuumed, shopped for groceries, and cooked. They mostly ate breakfast and lunch separately, but they always had dinner together. Should he tell her every time he decides to go out to the pool or fish off the dock? Will she automatically share with him what's going on with Martha's investigation? She was currently at the hospital visiting Martha.

Gil pulled an article of Lili's clothing out of the laundry basket and flipped it around, trying to figure out what it was. It looked like it was inside-out, so he pulled it through the other way. It still looked inside-out. Hmm. It seemed to be a skirt with shorts attached. He wondered what that was called. He pushed the shorts inside the skirt and it was inside-out again. He pulled it through the other way. Success!

He liked being in Florida for the winter. He liked living with Lili down here. He wondered what she thought about it? He had already booked the place for next winter, but could always cancel it up until mid-October. He decided to ask her what she thought about this whole thing. He came upon another perplexing piece of clothing. It looked inside-out, maybe. It had lots of straps, some twists in the cloth, and a couple of boob-holding cups. It was brightly colored with lots of flower patterns which camouflaged its shape, making it harder to figure out. He decided it was a shirt with a strappy back, an embedded bra, and a kind of twisted neckline. He wondered what it was called.

• • • •

AT THE HOSPITAL, LILI took the elevator up and found Martha's hospital room. She spoke to the officer standing guard. He checked his notebook and told her she was cleared to go in. She asked about arranging for other visitors and was told to check with Detective Arias to get them on the list. She walked in and saw that Martha was awake, but still had a breathing machine hooked up to her neck, along with heart and oxygen sensors. It had been a week since the surgery to repair her neck. Her hair was disheveled. "Hi Martha, I came to see how you're feeling."

Martha pointed to the wheeled table that held a notepad and pen, which Lili handed to her. She wrote a whole paragraph. "I'm still a little doped-up on painkillers, so my neck doesn't hurt right now. But I don't like the painkillers. They make me feel depressed and a little nauseous. The nurse said they need to keep me on them a little while longer or I'd be in a lot of pain. I also have other bruises on my body from the fight. Thanks again for shooting the bastard. I don't remember it."

Lili read it and tried to stifle the urge to laugh and cry. "I'm so glad I could help. I think you were unconscious by the time I got there. You're lucky."

Martha scribbled some more. "I could have been luckier!"

Lili chuckled. "Well, you must be feeling better if you're cracking jokes. When can you get out of here?"

Martha wrote. "The doctor said they'll remove the breathing tube tomorrow, but then they'll need me to stay a couple of more days. Detective Sammy questioned me this morning. I was too woozy the last time he came. Read the last few pages, since I know you'll be interested."

Lili read Martha's replies to the detective. She described what happened. Lili was proud that Martha was able to disarm her assailant. She has no idea who he was or why anyone would want to kill her. Nothing suspicious had happened to her over the past days or months. She has no children or relatives. She was an orphan.

Martha motioned for Lili to give her the notepad. She wrote "I don't want to go back to the condo. When I get out of here, I want to fly home. Can you help me?"

Lili took a deep breath and said, "Of course I'll help you. I'll get us a flight when you think you're ready. I'll get you a hotel room until then. Me and the girls will get your things packed up and arrange for your car to be shipped back to Portsmouth. Is there anyone we can call?"

Martha teared up. She wrote, "I don't have any family. I'll tell you about that some other time. My neighbor Barbara back home is my best friend. Here's her number. Thank you."

FOUR

Lili followed as an airline assistant wheeled Martha off the plane and into the terminal at Boston's Logan Airport. Martha's neck was bandaged, but she was breathing normally. She could croak a bit, but she still needed her writing pad to communicate.

After getting their bags, a skycap wheeled their luggage to the C&J bus. Lili wheeled Martha out the door, but Martha was able to climb into the bus on her own. She was a little shaky, but she hobbled down the aisle and plopped into a seat. Lili sat down next to her and handed Martha her bag and a cup of ice water with a straw. Martha drank a few gulps and wrote, "I'm starting to feel a little stronger just moving around some."

Lili smiled at her and asked, "How long is the bus ride?"

Martha wrote, "Just a little over an hour."

It was a really nice bus. Once they got going, both women settled in for a nap. Lili woke up a bit later and watched the bus drive through the Boston suburbs. Eventually, they reached I-95 and quickly cruised up to the Portsmouth bus terminal. The late-March air was brisk under mostly cloudy skies. Lili summoned an Uber and they reached Martha's house a few minutes later.

Martha lived in an older two-story white house with a one-car garage. The snow was gone, and the lawn was mostly green. The trees were bare and no flowers were yet in bloom. Lili brought in the luggage, and Martha showed her to the guest bedroom. It was cold, so Martha turned up the thermostat. The radiators started making a clunking noise. When Lili entered the kitchen, Martha pointed to the electric tea kettle and Lili said she'd love some.

Lili sat on a comfy chair in the living room and texted Gil that they'd arrived.

"How's the weather?" Gil texted.

"Cloudy and cool. Trees are still bare."

"Well I can't wait till we're together again and I can keep you warm."

Lili chuckled.

Crash! Lili went to the kitchen and found that Martha had dropped a mug and it shattered. Martha was white as a ghost and pointing at the phone list on the refrigerator. Lili asked, "What's the matter?" She found Martha's pen and pad, and gave it to her.

Martha wrote, "Someone's been in here! The phone list is backwards."

"Wasn't your neighbor here to check the house? Maybe she moved it. Which house is she in? I'll go get her."

Martha wrote, "101. Barbara."

Lili came back with Barbara in tow. She went over and gave Martha a hug. "Oh, you poor dear! How are you feeling?"

Martha wrote, "I can't talk yet, but it doesn't hurt too much."

Lili said, "Martha noticed that the phone list on her fridge is turned around. Did you move it while you were checking on her house?"

"Oh dear! No, I'm pretty sure I didn't touch it. All I did was walk around the rooms and check that the doors and windows were locked. Maybe you put it back that way before you left?"

Martha shook her head. She walked over to her desk and sat down. She looked around at the piles of papers, pulled open the drawers, and wiggled the computer mouse. The computer was off. She knelt down by the side of the desk and turned on the power strip. She pushed the power button on the tower and the computer booted up. Martha wrote, "I don't know what it is, but something doesn't feel right."

"Let me look around, a little," said Lili.

Lili walked from room to room, went down into the cellar, and out into the garage. Nothing looked out of place.

Lili returned and said, "I don't see anything strange, do you?"

Martha wrote, "Maybe I'm just being paranoid."

"Let me make a call." Lili called a digital forensics guy she knew at the Massachusetts Crime Lab. "Hi Ricky. How do I tell if a computer was booted up at some time in the past?"

Ricky started rapidly reciting some techno-speak steps to perform. Lili asked him to hold on for a minute. "Martha, let's take a look at your computer. Would you sign on please? I have a friend from the Massachusetts State Crime Lab on the phone and he'll guide us through this."

Martha got up and let Lili go to work. Lili went through a sequence of steps as Ricky guided her. She described to Ricky the information on the computer, then thanked him and hung up her phone. "Okay Martha, your computer was booted up eight weeks ago. That was while you were in Florida and before the attack. Is there anyone who would have booted up your computer then?"

"Oh my god, somebody *was* here. There's nobody I know who would have done that. Barbara doesn't know how to sign on to my computer. Warren does, but there's no reason he would have been here. He's the only one who knows how to sign in."

"Who's Warren?" asked Lili.

"Oh, he lives across the street over there. He helps me with my computer."

Lili said, "I'll call him just to make sure. Is Warren's number on your phone list?" Martha nodded.

Barbara said, "I'll call him."

Barbara phoned Warren, chatted a little, and hung up. "Warren says he hasn't been here since last fall, when you were still here."

"So, we have enough evidence to show that someone broke into your house," said Lili. "I'm going to get the police over here."

· · · ·

THE THREE WOMEN ORDERED from 5 Thai Bistro. It was one of Martha's favorite restaurants, but she could still only eat soft foods. As they finished eating, the doorbell rang and Lili answered it.

"Hi, I'm Detective James Berniski from the Portsmouth Police Department, and this is Officer Childs." He held out his badge and Lili let them in. Officer Childs was holding a crime scene kit.

"I'm Agent Lili D'Amico with the Massachusetts Crime Lab. This is Martha Eames, the homeowner and this is Barbara, her neighbor."

"LeClerc," said Barbara.

"So, you reported a break-in here, and you think it's related to a crime in Florida?" asked Berniski.

Lili gave him the whole story. Berniski took a lot of notes and asked a lot of questions. "So, Ms. Eames, do you have any ideas about who would want to harm you or who may be after something in your possession?"

Martha wrote, "No! I'm just a retired widow who knits and watches TV. My husband George did secret work at Lincoln Labs, but that was years ago and he never brought anything home."

"What kind of work did he do?"

"He was a semiconductor scientist." Berniski's eyebrows rose.

"Well, what I think we'll do is gather evidence on the break-in here. Smart call on checking the computer. Officer Childs is a trained crime scene technician, so he'll try to determine point of entry and see if there are some prints we can lift, or any other evidence we could use. Tomorrow, I'd like Agent D'Amico here to come down to the station so we can brief the Chief. If this is really related to the Florida case, we may end up bringing in the FBI. They'll be able to look into Mr. Eames's secret work."

· · · ·

BACK IN FLORIDA, GIL, Francine, and Francine's husband Carl were nearly finished loading up Martha's car with her belongings. Gil and Carl were dripping with sweat, but Francine seemed fresh as a daisy. "So Gil, when are you going to head back up north?" asked Francine.

"In three days. Tomorrow, I'm going fishing with my friend who has a boat. How about you guys?"

"Oh, we're staying until the end of April," said Francine. "This whole situation makes me nervous, though."

"Well, it looks like somebody was after Martha, in particular," said Gil. "It wasn't a random home invasion, so I don't think you have anything to worry about."

"I'm sure you're right, but I'm still feeling nervous."

Carl said, "If anyone ever broke into our place, they're the ones that should be nervous. I'll bet you would beat them up. Or you would talk their ears off until they'd just run away."

"You haven't run away, yet."

"Yet."

"Gil, are you going to drive home or fly?" she asked.

"I'll drive. I enjoyed the trip down, but I'm sure it was a lot easier with Lili driving half the time. Hopefully, I won't regret my decision."

Gil drove Martha's car to the parking lot where a car-carrier truck would load it up for transport to New Hamsphire. Carl followed Gil so he could bring him back to Manatee Point.

• • • •

GIL, MIKE, AND BOB had set up their fishing rods on Bob's boat to slowly troll in the gulf. The water was pretty smooth. Mike pointed to the ten o'clock position where a school of fish was roiling the surface and a lot of birds were diving for them. Bob changed his heading to troll by the school. Suddenly, Gil's reel started zizzing. so

Bob cut the throttle. Gil grabbed his pole and set the hook, while Mike and Bob quickly reeled in their lines. Gil's fish changed direction, causing slack in the line. Gil took advantage of the situation to quickly reel in a lot of line. The fish changed direction again, peeling out the line. "Start the boat and follow it or I'll lose my line!" said Gil. Bob scrambled to get the boat started and headed in the right direction, while Gil moved quickly to the bow.

Gil was able to reel in line as the boat moved slowly toward the fish. Suddenly, the line started peeling again. The fish was diving deep. Gil was dripping with sweat and his arms were getting tired. Mike yelled, "Ahoy, 'tis the white whale! Man the harpoons!" Bob was laughing, but Gil was not.

Gil watched helplessly as the line on his reel dwindled. As it neared its end, the line went slack. Gil started reeling in furiously, and after a few seconds, he realized he'd lost the fish. When he finally reeled in all of his line, he realized that it had broken right at the end, where the steel leader met the braided line. "Nice fish." said Mike. "What brand of reel oil are you using?"

Bob and Mike set up to troll again, while Gil was rigging up another lure. "What kind of fish do you think that was?" asked Gil.

"Maybe a shark, but we'll never know," said Bob. Another reel started to zizz. "Bob, it's yours!" said Mike.

Bob cut the engine, while Mike reeled in his line. Bob ran back and pulled his rod out of the holder. He started to play the fish. It was a big one. Mike's line tangled while his lure was still in the water. The fish was fighting like crazy, but Bob got it close to the boat. "Get the gaff! Get the gaff!" yelled Bob. Gil got the gaff hook and ran to Bob. The fish seemed to have lost its energy to fight, so Bob eased it over to the boat. "It's a cobia," said Bob. Gil hooked the gaff into the side of the fish and pulled it up. The fish started wriggling violently, and Gil fell to the deck with the fish on top of him. Mike pulled out his phone to get it on video.

Gil was screaming, "Get it off me!" Bob grabbed the fish by the tail, slid it off Gil and dragged it into the cooler. Gil got up and found a towel to wash off the slime.

They decided to call it a day, so Bob headed the boat toward the shore. Mike said, "Wow Gil, you went viral!"

Mike handed Gil his phone. There was a Facebook video with the caption 'Fish attempts to mate with fisherman.' There were already over a hundred comments. "Oh brother, I'll never hear the end of this one."

FIVE

The next morning, Gil called Lili. She said, "Gil, I think we should take a break from each other. How can I ever compete with your love of aquatic creatures?"

"Ha, ha. I guess that was my fifteen minutes of fame."

"Did you get hurt? Did that big fish have teeth?"

"That big fish was a cobia. They just have small teeth. It was really good grilled, but I think they're high in mercury, so I may get taller or shorter as the temperature changes. I'm packing up today. I plan to leave really early tomorrow to avoid the traffic on I-75."

"Well, hopefully by the time you get to your house, I'll be back at mine."

. . . .

MARTHA'S DOORBELL RANG. She answered the door and found Officer Childs with a young woman. She motioned for them to come in.

"This is Keysha Spinks, a forensic locksmith out of Boston. She's going to take a look at your door-locks to see if they were tampered with."

"How interesting. A forensic locksmith. And a girl, too," Martha wrote.

Keysha smiled and asked, "When the break-in occurred, was the deadbolt locked, or just the doorknob?"

Martha wrote, "Oh, I guess just the doorknob. I only lock the other one before I go to bed." Keysha nodded.

They started with the front door. Keysha set up her equipment on the floor. She quickly disassembled the knob lock and took the inner workings apart. She put high-powered magnifying glasses on and examined the different pieces. Then she re-assembled them. She gathered her equipment and Officer Childs showed her to the back door. After a few minutes, the pair of them went down to the cellar to check that door.

"So, how are you feeling today, Martha?" asked Lili.

She wrote, "I guess I don't feel so afraid today. I don't know if that makes any sense because nothing has changed yet. I felt better that you were here last night."

"Well, I can't stay here forever. Let's see what the locksmith has to say, then I'll go speak with the Police Chief and you can decide what to do. Is it possible for you to stay with Barbara for a while?"

She wrote, "I'm sure she'd let me. I'll have to think about that."

Officer Childs came back with the locksmith. Keysha said, "The lock on the door in the cellar was picked recently. That's probably how the perpetrator got in. The lock down there isn't very good. Your deadbolts are pretty good on the front and back doors, but you don't use them when you leave because it's a hassle. Knob locks are not very secure. What I recommend is that I put a combination lock on the front deadbolt, and eliminate the knob lock. On the back door, I'll put a more secure deadbolt on and eliminate the knob lock. On the cellar door, I'll put a secure deadbolt. This way, you'll lock the back door and the cellar door using deadbolts from inside the house. Then you'll lock and unlock the front door using the electronic combination lock. It will be battery powered. The contract I have with police is to provide these locks for only wholesale and installation costs. I'll do the whole job for $375."

Martha looked at Lili. "That sounds like a good deal," said Lili. "Now I'm thinking about my locks at home."

Martha wrote, "Thank you Keysha. Please install the new locks. Will you show me how to use them?"

"Yes Ma'am. It'll only take me about an hour."

Officer Childs said, "Thank you Keysha. Ms. Eames, I've checked your window locks and they're pretty good. If you decide to install a security system, call me and I'll recommend some contractors for you."

• • • •

LILI DROVE TO THE PORTSMOUTH Police Department. It was located in a scenic area near a saltwater pond. Detective Berniski escorted her into the Chief's office. "Agent D'Amico, this is Chief Voorhees."

They shook hands and Lili said, "I'm here as a civilian, so please call me Lili." The Chief indicated that they should sit.

"So Lili, how did the Massachusetts State Police get involved in this?"

"Well, this year I started working part-time so I could spend the winter in Florida with my boyfriend. Martha was staying in the unit directly above me. We heard her being attacked, so I got my gun and shot the guy. He's dead. Martha had been strangled by him and was barely alive. When she got out of the hospital, I volunteered to escort her to Portsmouth. She still can't speak yet, so soon after her surgery. And, she doesn't have any family."

"You ever shoot anyone before?"

"No, but I don't feel bad about it. Martha would have been dead in a few seconds if I didn't shoot him."

"Any idea what's going on?"

"No, none at all. Martha's just a long-retired woman who doesn't do very much, from what I can tell. I only met her in January."

"Well Jim, what do you think we should do?" asked Chief Vorhees.

"I think Ms. Eames may still be in danger, so we should guard her house until she has a security system installed. We should probably pay for it because it'll save us money. I also think we need to call in the FBI since the break-in is probably connected to her attempted murder in Florida. In the mean time, I'll call this Detective, um, Arias in Florida and fill him in."

"Lili, what do you think we should do?" asked the Chief.

"I think we should do what Detective Berniski says. I'll stay long enough to talk to the FBI, then I'll go back home to Northampton, Mass."

"Sounds like a plan. Jim, you get the guards and the security system arranged. I'll call the FBI. Nice to meet you, Lili."

. . . .

CARRICK WAS PERCHED high up in a big maple tree, watching Martha Eames's house which was across the street. Cloudy skies were making the evening sky dark, but there was a street light nearby, making him a little more detectable. This was his initial watch, so he didn't bring his rifle. It was easy to identify his target because she had a bandage around her neck. There was a police officer stationed on the front porch, and another in the backyard. There was a middle-aged woman in the house with the target, maybe her daughter. He used a laser range-finder and measured his distance to target as 476 yards. No problem.

The fact that the police were on alert would make Carrick's job riskier. He decided just to observe this evening, then come back in a few days. The police won't hang around for very long, he figured.

SIX

The sky was getting lighter as Gil drove north up I-75 toward Ocala, Florida in light rain. There wasn't any traffic this time of the day. He left the interstate at Ocala, crossed over to US Route 301, then headed north up the middle of the Florida peninsula. Route 301 was a pleasure to drive, scenic with citrus groves and cow pastures.

The sun came up, even though it was still raining a bit. He put on his sunglasses and turned on the radio. "Folks, that was Bizzle, with his *Response to Same Love*. I played that to show faith and support for our leader, Ronnie D, and his quest to rid our land, and our whole nation, of those who have turned to sins of the flesh. Now we'll hear from Zach Williams with *Heart of God*." Gil pressed the 'seek' button to find a better station. He was conflicted about wintering in Florida, with its ultra-conservative and hate-stoking politics and religion. Gil wasn't a Democrat and he wasn't a Republican. Both parties had some good ideas and too many bad ideas. The ultra-liberals and ultra-conservatives were preventing the parties from working effectively together. It was exasperating.

He settled on an oldies rock station that was playing *Purple Rain*. The rain ended, and a nice rainbow formed. Gil thought that a lot of people in Florida must now hate rainbows, the nemesis of conservative politics. As he was getting close to the ramp for I-10, several magnificent swallow-tailed kites were swooping above the road.

· · · ·

DETECTIVE JIM BERNISKI and FBI Special Agent Mayet Elsayed sat on the couch in Martha's living room, adjacent to a love-seat that held Martha and Lili. Everyone was drinking coffee in mismatched mugs. Special Agent Elsayed was a striking young woman with black, frizzy hair tied back. "So, Agent D'Amico, what do you think is going on here?" she asked.

"I think someone wants to kill Martha." Martha began to tremble, so Lili gently put her hand on Martha's arm. I think if they were looking for something, the house would have been tossed. I have no idea why they're after Martha. I recommend digging into Martha's past and present dealings. She could have witnessed something that she isn't aware of. The killers came here first and, when they realized she wasn't around, they searched for indications of where she was. They located her in Florida, and a guy tried to strangle her. He kept at it even when he knew he'd be killed. Do you know who the attacker was?"

Detective Berniski said, "I spoke to Detective Arias yesterday, and they still don't have an ID on the guy down there. They believe he's from El Salvador, based on his tattoos."

Lili said, "Well, since Martha probably isn't involved with Central American gangs, somebody probably hired him to get to her."

Special Agent Elsayed asked, "Ms. Eames, who are your closest relatives?"

Martha wrote on her pad for a few minutes while Lili looked over her shoulder. "I don't have any blood relatives that I know of. I was adopted as a young child in England by Stephen and Elizabeth Stone. They had no knowledge of my biological parents. I have some cousins from the Stone family in England and Canada whom I met as a child, but I never stayed in touch with them when my parents moved to America. George and I didn't have any children. Early in our marriage, I had a baby who was stillborn. After that, I couldn't bring myself to try for another one. I had my students at school, and that was enough for me."

Elsayed read what she wrote and handed it off to Berniski. "Has anything changed in your life in the recent past? Any new activities, investments, acquaintances, that sort of thing?" asked Elsayed.

Martha wrote another paragraph. "I've been doing the same things for the past 15 years, living in Portsmouth and going to Florida for the winters. I'm 81 years old, so I don't do all that much. My husband George died three years ago, which was a big change for me. The only new acquaintances I have lately are Lili and Gil who came to Florida this year. If they didn't, I'd be dead!"

Elsayed read it, passed it on, and said, "I'm so sorry about your husband."

Lili said, "You're eighty-one? I thought you were like seventy-five. Wow, you're in good shape!" Martha beamed.

• • • •

THAT EVENING, GIL EXITED I-77 somewhere in North Carolina. He pulled into a gas station and filled his tank. He searched his cell phone for nearby hotels. Since he wasn't with Lili, he decided to go for something low-budget. All he needed was a bed to sleep in. He pulled in to the Red Bug Motel which looked like it was freshly painted, about twenty years ago.

In the front office, the desk clerk was a girl, maybe fifteen years old, listening to pop music on a radio. "I'd like a room for one night, please."

She pulled out a form and asked, "How many people?"

"Just me."

"Pets?"

"No."

"Please fill out your name and address, along with your license plate information." A woman dressed in a red and gold sari was arguing on the phone in the office behind the desk.

Gil filled out the form and asked, "Is there breakfast?"

"Yes, there will be a continental breakfast over there, from seven to nine. That will be fifty-nine dollars please." He pushed his chip card into the little machine and, after a few seconds, it asked him to remove his card. She handed him a receipt. Here is your key. Room 24." She showed him room 24 on a map.

Gil moved the car closer to his room, then lugged his bag up the stairs and found room 24. He couldn't remember the last time he got a metal key for a hotel room. The room was everything he expected. It had an odd, musty odor, perhaps like boiled seaweed that had cooled. He set his suitcase on the wooden luggage rack. The carpet was dark olive green, and lightly stained from an old roof leak. The queen-sized bed looked fine and the bedding looked clean. He lifted the mattress a little and didn't find any bedbugs or red bugs. The bathroom was very dated, but clean. The cover of the toilet tank was cracked. Actually, the whole place was very clean.

Gil freshened up and went outside to look for a restaurant. He preferred to find a local place rather than a chain restaurant. He searched on his phone and found two places within walking distance. The closest one was a traditional American diner. He checked it out, but there was only one customer there, even though it was dinner time. He crossed the street and walked down the road a little farther and found a restaurant called *Boca Chica*. It was hopping.

The girl at the counter told him to sit anywhere. Based on the posters on the wall, he gathered that it was a Dominican restaurant. He'd never had Dominican food before, so he was curious. He looked at the menu and it was very long. A server came by and he ordered chinola juice, which was passion fruit. When she brought that over, he ordered pollo horneado, which was rotisserie chicken, along with rice and sweet plantain. It was wonderful! Maybe when he and Lili look for a house together, they could find one near a Dominican restaurant. As he ate, Gil wondered if he and Lili were ready to move in together, permanently. They hadn't really talked about it since deciding to go to Florida together. What about getting married? They didn't need to rush into anything. They'd only known each other for about six or seven months.

When he got back to the motel, he called Lili and asked about her day. She filled him in on the case and told him she'd head home once Martha got an alarm system, maybe in a day or two. He told her about the Dominican restaurant and she said she'd never been. After they hung up, Gil grabbed the TV remote and sat in bed. The mattress was bouncy and sagged a bit in the middle. He searched the guide for a show to watch, but didn't find anything. He found his Kindle and resumed reading his science-fiction novel.

• • • •

LILI WAS KNITTING A sweater for her young niece. Martha was reading a magazine. She picked up her pad, wrote a bit, and handed it to Lili. "I just read an article about doing a DNA genealogy search. That detective asked me about my family, and I told her what I knew, but I guess that wasn't the whole story. I did a DNA test a couple of years ago and it showed that I do have some blood relatives in South America and other places in Europe, maybe. Could I show it to you? You're a DNA expert, right?"

"I do know a lot about DNA, but I'm not a genealogist. I'd love to take a look at your DNA results."

There was a knock at the back door which surprised Lili. A police officer was stationed back there, guarding the back steps. Martha quickly wrote that it's probably Barbara. Lili grabbed her gun and answered the door. "Oh, please don't shoot me until after you've tried my casserole," said Barbara. I made an extra one for you girls." Lili let her in and Barbara set her casserole on the counter. "Chicken and broccoli."

"Thank you, it looks great!" said Lili.

"What are you knitting?"

"It's a sweater for my niece. She's seven years-old."

"It's beautiful! I love those colors. I'm working on an afghan. Sweaters are too stressful for me. How are you feeling, Martha?"

Martha wrote on her pad and handed it to Barbara. "I feel fine, but my neck itches. I can squeak a little, so maybe my voice is starting to come back."

"That would be great, but don't rush it. Swelling takes time to come down." Barbara looked at Lili. "I was a nurse for almost forty years. Mass General. Well, I'll see you later. I've got a cake in the oven."

SEVEN

Gil woke up, but it took a few seconds for him to realize that he was in a motel room. He got up and put on jeans, since he'd be headed into cooler weather. He packed his suitcase and left a tip for the cleaner. He was feeling a little weary, partly due to lack of sleep caused by the concave mattress. After bringing his bag to the car, he went into the office to look for his continental breakfast. A middle-aged man behind the counter wished him good morning and Gil wished him one back.

On a small table in the corner stood an industrial coffee maker with pots of regular and decaf coffee. There was also an urn of hot water for tea and a selection of teabags. Gil poured himself some decaf into a to-go cup with cream and sugar. He put on a sippy-lid and a cardboard sleeve. Gil only drank decaf because of his recent struggles with insomnia. The continental breakfast consisted of a disappointing assortment of factory-made mini-danishes in plastic wrappers. Gil grabbed a couple and checked out at the front desk.

"How was your stay, sir?" asked the proprietor in a cheerful Indian accent.

"My room was very clean, but it didn't smell very good. Also, the bed needs a new mattress."

"I have emailed you your receipt. Have a wonderful day, sir."

At the car, Gil wolfed down the two pastries which had way too much sugar in them. The coffee was surprisingly excellent. He did a quick check of the weather and headlines to make sure there weren't any existential threats, then he got going. The sky was overcast, but it seemed like just some morning haze that would probably dissipate in an hour or so. He got back on I-77 and headed north.

• • • •

RIGHT AT NINE A.M., the doorbell rang at Martha's house. Lili peeked outside and saw the police officer chatting with a workman who apparently belonged to the security van parked out front. The technician introduced himself as Pappy. Lili introduced him to Martha, then walked him around the house, the cellar, and the garage. Pappy said, "I think we should put in a master alarm panel near the front door, an auxiliary panel near the back door, and sensors on all the doors and windows. Ms. Eames, do you have a smart cellphone?"

She nodded.

"That's good. If you agree, I can put in video cameras looking out at the front and back porches. When someone approaches, you'll be alerted on your phone and you'll be able to see who's there before you answer the door. I'll show you how to work everything. If there's an intruder, it'll automatically call for help. I'll also give you a necklace with a panic button on it, so if you have any kind of emergency, including medical or fire, you can get help. It's at a very low cost to you because the police department is subsidizing it. They won't pay for the video cameras though, because they're not strictly allowed in New Hampshire. But the police love them." Pappy showed Martha and Lili the work order on his tablet and had Martha sign it with her finger.

Lili called Gil for a brief chat to make sure he was okay. When she hung up, Martha handed her the information she got from the DNA-testing company. Martha wrote, "Since I was adopted as a very young child, I've always been curious about my ancestry. But when the results came back, they were confusing to me. So, I never did anything with them."

Lili looked through the report and got excited. "This is fascinating! Based on what you said, I expected that you would be mainly English, but you're not English at all. Your ethnicity come from the regions around Germany and Eastern Europe. It says you're mostly Jewish and Bavarian German, with a little from Holland."

Martha wrote, "But what does Ashkenazi mean? It sounds like Nazis."

"Hold on a minute, let me look it up." Lili found the Wikipedia article on Ashkenazi Jews on her phone. "It has nothing to do with Nazis. It's just the opposite. When the Romans conquered Israel about two thousand years ago, most of the Jewish people left. They dispersed in different directions. Ashkenazi Jews are the ones that ended up in Central and Eastern Europe—Germany, Russia, Poland, places like that. Did you know that you had Jewish ancestry?"

Martha wrote, "No, I'm not sure I even believe it. Why is Jewish even an ancestry? It's a religion. Why doesn't it say that I'm 50% Christian?"

"Those are good questions. It's true that Jewish is a religion, but I think it's also an ethnic group. Jewish people tended to live in close-knit communities for thousands of years. Christianity spans a lot of different ethnic groups. So, in this report they aren't referring to being Jewish as a religion, it's more of a common set of identifiable DNA features. Let's look at your identified relatives. You have quite a few here. The closest ones say they're in South America, but there aren't any in North America, and only distant ones in Germany or Holland. Did any of them contact you?"

Martha shook her head.

"Would you like to contact them?"

Martha thought a bit, then wrote, "I feel like I need to know more about these people before I contact anyone. This report doesn't really tell me anything about who these people are."

"I know a lot about genetics from my work catching criminals, but not a lot about genealogy. If you make me a copy of this report, I can bring it to a friend of mine who's a forensic genealogist. She usually works on legal cases, but I'll see if she can help you. It may cost a few hundred dollars, though. Are you interested?" Martha nodded. "Is it okay if Gil helps me on this? He's clever about a lot of things." Martha agreed.

• • • •

LATER THAT DAY, PAPPY trained Martha how to operate her new security system. He had her pretend she was leaving the house to go somewhere, then returning to the house, and what to do if the alarm goes off by mistake. He had her set the alarm for when she was going to bed for the evening. He showed her how to use her phone and tablet to view the video cameras. Martha paid him with her credit card on a gizmo he carried. After he left, the police officers spoke to her to make sure she was going to keep all of her doors locked while she was alone in the house. They were finished guarding her house.

Lili said she would be leaving in the morning, after breakfast. Martha wrote, "I feel like everyone's abandoning me! I liked having all these people around."

"Well, Barbara's still here, and you can video-chat with me anytime. Do you know how to do that?"

Martha shook her head. Lili showed her how to call her with video, and that she could text along with the video until her voice was back. Martha wrote, "Can I do this with the other people in my address book?"

"Sure, as long as they have a smartphone, a tablet, or a computer. If you need help, just call me."

Martha's eyes lit up and she wrote, "I can chat with my friends from all over, almost like they're here! This is wonderful!"

• • • •

LILI WOKE WITH A START. Did she hear something? She checked her phone on the bedside table, twelve-thirty a.m. Someone was knocking on the back door. She got her gun and ran into Martha in the hallway. "Stay here and get ready to press your emergency button. I'll go see who's knocking." Martha shook her head emphatically. She motioned for Lili to calm down.

They went downstairs and peered out the window. It was a young woman and what looked like three teen-aged kids. Martha carefully disabled the alarm and Lili opened the door. "Who are you? Where's Martha?"

Martha nodded and Lili let them in. "Martha, what's going on?" the woman asked.

"I'm Lili, Martha's friend. Martha can't speak due to a neck injury. Who are you? What's this all about?"

The woman hesitated. Martha got her pad and pen. "This is Vera. She's part of our underground railroad. I'll let her explain. Vera, Lili is okay. She's an agent with the Mass. State Police. She saved my life a few weeks ago in Florida."

Vera's eyes went wide. "Whoa! Can we get these kids to bed first? Then we'll talk."

Martha led the kids upstairs and showed them the bedrooms and the bathroom.

"Would you like some coffee, Vera?" asked Lili.

"No, thanks. I plan to go to sleep soon. So what's this all about?"

Martha came back down. Lili explained what had happened to Martha in Florida, with Martha contributing in writing. "So, Vera, what's this underground railroad?"

"We're called SafeUR, for Safe Underground Railroad. We started up about a year and a half ago because the conservative states started passing laws against gay and trans kids, and against abortion. The gay and trans kids are at risk because they get abused at home or they run away and get trafficked as sex workers, hooked on drugs, or even abused and killed. Pregnant girls often seek illegal abortions and die, or they're subject to criminal prosecution, or they run away, unprotected. Our lawyers forbid us from transporting these kids over state lines, which could be a federal offense. So, they are driven to the state borders where they walk across to the next state and another car picks them up."

"Where do they go?"

"We tap into a large network of supervised housing, churches, and foster homes. Every kid is assigned to a professional social worker who helps them develop a plan. We make sure their families know they're safe. Some will go back home after an abortion or childbirth. Most of them won't go home until they're adults, if ever. We find them jobs, on farms, in restaurants, or at resorts. We enroll them in school, get them health care. We've already moved thousands of kids into the network."

"Wow, thousands of kids, already?" Lili considered this for a moment and said, "So Martha, you didn't think to tell me or the FBI about this? You don't think this could be related to why somebody is trying to kill you?" Martha shrugged. "Unbelievable!"

Vera said, "Since we started, we haven't had any cases of violence, that I know of. Martha's just a SAW house, a Stop Along the Way. I'll have to feed this attack situation up the chain. Are these kids safe here?"

Lili said, "Well, now we have an alarm system, so I think they'll be alright for tonight. When will somebody be picking them up?"

Martha wrote, "The pickup will be between 9:30 and 10:00 am."

EIGHT

Gil stopped for gas along I-81 at a place called Stephens City, Virginia. While he was wolfing down a hot dog, he noticed a poster for the Shen-Valley Flea Market in a place called Doubletoll. He inquired at the gas station's mini-mart, and the lady told him it was just ten minutes down the road and it was open. *Why not? I've got to stop and smell the roses, right?* he thought. He pulled into the flea market and parked. It was cool out, but there was a building with vendors inside, and some vendors were under tents outside, too. There weren't very many shoppers, though.

Gil wasn't really a collector of anything, but he thought that maybe he could find something that would interest him. There was a good bevy of women hovering around a tent full of children's clothing. A few old guys were chatting around tables full of old tools, knives, belt buckles, and other guy stuff. One vendor guy had collections of random items. He had a large collection of corks, a nice collection of cobalt-blue glassware, and fancy collections of canes and hatpins. This vendor had other interesting things as well, but one unique collection caught Gil's eye. "People collect lawnmower pull cords?"

The vendor smiled, and was only missing one tooth in front. "Well, I did. It's all about the handles. The wooden ones and the red ones with logos are worth the most. They're not all from lawnmowers. Some are from outboard motors and Weed Whackers, things like that."

Gil decided that he wasn't going to be a collector. As he looked around at the various vendor booths, he realized that he didn't know enough about Lili's likes and dislikes to buy her anything. He decided he should go shopping with her a few times and pay attention, which would be easier said than done. Another thing he noticed was that a significant amount of antique items were things his family had when he was young. He himself was an antique, he realized. He enjoyed the flea market as a respite, but he soon got back on the road.

• • • •

GIL WOKE UP CONFUSED for a few seconds until he remembered that he was in a sketchy motel on the outskirts of Harrisburg, Pennsylvania. He was very weary, even though he'd slept okay. He stared at a water stain on the ceiling where some paint had fallen onto the carpet. There was no breakfast at this motel, so he got dressed, checked out, and headed out to find a diner.

There were two diners across the street from each other just down the road. One was packed and the other had only two cars parked in the lot. He went into the crowded diner and sat at the counter. He ordered decaf coffee, fried eggs, and corned beef hash, vowing to eat healthy food when he got home. He checked the news on his phone, and read about Putin planning to put nuclear weapons in Belarus. Gil was dispirited when he thought about the state of the world. After breakfast, he got back on I-81 and headed east toward I-78.

• • • •

MARTHA WAS MAKING COFFEE when someone knocked on the back door. Lili saw that it was only eight-fifteen, so she looked out the window, and it was Barbara carrying some food. Lili let her in. "I brought three quiches, two Lorraines and one spinach and onion." Barbara stayed to help serve.

Martha wrote a note and handed it to Lili. "Would you go wake up the kids and tell them that breakfast will be ready in a few minutes?" Lili did that while Martha put some bread in the toaster and got some orange juice out of the refrigerator.

The kids didn't speak much at breakfast, but thanked the women for their meals. They all looked nervous and sad. They went back upstairs to get their belongings ready for the next phase of their journey. Lili wanted desperately to know their stories, but figured they were told not to say anything to anyone because it was dangerous for them. A middle-aged woman named Nancy came for them at the back door, and they left by cutting through the back yard.

As they were cleaning up after breakfast, Lili said, "You know we're going to have to tell the FBI about this." Martha got upset and shook her head vehemently. "Martha, we don't have a choice. Someone could be after you because of this underground network. Maybe you helped their child run away."

Martha wrote, "If we tell the FBI, they'll have to investigate the whole network! They'll shut us down!"

Lili said, "Let me talk to Special Agent Elsayed, and see if we can come up with a way that won't undermine the network. We have the advantage that the President and his administration would probably be in favor of keeping this network going." Martha looked dejected, but nodded her head.

Barbara shrugged and said, "Well, I guess I'll head back home. Is there anything you need from me?" Martha shook her head and wrote, "Thank you!"

Lili said, "I'm going to get my stuff together and head home. Is there anything you need before I go?" As the front door shut behind Barbara, Lili heard a loud thump at the front of the house, a gunshot in the distance, and then it sounded like someone fell. "Martha, lie down on the floor and don't get up till I say!" Lili looked out the front window and saw Barbara lying still on the porch floor. She went to the door and there was a dent in it. Blood was splattered on the windows near the top of the door. She went back to where

Martha was lying down on the living room floor, pulled out her phone and called 911.

. . . .

CARRICK LOOKED AT THE target through his scope to verify his kill shot. It went through her left eye, just a little off. He took a picture using his scope camera. He climbed down out of the tree, disassembled and packed his rifle, and checked the area for anything he might have left behind. In a minute, he was on his way back through the woods.

NINE

The EMTs had to sedate Martha, and an ambulance took her away, with a police cruiser following. Detective Berniski and Lili were in the kitchen. He said, "I was told to just secure the scene and wait for the FBI. They've got the ball now, and I think that makes sense for a change. I don't think this is a local crime. What do you think is going on?"

"I think somebody is still trying to kill Martha. Barbara came in the back door with some quiches this morning. Whoever the sniper was, they wouldn't have seen her enter the house. When she stepped out the front door, the sniper thought it was Martha."

"I think you're right. Barbara was wearing a white turtleneck under her coat which would have looked like Martha's bandage. We think the shooter was probably in a tree in the woods behind the houses across the street. We're taping the woods off now, so the FBI techs can search."

"Thanks for putting up that screen so passers-by can't see poor Barbara. We'll have to figure out what to do with Martha. She can't stay here. I hope the FBI will be able to hide her."

· · · ·

GIL WAS CRUISING ALONG I-78, making good time. Pretty soon he'd enter New Jersey and take the exit for I-287 and head north. His phone rang on his dash-screen. Detective Karen Tindall? He hit the touchscreen to accept her call. "Hi Karen!"

"Hi Gil, how are you doing?"

"I'm fine, how are you?"

"I'm good. We're wondering if you could help us on another case. It's a really weird one and we could use a robot. Are you in your car?"

"Yeah, I'm in Pennsylvania, driving home from Florida."

"Oh, is Lili with you?"

"No, she had to fly home early to help a friend. So, you need a robot? I'm interested."

"Well, the short version is that someone broke into a few buildings and broke through their cellar walls to build some tunnels. As far as we know, there's no rhyme nor reason for these tunnels. They aren't safe for us to go looking around in there. The robots that the bomb squad and the fire station have are too big to fit. We put a fiber optic scope in there, but it didn't give us a good picture of what might be going on. What do you think?"

"Maybe people are desperately trying to escape from Greenfield."

"Oh brother."

Gil's mind was going a mile a minute with ideas for tunnel-exploring robots. "This sounds like fun! I know I can help you with this. I'm going to need a break for a few days after driving home. Can it wait until Monday?"

"Monday would be great. This has been going on for at least six months. There haven't been any confrontations or anything violent and no amorous fish involved, so you shouldn't get hurt this time, I hope.

"Word gets around."

"Have a good drive home." She clicked off.

Gil's newfound excitement seemed to accelerate his need for a rest-room break.

• • • •

SPECIAL AGENT MAYET Elsayed, Detective Jim Berniski, and Lili sat in Martha's living room to discuss the case. Mayet listened as Lili described the shooting and Jim explained what he found when he arrived. He said, "I firmly believe that this isn't a local issue and that the FBI should have the lead on this, overall. We'll help you in any way you need."

Mayet raised her eyebrows at Berniski's unexpected cooperation. "Thanks, Jim. At this point, since the crime scenes are limited to the forest and the house, and my crime-scene technicians are here, I think you can re-open the road. It would be good if your guys would complete canvassing the neighbors to see if there were any witnesses. Also, you guys can guard Martha at the hospital. Also, could you track down next of kin and notify them? Is that okay?"

Jim was pleasantly surprised that Mayet was freely delegating the local part of the investigation to him. "Sure. I'll let you know who they are and what they say. Also, I think we should pursue the angle that Barbara LeClerc might have been the target. I doubt it, but it should be looked at."

"Good point. Good idea. You go ahead and pursue that."

"I'll get this stuff going now." He got up and went out the back door.

"Um, Special Agent Elsayed, there's something else you should know about," said Lili.

"Please call me Mayet. May I call you Lili?"

"Sure, of course. Last night I found out that Martha's involved in an underground railroad."

Mayet looked confused. "You mean like the ones that helped slaves escape?"

"Yes, except this one is helping gay and transgender kids escape from states where their lives are in danger. Pregnant girls, too. Last night, just after midnight, a woman showed up and dropped off three kids. The kids stayed the night, had breakfast, and then moved on with a different woman. Last night's woman said that they're trained not to transport the kids across state borders, so they have them walk across the border and they're picked up by a different person."

"And you think this could be why Martha's being targeted?"

"I don't know. The motive isn't clear, but it's certainly worth looking into. The woman said that Martha is just a 'SAW,' a Stop Along the Way. These kids are eventually brought to supervised housing or churches, and they find jobs for them and keep them safe. Anyway, Martha and the other woman were worried that telling the Police or the FBI about this underground railroad would threaten their network. The woman said they already have thousands of kids in their network."

"Wow, thousands of kids?" Mayet thought for a few seconds. "There are huge political ramifications with this underground railroad. I agree that it must be protected. I will discuss this discreetly up the chain. You know that I'm going to have to arrange to put Martha into the Witness Security Program, right?"

"I know you'll probably do some Federal kind of thing, but one idea I have is to offer to take her to my boyfriend's house in upstate New York and stay with her there. It would be difficult for her to be tracked down there, as long as she has no contact with her friends and no electronic traceability."

"Well, I don't think that'll fly, but I'll consider it."

· · · ·

AFTER THE POLICE AND the FBI left, Lili spent an hour cleaning up the blood from the front porch. She called Detective Berniski and asked if she could visit Martha in the hospital. He told her that she was in a hospital in Dover, since whoever is after her probably wouldn't think to look for her there. Lili called Gil to tell him what had happened. He was stunned. He said he was passing Poughkeepsie, just a couple of hours from his house, and that he had a request from Karen to consult on a case.

At the Wentworth-Douglass Hospital, Lili was allowed access to Martha's room. Martha was dozing, so Lili just sat there for a while, trying to calm herself down. After a while, Martha's eyes opened and blinked a few times. She glanced over at Lili and tears just started to roll down her face.

TEN

Gil finally got to his house in Saratoga Springs, New York. The weather was cold and gloomy. There were still a few patches of dirty snow around his house. He was completely unsettled because of the sniper situation. He felt like he needed to go to Lili and be with her, but first he needed to unpack his car, shower and eat, but he was too tired to do any of those things. He settled into his recliner and phoned Lili. "I feel like I need to go to you and provide moral support," he said.

"I'd love that, but I'm heading home today. The FBI is putting Martha into witness protection right away. I really just want to go home and get my life settled again. When are you going to Greenfield?"

"I told Karen I'd be there Monday."

"Why don't you just come stay with me in Northampton?"

Gil panicked for a second, thinking that he might be casually making a big decision, but he shrugged and said, "Sure, good idea." All the fretting he'd been doing was instantly solved by Lili's simple idea.

• • • •

GIL DRAGGED HIMSELF out of his recliner and started to unpack the car. He realized that he had all of Lili's stuff, including her bike. He sent a text to remind her of that, and she replied with two exclamation points. He was going to have to head to her house as soon as posible. He also texted his daughters to let them know he was home. Julia invited him to come to dinner.

When he got to Julia's house, Ziggy and Dez were jumping on the couch while watching an episode of *Dora the Explorer*. Jazz was in another room reading a book. Jazz was a moody ten-year-old, already in training to become a teenager. Julia came out of the kitchen to give her father a hug. "How was Florida? How was shacking up with Lili? Are you going back next year?" Mike came out of the kitchen to listen.

"Well, Florida was definitely nicer in the winter. I felt chilly when it got below about seventy-three degrees. But, there's something about the culture down there that makes me uncomfortable. I don't know how to put it into words."

"The politics?" Mike asked.

"There's that, but that's not what I'm talking about. One example is that there's a lot of talk about contractors doing substandard work. I was told that a lot of them are from Boston. It's almost like Florida is a place for people to go and misbehave in many different ways. But, that's just my initial, paranoid impression. I've only been there for one winter. We plan to go there again next winter."

Mike said, "So, tell me more about this shooting. How's Lili with that?"

"Oh boy. I told you that Lili had left early to accompany our new friend Martha home to Portsmouth after someone tried to strangle her, right? Well, a couple of days ago, while Lili was there, a sniper shot and killed Martha's neighbor as she was leaving Martha's house."

"*What*?" Julia yelped. "Oh my god! What is happening?"

"Apparently, someone is very determined to kill Martha. The FBI got involved and Martha's going into witness protection. Lili's heading home to Northampton today."

"Holy shit!" said Julia.

Ziggy wandered in and said, "You swore, Mommy."

"Oh, I'm sorry. Naughty me!"

Dinner was baked-stuffed haddock with seasoned rice and asparagus. Julia seemed nervous and distracted while she was serving. When she went in the kitchen, Mike gave her a hug to calm her down.

"Dezzy, do you like fish for dinner?" Gil asked.

"I love fish with crumbly crackers. But I don't like 'sparagus.'"

· · · ·

AFTER DINNER, GIL HELPED Julia and Mike clear the table. He said, "Tomorrow or the next day, I'll head down to Lili's place for a while. Most of her stuff is still in my car."

"Oh, right." said Julia.

"Also, Karen Tindall asked me for some help on a case."

"What! You nearly died last time!" said Julia.

"This isn't that kind of case. Apparently, somebody's been digging tunnels around Greenfield, so they need me to make a robot to investigate the tunnels. No one's been hurt and nothing's been stolen, as far as they can tell."

"That's weird. I guess that doesn't sound too threatening. And you'll be staying with Lili in Northampton?"

"That's the plan." Julia smiled to herself.

· · · ·

THE NEXT MORNING, GIL dressed to play pickleball at the gym, but his foot was killing him. He tried to ignore it, but it was really bad. Maybe he had a fracture. He ate breakfast, changed into a shirt and jeans, and headed over to the prompt-care clinic.

"You probably have gout," said the doctor.

"Gout? What's gout?"

"It's a buildup of uric acid in your blood. It creates crystals in your joints that are very painful, as you've discovered. Gout is aggravated by foods that are high in purines, such as red wine, beer, shellfish, red meat, and others."

"My diet isn't really high in any of those things."

"Well then, you're going to take some pills to treat it. No big deal. I'm going to sample the fluid in your foot to confirm it. We'll also do a blood test today to determine the uric acid levels in your blood. We'll see if the gout recurs once you are educated on prevention. If it keeps coming back, your Primary Care Physician will figure out the best long-term medication for you to take. Here's a pamphlet."

ELEVEN

Lili's garage door was opening as Gil pulled into the driveway of her townhouse. He got out of the car and she ran over to give him a big hug and kiss. "Welcome to Northampton!" she said.

"It's a strange feeling, but I'm thrilled to know how much I've missed you over the past week," he said. Lili beamed.

Gil was still limping a bit from his gout as they unpacked the car and brought everything into the house. As Lili was putting her clothes away, Gil wheeled his suitcase into her bedroom and said, "This whole situation is very disorienting."

Lili shut the blinds, pulled him close and said, "Let's get you oriented, Mister."

• • • •

GIL WAS IN LILI'S GARAGE playing with his radio-controlled inspection vehicle. It was about a foot and a half long, and had a basic tank-like chassis where attachments could be added. It also had a control panel with video and GPS outputs. So far, Gil had only added a camera. Lili came in and said, "I talked to my boss, Cherise. She asked me to come in for a formal debrief about the shooting tomorrow morning, then I have to set up a mandatory psych appointment."

"Sounds like what you expected would happen."

"Yeah. I'm kind of looking forward to it."

"Which part?"

"Both, I guess. It worries me that I seem to have no emotional reaction to taking a human life, but I don't feel anything but relieved that I got there in time. I hope it doesn't mean I'm a sociopath."

"I don't think so, but if you are, please don't have that cured. I love you just the way you are."

. . . .

GIL WAS SHOWING DETECTIVE Karen Tindall his radio-controlled inspection vehicle in the parking lot of the Greenfield Police Department, while a couple of officers looked on. Karen was wearing her police uniform, without the hat, as she normally did. Chief Manny Reyes came outside and shook Gil's hand. "Thanks for coming, Gil. I figured this would be right up your alley."

"Thanks for thinking of me. What retired guy wouldn't want to come here and play with toys? Hopefully, no bad guys will pop out of these holes."

"Yeah, speaking of that, did Detective Tindall get you to sign that waiver?" Karen rolled her eyes.

Gil laughed. "I signed the waiver, Chief. It's a good thing I get an armed guard."

Karen drove Gil and his gadget to their first location. "First, we're going to the Arch Street Salon. That hole was discovered in January by the property owner during a routine inspection. The building has a hair salon with some apartments upstairs and a cellar with a stone foundation. Apparently, the tenants received notices that some foundation improvement work would be going on during the week between Christmas and New Years. The salon was closed and most of the tenants were gone that week. Obviously, the notices were fraudulent."

"That sounds ballsy." said Gil

Karen went into the salon to let the workers know we'd be in the cellar. Gil brought his gear in through the back door. The cellar had poor lighting and a damp, moldy smell. The cement floor was probably poured many decades ago, but after the original foundation was constructed. In some places, the cement had been splashed over the lower foundation stones. An old furnace with a large, rusty-black oil tank stood to one side.

A hole, about two feet square, had been knocked out by removing some foundation stones. The removed stones were stacked in a corner. "They left the place very tidy," said Gil. How nice of them, he thought. Gil stuck his head in the hole and looked around with a flashlight. "There's a larger area, big enough to move around in, with three tunnels leading out."

"We decided not to go into that space. I didn't seem safe. The structural supports aren't standard, and there's no ventilation. We tried to use an inspection scope, but it kept getting buried in the soft dirt."

"Is there anything nearby that the tunnelers would be interested in? Any bank vaults or jewelry stores?"

"There's a Sherwin-Williams across the street, and a few houses. We're right next to the railroad bridge arch. That's about it."

"Well, let's see what we can see." Gil set up a spool of parachute cord and secured it to the robot, in case it got stuck. He placed the machine into the hole and opened his control panel. The panel was professional-grade, protected by a yellow water-tight case with a large laptop screen. Definitely not a toy. Gil said, "What shall we name this thing?"

"How about Danica?"

"The race-car driver? Excellent!" Gil steered Danica into one of the tunnels. Karen watched over his shoulder. "The tunnel is very consistently shaped. It's reinforced with some kind of intricate structure. I think some machine must have done the digging. I wonder where they put the dirt."

"There was a fresh dirt spot outside," said Karen. "Maybe they had a dirt pile and took it away in a truck."

"This whole excavation looks fairly sophisticated." He steered the robot about thirty yards and the tunnel ended. "Dead end." He backed Danica back to the entry space, and went down the next tunnel. This tunnel ended at a curved wall. "This structure looks like the kind of clay sewer piping used in the old days." Gil sent Danica down the third tunnel. "Whoa," he said. The tunnel led to a cement wall which seemed to have a modern cement storm drain structure. The tunnel then veered to one side and followed the structure along Arch Street.

As Danica moved forward, Gil noticed several small excavations spaced along the tunnel's dirt floor. The tunnel floor was soil that was eroding in areas where there were puddles of water. "Danica is waterproof, so we don't have to worry about the water." Gil steered Danica through the tunnel which circumvented large, vertical cylinders every so often. "I assume these cylinders are storm-drain catch basins," he said. After about 250 feet, the tunnel angled up about 30 degrees and ended. "Maybe a man-hole."

Gil steered Danica back to the cellar. As Gil was reeling up his parachute cord, he said, "This whole area was intricately engineered. The support structure seems like it was expanded into the tunnel, like a Slinky toy. I'd say it might be beyond state of the art. I think we're looking for a startup company or maybe some grad students. But, I have no idea what they're up to. I think we should contact the civil engineering department at UMass and see what they say."

"Can we find that person-hole?"

Gil laughed. "Right, maybe access hatch? Anyway, I saved the GPS coordinates so we can find it." When they left the building, Gil looked at the GPS app on his phone. "It's near the dead-end on Oak Street." They drove around the residential neighborhood and parked at the end of Oak Street. They walked into a wooded area and found a capped access pipe poking up from the ground at an angle. The cover was made from a lightweight composite material, and was padlocked. "The cover and support structure were 3-D printed. You can tell by the little ridges," said Gil.

Karen went back to her car and got a bolt cutter. She put on a pair of latex gloves and cut the lock, placing it in an evidence bag.

She shined her flashlight down the access hatch and said, "It looks like the tunnel just ends here. I'd better lock it. It should be safe, since we know no one's down there right now." She removed a pair of handcuffs from her belt and locked one end through the cover. "I'll get this dusted for prints. You know, if this tunnel is following the storm sewers, we could get a map from the Department of Public Works."

"Sounds like a plan."

• • • •

RACE JOHNSON WAS GREENFIELD'S Engineering Superintendent. He had his assistant, Rona Polo, print out a map with the layout of the storm drain system that included the Arch Street area. Gil marked the area he inspected, then he showed Race and Rona the video. Race said, "Wow, that's pretty advanced. It's definitely not kids."

"Do you guys have any idea what's going on here?" asked Karen.

"You said there are other tunnels?" Rona asked.

"There are two others we know about. One here, and one over here," Karen said, pointing at the map.

Rona shrugged. Race said, "I don't see any logic for the tunnel locations on this map. I have no idea what could be going on, but I'll ask around."

"Well, we're going to inspect the other tunnels. Would you like to watch?"

"Rona, why don't you go over and watch once they're set up," said Race.

• • • •

THE NEXT TUNNEL BEGAN in a house on Lincoln Street. Cheryl Needham was the homeowner. "I found this when I came home from Florida last week."

"Where do you go in Florida?" Gil asked.

"I have a house in Naples. It's too big for me, since my husband passed. So I'll probably sell it and get a condo."

"I was in Sarasota this winter," said Gil.

Rona, Karen, and Cheryl watched over Gil's shoulder as he guided Danica along the tunnel toward the south. The tunnel followed a cement storm-drain pipe, similar to what they found on Arch Street. At one point, the floor became very muddy and the tunnel branched off to the left. Gil steered Danica to inspect the branch tunnel, which was free-standing, since the sewer pipe had no corresponding branch. The floor of the tunnel was wet and puddled in places. It continued for about fifty yards and dead-ended.

Gil steered Danica back to the main tunnel. After fifty yards or so, there was another wet branch tunnel. It dead-ended after about forty yards. The main tunnel ended at that branch, but there was no access pipe. "The fact that there are wet branches is interesting, but I have no clue what it means," said Gil.

"Cheryl, would you mind leaving this hole the way it is while we continue to investigate?" asked Karen.

"Okay, but it's kind of creepy. I think I'll just move this bin over to block the opening for now."

"Rona, could you send me the maps of the sewer system?" asked Karen.

"Sure, if Gil would send me the info on Danica. We sure could use one of those."

· · · ·

THE LAST TUNNEL THEY inspected was on Pond Street, in the cellar of a Victorian-style mansion converted to apartments. This tunnel was just like the one on Arch Street, with no surprises. There was an access cover on a vertical section of the tunnel, between two houses on the other side of the street.

Back at the Police Station, Karen pinned a big map of the entire city's sewer system on the wall in one of the interview rooms. Gil highlighted the tunnels they'd inspected. Karen and Gil stared at the map. "There have to be more tunnels," he said.

"It seems like someone is looking for something. Whatever it is, it must be worth the expense of doing all of this," Karen said.

"What's the simplest explanation?"

"Somebody robbed a bank and buried the loot," she replied.

"That's pretty good. I was drawing a complete blank. We should make a list of whatever possible explanations we can think of. Maybe they are environmentalists searching for the source of some pollution."

"Or, somebody was murdered, and their body was buried during installation of the sewers."

"A startup company is testing a new underground inspection system," said Gil.

Karen said, "Let's just think about it for a while and add to the list over the next few days. It would help if we could figure out where to look for more tunnels."

"Can we put some kind of surveillance camera near the entrances to find out who's doing this?" asked Gil.

"I'll ask. Judges don't like to issue surveillance warrants unless somebody's likely to get hurt. But there has been someone breaking into houses and damaging people's cellars."

TWELVE

G il and Lili went out to dinner at Fitzwilly's in Northampton, not far from Lili's home. Lili said, "I didn't need to worry about the shooting debrief. Cherise said it was probably the most justifiable shooting she's ever heard of. Everybody basically congratulated me. It felt a little strange."

"Did you meet with the psychologist yet?"

"Yes, I met with Dr. Gary Percival, a guy with two first names. He was nice. He kind of explored to see if I had any inner demons. He concluded that my greatest source of anxiety was having you stay in my home."

"Should I move out?"

"A little anxiety can be a good thing." She batted her eyelashes. "So tell me about these tunnels."

Gil described his day searching the tunnels under Greenfield. "We're developing a list of possible motives. Like, maybe someone is planning to take over as the Lord of Greenfield and make all the residents their vassals."

"It seems a little like an archaeology dig."

"Hmm, that's possible. I'll add it to the list."

"Are you having the structures analyzed to figure out where they were made?"

"Do you think it would do any good?"

"You might learn something. I don't think they'd want to burden the lab with DNA testing for this type of crime. Speaking of which, Cherise asked if I'd come in part time to analyze a backlog of DNA evidence. I start on that tomorrow. I'll do mornings. It should only take about a week."

"Well, that's definitely important. I won't have much to do until some more tunnels are discovered. I have to go back home on Sunday, anyway. On Monday I start my series of doctor and dentist appointments that I put off during our winter away. Would you like to visit me in Saratoga?"

"I'd love to! I haven't met Julia and her family yet. I enjoyed meeting Amelia when we were in California. I'll come out after I finish the DNA backlog."

. . . .

LILI AND GIL WERE DRESSED for dinner out. Somehow, they got corralled into pushing Ziggy and Dez on the swings. Ziggy, at seven, didn't need a push, but he liked Grampy to push him anyway. Dez was five, and she was already best friends with Lili, though they'd only met an hour ago. Jazz was sitting on the deck, scrolling through her phone and casting furtive glances at Lili.

A short time later, Lili's eyes lit up as they approached the impressive stone building that housed The Olde Bryan Inn. "Established 1773?"

"I think they've updated the menu since then," said Gil. They waited in the bar while the maitre d' checked on their table. Lili chuckled as Ziggy stared, mouth agape, at the huge painting of a naked woman lying on a settee with a swan standing on her. "I feel the same way he does," said Gil.

Once seated, the younger kids colored their children's menus as they waited for their meals. "So, what attracted you to Grampy, Lili?" asked Julia.

"Well, he's cute and he makes me laugh." Jazz snorted as she tried not to laugh. Gil blushed.

"I can see why you're attracted to Lili. She's very pretty," said Julia.

"Yes she is," said Gil. "Plus she's a trained police officer who carries a gun, so I have to do whatever she says." Ziggy laughed and Lili rolled her eyes.

"So, Julia, what's it like working at your airport?" asked Lili.

"Sometimes it's very chaotic and sometimes it's completely dead. But the pilots and the staff are very nice, kind of like a family. Once in a while there's an emergency of one kind or another, which makes it exciting."

"Do you know how to fly?"

"I got my private pilot's license years ago, but I'm happy to work on the ground. I keep my physicals and my check rides current, in case I need to fly for some reason."

"Do you think you'll ever go back to flying?"

"I don't see myself doing that right now, but who knows what the future will bring?"

The server brought their meals.

"Jazz, I hear you're a gymnast. Do you do that through your school?"

Jazz blushed. "Um, no. There aren't any sports at my school. I go to gymnastics at a gym."

"What grade are you in?"

"Third."

"Wow, you're starting sports early. That's really impressive."

"So Gil, what's with those tunnels in Greenfield?" Mike asked.

"It's the weirdest thing. Somebody broke into homes, busted through their foundations, and built these person-sized tunnels with futuristic walls that look like Slinkys. The tunnels follow alongside the sewer pipes until the pipe has a junction, then they stop. They put in plastic manholes where they stop. We have no idea why they were built or who may have built them. Any ideas?"

"Maybe a new superhero is making a lair!" offered Ziggy.

"Or an arch-villain." offered Mike. Gil added those ideas to his list.

• • • •

IT WAS SUNNY, BUT VERY cool, as Lili and Gil pedaled north on the Warren County Bikeway. There were hardly any other people on the trail, except for the occasional dog-walker. They rode at a fairly rapid pace, and both of them felt good. They'd been biking together regularly in Florida, and both enjoyed it. Lili whooped at the view as they went over a pedestrian bridge, high above a busy road.

The trail was mostly flat and paved, with a few minor road sections. Part of it ran through residential neighborhoods, but most was through scenic areas. They rode by Round Pond, then between the *Six Flags Great Escape* amusement park and Glen Lake. The trail led north close to Route 9, then up a gradual hill. As they crested the hill, they stopped to behold a magnificent view of Lake George that opened up in front of them. Lili laughed with joy at the sight of it. They coasted down to Million Dollar Beach and took a break. There was a stiff breeze coming off the lake, so they sat on some boulders with their backs to it.

"This is a great trail," said Lili. "Should we ride through town?"

"There won't be much to see in April. Most of the businesses are closed. I suggest we come back in the summer for that. We could take a dinner cruise."

They drank some water and ate their apples while soaking up the sun. "This robot of yours, does it have any way of gathering evidence? It seems like you've done cursory tunnel inspections that got you an overall picture of what's down there, but I think you should do a more detailed inspection to look for evidence. You know, if your camera shows a scrap of something, the robot could bring back a clue. You need to point the camera down at the ground more."

"You're right about that. Good ideas. I could add a grabber arm to it. I'll have to take a closer look at the video, too."

"I could help you with that."

"Great! Right now, the biggest lead we have must be the tunnel structures themselves. I'm going to ask some UMass engineering professors and see if they know whose work this could be."

• • • •

LILI HAD BEEN SCRUTINIZING the tunnel videos on her tablet for over an hour, while Gil was emailing college professors from his computer workstation. "I just emailed my brother Randy. It's his birthday," said Gil.

"Where does he live?"

"He's in Boston. We're not close. He's a racist. He really doesn't like black people. Some of the stuff he posts online is over the top. I don't know how he got to be like that." Gil got up, stretched and asked, "Can I get you something to drink?"

"Do you have any orange juice?"

"How about a V8? That's what I'm having."

"Sure, that would be great." While he was in the kitchen, Lili heard beeps and saw a sudden flood of emails fill his computer screen. "Gil, you're suddenly getting a whole lot of emails."

He hurried back in and handed Lili her drink. "Jeez, what's going on?" He started reading the responses. "People are referring me to Rensselaer Polytechnic Institute. An architecture professor from RPI is asking me to call him right away. Gil punched a number into his cellphone. "May I speak to Professor Fallaci? This is Gil Novak."

"Please hold a moment," said a woman.

"Hi, Mr. Novak? This is Carlo Fallaci. Thanks for calling me back so quickly." He had a distinct Italian accent.

"This is about a missing student?" Gil asked.

"Yes, the tunnels you showed in your videos are definitely the work of Katrina Ryu. We call her Roo. She's been missing for months. You say this tunnel is in Massachusetts?"

"Yes, it's part of a police investigation."

"Then she must be alive! This is amazing! I'd like to meet with you, if I could. There is an FBI agent that will want to meet with you, too. Would you be available this afternoon to meet in Troy?"

"Sure, no problem. I'm in Saratoga. I'll give you my phone number."

THIRTEEN

Gil found his way to the Greene Building at RPI, an unimpressive structure for a School of Architecture, he thought. He was ushered into Dr. Fallaci's office by the professor himself. The room had an old conference table along with the professor's desk. "Please Mr. Novak, have a seat. Could I get you some coffee?"

"Please call me Gil. If I could just get some water, I'd be happy."

"Please call me Carlo. I'll be right back with your water." Carlo left the room and Gil looked around. He saw an impressive variety of building designs, most very complex and some quite artistic. Carlo brought back a large paper cup of water and an FBI Agent. "Gil Novak, this is Special Agent Davis from Albany."

Davis showed his badge and Gil said, "I'd like Detective Karen Tindall to join us by videoconference, if that's okay. She's from the Greenfield, Mass. Police Department and this is her case. I'm just a lowly consultant."

"You have a pretty high security clearance for a lowly consultant, Mr. Novak," said Davis.

"That's from my work before I retired. I was a robotics engineer up in Saratoga." Gil worked with Carlo for a few minutes to set up a video-link with Karen.

Karen's face came up on the screen. "Hello, I'm Detective Karen Tindall from the Greenfield Massachusetts Police Department." She held her credentials to the camera.

"I'm Carlo Fallaci, Professor of Architecture at RPI."

"I'm Special Agent Jameson Davis from the FBI's Albany office." He showed his credentials to the camera.

"And I'm Gil Novak, consultant to Detective Tindall."

Agent Davis said, "Professor Fallaci showed me a video of a tunnel in Greenfield that he is convinced is the work of Katrina Ryu.

Ms. Ryu was reported missing by RPI and by her mother in June of 2022, almost a year ago. None of our leads panned out and we haven't heard anything, even though there is a substantial reward offered for information leading to her recovery. Detective Tindall, what is the nature of the crime you are investigating?"

Karen smiled and said, "We're actually investigating what seems to be a minor matter. Somebody has illegally entered three buildings in our city, broken through the foundations, and dug several tunnels. These tunnels don't lead to anything in particular, as far as we can tell. The structure of these tunnels is very unusual."

Gil asked Karen to display a picture from one of the tunnels. "I inspected the tunnels using a small remote-controlled robot," said Gil. "The tunnel structures seem to be made of a composite material formed into an expandable mesh. The mesh would have been brought down in a compressed form and expanded into the tunnel. Each tunnel has a series of these meshes. The fact that these tunnels don't collapse using such a gossamer structure is impressive to me. One unusual feature I observed is that, rather than being complete cylinders, the tunnels are open at the bottom. This tells me that the people passing through these tunnels wanted access to the ground below."

Karen said, "We were able to take a sample of the tunnel structure from one of the openings. The tunnel is made from a material composed of wood and plastic called a PLA. The lab couldn't match it to any of the more popular commercial forms of wood-plastic composite."

Agent Davis asked, "Professor, what makes you think this is the work of Ms. Ryu?"

Carlo brought up some pictures of projects done by Katrina Ryu. Some were designs and others were physical models. "Most of our students focus on building designs. Roo, however, seemed to be fascinated by access-ways, tunnels, and entryways. She did some work on establishing an engineering process for designing expandable mesh structures based on their structural design, material of construction, and installation. She surprised our community by how strong she could make these structures with very little material. I'd say she's somewhat of a genius. A very unusual personality."

"In what way?" asked Karen.

"She's like a force of nature," said Carlo. "Whatever she worked on, she would have very energetic and enthusiastic interactions with a variety of professors, architecture students, engineering students, building inspectors, and even researchers from other colleges in a variety of disciplines. Her results were always fascinating and amazing. But, she didn't seem to form ongoing relationships with any of the students or staff here."

Agent Davis said, "We found no evidence of relationships with anyone other than her mother. She was estranged from her father who repatriated to South Korea when she was a young child. Katrina was born and raised in New York City. She has no siblings, except maybe some half-siblings in South Korea. We couldn't find information on any friendships at all, even from high school. No hobbies, either."

"Besides the structures," Gil said, "the process for excavating these person-sized tunnels is unknown. Professor, do you have any contacts that could figure out how they would have dug those tunnels?"

Carlo thought for a few seconds and said, "I would have to put that question to our Civil Engineering department, but we may have to ask people from some of the mining schools about that."

Agent Davis said, "Professor, please put the question out there and see what you can find. Detective Tindall, the FBI has no specific interest in your crime investigation, other than finding Ms. Ryu. So, please keep me in the loop if you find something that may help us. I'll update her mother. This will give her hope."

Karen asked, "Agent Davis, have you spoken to her father? Maybe he knows something."

"I spoke to him at the beginning of our investigation and he'd had little contact with his daughter. But it may be a good idea if I follow up with him. I think I'll also contact Ms. Ryu's half-siblings, perhaps through the American Embassy in South Korea. I don't know if they've ever even heard of her."

• • • •

LILI AND GIL STROLLED along the wide sidewalks of Broadway in Saratoga Springs, while he filled her in on the FBI meeting. It was an unusually pleasant evening in April and a lot of people were out and about.

"That's twice we've encountered the FBI lately." said Lili. "Your case is now two cases. The strange tunnels in Greenfield and a missing genius. If I were the FBI, I'd try to find out where this Roo was getting her money. Somebody must have hired her for something. Tunnel building in Greenfield must have cost quite a bit."

"They say her accounts show no activity. They didn't even have any indication that she was alive until yesterday. So, I don't know how they'd trace money."

"Maybe Karen will find out where they bought the tunnel materials. It sounds like it's rare stuff."

"I'll give her a call tomorrow." Gil was quiet for a minute. "I wonder how Martha's doing. I can't even imagine what her life is like now."

"Yeah, unfortunately I don't have any way of finding out. The US Marshals have her and I'm sure they won't divulge any information, even to the FBI. I can only guess that she's kind of going with the flow. It's not like she has a lot of close ties to people. She always seems to be kind of cheerful, but her friend Barbara getting killed must have been a huge shock."

"I wonder if we'll ever even see her again."

"Maybe we'll find out in Florida next winter."

They found a table at *Boca Bistro* and ordered some wine and a paella to split. "I think I'll go back to Northampton on Friday." said Lili. "When do you think you'll come down?"

"Maybe Sunday. I have an eye appointment Friday and I want to hang out with the kids on Saturday and watch Jazz's gymnastics."

FOURTEEN

L ili was driving through the rain on the Mass Turnpike when the phone rang through her car console. It said 'SA Mayet Elsayed.' "Hello, Mayet."

"Hi Lili. Have you heard from Martha Eames?"

Lili hit the rumble strip in the breakdown lane and quickly recovered. "How could I hear from Martha? She's in WITSEC."

"She's gone," said Mayet. "The US Marshals were compromised. A Marshal guarding her was injured in a shooting, wherever they were staying. They transferred her to another location, but then she disappeared. They didn't catch the shooter."

Lili was stunned. "How could this happen? This is a disaster!"

"I'm sorry. I'm as angry as you must be. But, based on video-surveillance, it seems that Ms. Eames left of her own accord. Do you know where she would go?"

"Well, I think she's very smart. I don't think she'd go home. If I were her, I'd go into that underground railroad of hers."

"That's what I thought. How can I find her there?"

"It's probably more secure than WITSEC. I don't think you could find her there, but we may be able to find out if she entered their network. Based on my understanding, they don't keep track of where anyone ends up. It's a blind system."

"Well, she might try to contact you. If she does, will you let me know, please?"

"If she contacts me, I'll let you know, but I don't think we'll find her. The best I can do is to try and establish a way of leaving her a message. I don't think it would work if the FBI or the US Marshals try to contact her. But I'm her friend. Who could possibly be after her that could compromise the US Marshals?"

. . . . .

LILI WAS BESIDE HERSELF as she continued to drive. *Martha survived a second attempt on her life. The people guarding her were compromised. The US government! So, she's on her own, somewhere. She would have contacted SafeUR. She would have been given a place, a time, and a contact with a false name. She would have been driven to some 'stops along the way,' with different drivers. Ultimately, she would have been delivered to a final destination.*

She would end up in a safe place to live and work to support herself. She doesn't have access to her savings or her Social Security, or whatever other income she previously had. The network must have some way of keeping people from divulging their names to the IRS. False names? Working under the table?

Martha's pretty old. What did she do before she retired? She was a school teacher. She must be taking medications. How would she get those? She could be in Denver, Phoenix, LA, Newark, or anywhere. I don't think I can find her. How can I leave a message for her?

All these thoughts kept rolling around in Lili's head until she got home. She felt exhausted. A glass of red wine with her tuna sandwich helped her to relax a bit. She called Gil and filled him in. He didn't have any great ideas, but he said that maybe Martha would contact her. That might be the only thing she could do. Wait for Martha to contact her.

Lili unpacked and started a load of laundry. She got the mail from her mailbox. It was mostly junk, except for a couple of bank statements and auto-paid bill receipts. Why was she still getting hard copies of electronically paid bills? She'd have to go online and fix those. What a pain. As she went to file her paperwork, she saw the folder on her desk with Martha's DNA test results. She'd promised Martha that she'd have her forensic genealogist, look into it. She texted Jeanie Peridot and asked her if she'd look at a friend's DNA test results to find out who her relatives are.

· · · · ·

GIL AND MIKE STOOD by the wall of the gym, watching Jazz perform her gymnastic events. Gil could see Ziggy and Dez through the large hallway windows fooling around in the building, with Julia keeping a watchful eye. Jazz had a determined look in her eyes as she ran across the floor mat as fast as she could, then launched into a series of cartwheels and roundoffs, some with one hand, some with no hands at all. It made Gil both proud and nervous to watch her flying through the air. She was amazing, better than the other girls her age. Julia was trying to help manage the event, while watching her other kids and trying to catch some of Jazz's routine.

Next, Jazz was up on the balance beam. She did a series of moves followed by an intricate dismount, and she totally stuck the landing! Gil knew how important that was from watching the Olympics every few years. He wondered whose genes Jazz had inherited that enabled her to do these things. Certainly not his. Probably not those of Cynthia, his late wife, either. His memory stirred as he thought about the way Cyn moved so gracefully, but she wasn't the athletic type. His heart ached for her at moments like this.

While Jazz waited for her next event, Gil thought about Martha's predicament. It overwhelmed his mind whenever he thought about it. Two attempts on her life, witness protection compromised, two people shot and killed, and another injured. She's eighty-one years old! And now she's on the run. Poor Lili, all wrapped up in this. She's got to be going crazy. Gil thought that he should be with her for moral support, if nothing else. He'd go to her tomorrow.

• • • •

GIL GOT TO LILI'S HOUSE before lunchtime. He knocked on the door and walked in as he said hello. "We're in here," said Lili.

In the living room, Gil found Lili and a younger woman sitting next to each other on the couch. There was a mess of papers spread out on the coffee table in front of them. Lili popped up and gave Gil a kiss. "This is my friend Jeanie Peridot. She's the forensic genealogist I've told you about." Jeanie blushed and coyly said hi.

Gil got a bit flustered. Jeanie was supermodel-gorgeous. "Oh right. Martha's stuff."

"Yes, I thought I'd get her genealogy looked at, like I promised her."

"I like doing these personal studies as a break from looking for criminals," said Jeanie. "Usually I get lots of old pictures and some old documents to help. But apparently, Martha was adopted as a baby and had no family history that she knew of. Maybe we can find some for her."

"Well, don't let me distract you. I'll just get some water. Can I get you anything to drink?"

"No thanks, we're all set," said Lili. "So, where were we? Oh yeah, Martha said that her maiden name was Stone. She was adopted from an orphanage in England. Gil came back into the living room and sat down to listen.

"Was Stone an adopted surname or her birth surname?"

"I don't remember what she said, exactly. It could be either."

Jeanie typed some notes into her tablet computer. "When I look at the DNA results, the results with the closest matches are from South America, and one from The Netherlands. The matches aren't that close, though. Some have German names and some Spanish or Portuguese. As you said, the results show that she's forty-two percent Jewish and twenty-eight percent Bavarian. A lot of Jewish people have German names. Quite a few German and Jewish people went to South America during and shortly after World War II. What I think I should do first is to upload her DNA results to see if there are matches with the other ancestry DNA companies. We'll see if we can find some more closer matches. That will give us a more thorough picture. Once we get those results, I'll get into record searches and see if we can build her ancestral narrative."

They gathered up the papers and Jeanie got ready to leave. "It'll take me a few weeks to make some progress on this. I'll let you know." Jeanie gave Lili a hug. "It was nice to meet you, Gil."

· · · ·

"YOU GUYS SEEMED VERY cozy on the couch there," said Gil, with a concerned look on his face.

"You're jealous!" said Lili, smiling. She skipped over to Gil and put her arms around his neck. "You have nothing to worry about. I'm a very monogamous person. If I ever wanted to move on, I'd tell you before I did. And, right now, I don't see that happening." She looked at his expression and said, "Jeanie is pretty hot, though, isn't she?"

"Oh yeah."

"She's very into women, though, so you're out of luck."

Lili's phone rang and she began chatting and laughing. Gil scrolled through the latest news on his phone. Lili's call ended and she said, "That was my sister Amy. We've got a wedding to go to next June-ish on Long Island."

"What's Amy like?"

"She's the ultimate material girl. Her husband Phillip is a broker on Wall Street. She's very into lots of makeup and jewelry, stuff like that. She made her daughter Darcy's engagement seem like an impending business merger. She kept going on about her fiancé's family's financial and social status."

"I'm not going to like that."

"Me neither, but they're family. We'll just think of it as a satire. I'm sure the food will be good."

FIFTEEN

Gil was buzzed into the main area of the Greenfield Police Station, where he walked over to Detective Tindall's desk. "Hi, Karen! You really have video of the tunnel people?"

"Pull up a chair. The judge wouldn't sign off on surveillance, so I did the next best thing. I asked the people living adjacent to the tunnels to keep an eye out for suspicious activity out there. Cheryl Needham's son installed a few video cameras around her house. I had to zoom-in the video a lot, so the picture isn't very clear. But watch this."

Gil saw a grainy picture of a person in the woods. He was walking around holding something. They watched for a couple of minutes and Gil asked Karen to zoom out a little. He grinned and said, "I think I know what he's doing. He's dowsing."

"Dowsing?"

"To dowse, a person holds an L-shaped rod in each hand and, when the rods move, they're over a water source, a pipe or conduit, a buried body, or whatever they're looking for. I worked with a guy who used dowsing to find buried pipes or wires before excavating. He swore by it. I think it's a bunch of malarkey, but I actually tried it once with that guy. I walked for a few yards and the rods suddenly moved toward each other. It was creepy. But, I never found out if there was anything under there."

"Well, this video won't get a judge to authorize any surveillance," said Karen. "But what we do know, if these people are, in fact, dowsing, is that they are looking for something under the ground in that area. Why wouldn't they just use a metal detector?"

"Maybe because what they're looking for is either not metallic or buried too deep. If the dowsing gives them responses, they would dig down. If not, they might try using ground-penetrating radar. I don't know anything about buying or using that type of equipment. I'll have to research it. If it's really expensive, these guys may hire another PhD student to make one for them. They seem to have quite a bit of money, based on their tunneling escapades."

"Well, why don't you look into that. I'll put some surveillance on the area and maybe we'll catch these people."

Gil's cell phone rang with a rousing rendition of *By The Beautiful Sea* which made Karen giggle and shake her head. "Hi, Professor. Sure. Hold on, can I put you on speaker? I have Detective Tindall with me." He fumbled with his phone for a few seconds. "Okay, so you say you have information on the tunneling method?"

"Yes. Professor Clive Fassbender from the Colorado School of Mines sent me some information. He said that the people you're after probably used a small boring machine of a type used quite routinely. The machine would have a rotating head that bores through soil and rocks. Water is pumped into the head of the machine which mixes with the soil and crushed rocks and is pumped out the back as a slurry. He said that it's unusual to use an expandable mesh tunnel material. He'd never heard of that. He also said that tunneling along the sewer piping was a smart thing to do because that soil would have been previously excavated and back-filled, making it easy to tunnel through. I'll email you the information he sent me. I hope this helps."

"I'm sure it'll help, Professor. There couldn't be too many of these boring machines around here," said Gil.

"Thank you so much, Professor. You've been very helpful," said Karen.

Gil ended the call. "I'll look through the material he sent over. I'm curious about those machines. I wonder how they steer them."

"That's funny. I'm not the slightest bit interested in those boring machines."

"You can't make dad jokes, you're a mom."

"By the way, you and Lili are invited to dinner at Eddie Locke's place tonight. Lili has all the details." Eddie Locke was an old high school classmate of Gil's.

"That sounds like fun. Is he still dating Pam Leone from our last case?"

"As far as I know, he is. So, how was it shacking up in Florida with Lili?"

"It was a little surrealistic. Sometimes it felt like I was with Cynthia, then suddenly I'd realize I was with a stranger. Other times it felt like I'd been married to Lili for years. We were definitely thrown into a mode of getting used to each other's idiosyncrasies very quickly."

"What idiosyncrasies?"

Suddenly Gil started moving his arms up and down saying, "Danger Will Robinson! Danger Will Robinson!"

Karen looked at him like he was crazy.

"Sorry. That's from my generation. It was from an old kid's show called *Lost in Space*. Whenever the boy in the show, Will Robinson, was about to get into trouble, his robot pal would launch into that warning. Anyway, I'd have to be crazy to start telling you what I think are Lili's idiosyncrasies."

Karen grinned. "I guess you are a smart guy, just like the Chief says."

· · · ·

GIL AND LILI ARRIVED at Eddie Locke's place at 6:00. It was an attractive ranch-style house with dark brown cedar siding. As they approached the front door, they were surprised to find it to be made of stainless steel, with no apparent door knob. As Gil was about to knock, the door automatically opened with a hiss. The top half of the door slid up and the bottom half slid down. They looked at each other, shrugged, then walked in. They were shocked.

The entire living space looked like the inside of a spaceship from a science-fiction movie. The walls, ceilings, and floors were shiny gray and cream colored. All the wall and ceiling corners were curved. The furnishings were ultra-modern, and most were attached to the floors and walls, with leather cushions in muted colors. The television was an enormous screen that took up a whole wall of the living room. Another entire wall was comprised of an aquarium filled with colorful fish, some up to a foot in length.

Eddie approached and said, "Welcome aboard, Gil! You remember my friend Pam?" Eddie and Pam were wearing matching coveralls.

"Yes, of course. Hi Pam. This is Lili, whom you may remember."

"Of course, hi! We're so glad you could come."

"Eddie, your house is unreal!" said Gil. "I've never seen anything like it, except in the movies." He handed Eddie a bottle of wine.

"Thanks, buddy! This style is typical of the living quarters on my starship. Oh, I almost forgot." Eddie went over to a tablet computer that was built into his kitchen island and turned on some new-age music.

Lili was enthralled. She walked around looking at the curious collection of house plants and artwork. A woman's voice out of nowhere said, "Approaching." A view of people walking toward the front door appeared on the video screen. The door opened with a hiss, and Micky Tindall walked in with his wife Jane. Karen and her husband Jeff followed along. Karen's father-in-law, Micky, was also a classmate of Gil and Eddie's. There were hugs and greetings all around.

Eddie said, "We've made some special drinks for you tonight. The blue and green ones are alcoholic and the pink one is lemonade. Please help yourselves to some hors-d'oeuvres over at the Science Station." The brightly colored drinks in glass pitchers matched the futuristic theme of the house. Even the appetizers looked futuristic, with perfectly cut sandwich wedges of salmon surrounded by cream cheese and stripes of sliced cucumbers, circles of bread topped with spirals of thinly-sliced avocado, and small cones of bread filled with chicken salad and cranberry sauce.

Gil brought Lili a blue drink, while he stuck with the pink lemonade. She took a sip and flipped her hand open by her head, the universal sign of her head exploding. "This drink is sweet, tangy, and loaded with alcohol. I think the blue is Curaçao liqueur, which tastes orangy. If I drink more than one of these, I'll be lost in space."

Karen came over to them and looked around to make sure nobody could hear them. "Lili, have you heard anything from your friend in Witness Protection?"

"There was another attempt on her life! Her guard was shot and she took off. Nobody's heard from her since."

"You have got to be kidding! Somebody found her in WITSEC? How is that even possible?"

"I have no idea. I'm hoping she'll contact me, somehow. Though, I'm not sure what I'd tell her if she does."

"Either they were tracking her the whole time since she entered the program, or the US Marshals are compromised at some level," said Karen. "Neither scenario seems plausible."

"She could have tried to contact a friend, but she doesn't seem to have any around here, especially since her neighbor was killed. Her Florida friends haven't heard from her. She doesn't have any close family either."

Gil said, "The whole situation is even more bizarre than tunnels under Greenfield, and definitely scarier." Gil saw Eddie talking to Micky, so he went over to join the conversation. "Hi Mick."

"Hi Gil, do you remember Alice Hayes?" asked Micky.

"A little. She really wasn't in any of my classes."

"Well, after high school, she worked as a stripper at Burgo's Tavern in Sunderland. She just retired as the CEO of a big cosmetics company in New Jersey."

"So, we should encourage more girls to get that sort of work experience as a pathway to success?" asked Eddie.

"I really don't think that's a good idea, but good for Alice." said Gil.

"So, what's up with the mysterious tunnels?" asked Micky.

"I think that they may be examples of quantum tunneling. Created by advanced beings from another dimension," said Eddie.

"Well, I'll have to add that to our list of possibilities. But, I can't really talk about an ongoing investigation," said Gil.

"Excuse me, gentlemen," said Eddie. "I have to help get dinner ready to serve."

Pam requested that everyone refresh their drinks and make their way to the dinner table. The dining room had subdued, bluish lighting and, in the middle of the table, lay a large, cream-colored hemisphere. Pam pressed a button on the wall, and the top of the hemisphere lifted, casting white lights onto the tabletop. Suddenly, the sides slid out in segments, like oranges slices. The segments lowered to the floor, becoming the chairs. The table and chairs had purple accent lighting underneath.

After the women had decided where everyone should sit, they all sat down. Eddie and Pam brought out platters that contained matrices of cube-shaped foods. Each platter held different colored cubes, and each cube was about three inches on each edge. The platters were labeled: green cubes were broccoli and spinach, white were rice, orange were sweet potatoes, and there were also chicken, beef, and salmon cubes.

As people took food and passed around the platters, Eddie explained, "That's the way they come out of the food synthesizers."

"Well, actually that's the way they come from a company called SQUAREAT in Miami," said Pam. "We had a friend ship them to us in a refrigerated truck."

Lili tried a green cube. "It's really good!"

"They are all nutritionally balanced portions that are easy to store and last for two weeks in the fridge," said Pam.

"And the farm is very neat and compact, with a variety of square animals, birds, and plants." said Eddie. The guests chuckled.

"Well, I guess were all getting a square meal today," said Jane. There were a few groans in response to that comment, but the table had a constant buzz of excitement as people tried the variety of food cubes.

As everyone finished their meals, Gil and Micky helped clear the dishes. Pam and Eddie brought several trays of futuristic-looking pastries to the table. They were all very colorful in cylinder, triangle, and cone shapes. Pam went around offering scoops of vanilla ice cream.

"Oh, these are fabulous!" said Karen. Where did you get them?"

"I went to a wedding cake designer in Northampton, said Pam. She's a friend of mine."

"This is the most interesting dinner I've ever had in my life," said Gil. "It's been wonderful." Everybody chimed in to agree.

After dinner, some opted for another drink, but more opted for coffee. Gil, Lili, and Karen were chatting with Pam. Eddie called for everyone's attention. "I would like to thank you all for coming. I hope you've enjoyed my star cruiser, but I'd like you to consider this. Earth is really just a spacecraft hurtling through space at unimaginable speed. We've been lucky enough to be safe from the dangerous space environment by residing within our atmosphere. Unfortunately, we've been polluting our atmosphere at increasing rates for the past couple of hundred years. Hopefully we will soon remedy that situation and survive. If not, earth will continue to hurtle through space without us. Thank you." Everyone clapped.

SIXTEEN

Sergeant Dwayne Phillips parked his cruiser in the small parking lot off Mountain Road in Greenfield. He got out of the SUV, paused, and listened to the sounds of the night. It was cold out and very quiet, except for the occasional rustle of leaves. Probably mice, he thought. Phillips took a hard-case out of the back seat and set up a small drone and its remote controller. This drone had infrared imaging and he had tested it once at night, but he hadn't yet used it in the field. On such a quiet night, he was concerned that he might spook the object of his surveillance. He decided to fly it at an altitude of 400 feet to minimize the noise and maximize the view.

He launched the drone straight up into the air and, when it was up to altitude, he could barely hear it. He moved it slowly north, toward Cheryl Needham's house, as he scrutinized the image on the controller. He lowered it to 300 feet over her house and looked more closely. Nothing. He raised it back up to 400 feet and moved it slowly to the west, toward Pond and Oak Streets. There! He saw a hint of red by the woods on Oak Street. He hovered over it and lowered the drone to 300 feet. A fox.

Phillips raised the drone back up to 400 feet and moved it slowly to the east, back toward his parking lot. There! A person in the woods just east of Parkway Street. He grabbed the radio mic from his shoulder and said, "This is Phillips. I'm doing drone surveillance on Mountain Rd. I need a unit to Parkway Street, halfway between Crescent Street and Highland Pond, quiet approach. I'm observing one suspect on the hill to the east of the road. Suspected to be involved in the tunneling caper. Suspect not expected to be armed or dangerous."

After a few seconds, Russ at dispatch said, "I have unit four headed over with Voorhees and Gorski. They should be there in a couple of minutes."

A minute later, Phillips observed the cruiser approaching slowly from the north, the wrong way down Parkway, which was a one-way dirt road. They had their spotlight on. "Unit four, Phillips. Suspect is about thirty more yards on the left, about twenty yards into the woods." Suddenly, the suspect took off. "Unit four, suspect is running to the north. Behind you now. I lost visual. There he is. He just crossed Parkway and is headed west toward Chestnut Hill."

"This is Voorhees, I sent Gorski into the woods. I'm driving over to Chestnut Hill."

Phillips watched Gorski run into the woods toward Chestnut Hill. He lowered the drone for a better view, but he lost the suspect. He increased the drone's altitude, but still couldn't see him. He observed the cruiser heading up Chestnut Hill. The cruiser reached the street's dead end. Voorhees jumped out of the vehicle and headed into the woods. A minute later, the two officers met in the woods and searched the area. Shortly thereafter, they ran back toward the cruiser. "We lost him. He's not here.

"I don't see him on the drone, either."

The officers left the woods. "Ouch!" said Gorski. He shined his light at this feet, revealing that he'd kicked a storm drain grate that had been moved from its basin. "I think he went into the sewer."

"You need to drive around to find where he comes out," said Phillips. "I'm coming down to help search."

Phillips retrieved the drone, put the equipment back into his cruiser, and drove to the patrol unit. Voorhees and Gorski found two more grates out of place on Highland Avenue. "I think we lost him," said Gorski. "Whoever he is, he's pretty clever."

• • • •

PHILLIPS PHONED KAREN. "I'm pretty sure this guy got away by now. I'll just have patrol make sure all the storm drains are covered."

"In the morning, we'll look at your drone footage and the storm-drain map again," said Karen. "Maybe we can figure out what he was doing."

• • • •

KAREN AND GIL WERE drinking coffee and staring at the storm-drain map in the conference room. Karen pointed at the map and said, "According to Dwayne, they found a grate removed from here on Chestnut Hill, and two over here on Highland Avenue," said Karen. Why do you have a confused look on your face?"

"There's something strange about the drain system arrangement. Mostly, the storm drain piping follows the roads, which I'd expect. But then there are some places where there are extra pipes, extra manholes, and some pipes that directly cross properties at unexpected angles. I'm wondering why. I almost seem to remember something about that. I'll ask the engineer, Rona Polo. Do you have her number?"

Gil made a quick call to Rona, who she said she'd find out and get back to him.

"I'm going to have someone search the area along Parkway Street with a metal detector and see if we can find anything," said Karen.

"Lili suggested that we search the new tunnels more closely and look for evidence," said Gil. "Let's start with the one on Oak Street."

• • • •

GIL SET UP DANICA AND steered her down the manhole at the end of Oak Street. He guided the robot, slowly moving her in a zig-zag path to carefully search the entire floor of the tunnel. At first, the tunnel's floor was dense clay, and very rocky. After a while, there was a transition to soft soil with only a few rocks. He thought it must be construction backfill from laying the sewer pipes, as the mining professor had mentioned. He steered Danica all the way to the cellar wall at the Arch Street Salon. Nothing. He inspected the dead-end tunnels as well. As he steered the robot back toward the entrance, Karen called out, "Wait, stop. What's that?" Danica moved forward a few feet and turned to one side. "It looks like a stone, but it's greenish."

Gil fumbled around a bit trying to grasp the stone with the robot's arm, and he finally got it. He had the robot release the item in a small plastic bin he'd installed. He steered Danica back out to the manhole and lifted her out. "It looks like an old piece of metal," he said. "We'll have to clean it up and see what it is."

Karen put on a rubber glove, snatched the item out of Gil's hand, and dropped it into an evidence bag. "I'll send it to the crime lab."

SEVENTEEN

Gil met Lili in Northampton to play some pickleball. It was chilly out and threatening to rain. They volleyed a bit to warm up, then they started a singles game until another couple showed up. Gil invited them to play and they all introduced themselves. Sue and Rich Fontaine were retirees who'd moved to a condo in town several years ago.

After Sue and Rich warmed up, they played girls against the guys. It was a lively game, but the girls prevailed. While they were taking a break, Gil found a message from Rona Polo on his phone, so he called her back. "Hi Rona, did you find anything?"

"Hi Gil. I actually found something interesting. The storm-drain system isn't just for stormwater. It encompasses several brooks running through the town. They were buried during the 1800s, as the town developed. The storm-water and the brooks all drain into the Green River."

"Huh, I remember something about that. When I was a kid, the field behind the junior high school had a sinkhole. My teacher told us that a culvert collapsed. A brook was flowing under the field through a series of culverts. It was called Graves Brook because way back in the pioneer days, a couple of settlers were killed by Indians and buried there."

"There is a Graves Brook on the map, but that's up by Highland Pond. The biggest brook is called Maple Brook. Also, Cherry Rum Brook is partially covered with culverts, but isn't connected to the system."

"Do you have a map that shows the brooks?"

"Sure. I'll send it through to Karen."

Lili poked Gil in the ribs and told him to hang up and get back to the game.

• • • •

A STEADY RAIN WAS FALLING by the time they got back to Lili's house. Gil followed Lili into the house and called Karen. "Did Rona send you a new map?" he asked.

"Yes, she did. What's it for?"

"It turns out that the storm-drain system was also used to accommodate the flow of several brooks in town. The brooks were buried to accommodate the town's development. One of the brooks was called Graves Brook because a couple of settlers were buried there after being killed by Indians. Maybe the tunnelers were looking for the graves?"

"That's a lot of effort and expense to find old graves." said Karen.

"Maybe they think the dead guys had something of value. I'll look into it."

"The object we pulled out of the tunnel looks like a button. The lab x-rayed it. They're soaking it in an acid solution overnight so we can get a better look at it. I don't think it belongs to our culprits, though. Maybe it's from those graves."

"Yeah, maybe it's cursed!"

• • • •

LILI HAD A MISCHIEVOUS smile on her face. "Martha sent me a message!"

"How?"

"There was a small note taped to the window above the kitchen sink that said, 'Back Porch.' I opened the back door and there was a blank envelope between the back door and the screen door."

"What did the message say?"

"WITSEC not safe. Someone tried to kill me again. I still have no idea why anyone is after me. I'm safe in my network and having a good time. If you want to contact me, please be careful. Assume you are being watched. Then she explained how I could send her a message."

"That's very helpful. I'm glad she's okay."

"I have to figure out what to do with this. I'm not sure if I should tell the FBI."

"What was that FBI agent's name?"

"Elsayed. Mayet Elsayed."

"If you called Agent Elsayed and told her about Martha's message, do you think that would put Martha in more danger?"

"Well, the US Marshals are definitely compromised. Martha was with them when they were attacked. Whoever is after her had a link into at least one branch of the Federal Government. The FBI could be compromised, too. There's no reason to think that Special Agent Elsayed is compromised, because she wouldn't have had any links to the US Marshals. We know she already assumes that Martha is in her underground railroad. Maybe I'll call Mayet and just tell her that I am able to contact Martha, but I can't tell her how. What do you think?"

"I think that's a better plan than not calling her. You should hide or get rid of Martha's message, though. What if someone breaks in and finds it? Wait, come to think of it, what if your house is bugged?"

Lili's eyes went wide and she slapped her hand over her mouth. She grabbed a pad of notepaper and wrote, *"Get your stuff, we're getting out of here!"* They quickly gathered up their clothes and toiletries and left in Gil's car. Lili used a notepad to write down some key phone numbers from both of their phones, after which she removed the batteries. They drove to Walmart and bought four prepaid phones.

Lili called Special Agent Elsayed. "Hello, this is Agent Lili D'Amico regarding the Martha Eames case."

"Yes, how are you, Lili?"

"Right now, I'm worried that I could have put myself and my boyfriend in danger. I just received a note from Martha and I read it out loud to my boyfriend, Gil Novak. He asked what if my house was bugged, and I realized that I'd never considered that. We left my house in Gil's car, and I took the batteries out of our phones. I'm using a prepaid phone right now. Have you checked your phone?"

"Supposedly, my phone cannot be compromised, but I'll double check. What did Ms. Eames say?"

"She says she feels safe in her network. She also told me how to contact her, which I prefer not to share with you."

Agent Elsayed paused for a few seconds and said, "I think that's okay, given the circumstances. If your house is bugged, would anyone who was listening have heard you say how to contact Ms. Eames?"

"No, I haven't told anyone."

"Would it be okay if I have your house and car checked for surveillance equipment?"

"Yes please. What about my phone?"

"Is it a work phone from the State Police?"

"Yes."

"Why don't you talk to your boss and see if that can be arranged. If we find that you've been under surveillance, we can check your boyfriend's house, car, and phone, as well. It might be good if you told somebody else how to contact Martha in case you become unable to."

EIGHTEEN

Lili and Gil spent the night in a beautiful bed & breakfast in Amherst. They were close to the city center which allowed them to walk to dinner and enjoy the evening. The following morning, Gil dropped Lili off at the Crime Lab in Springfield, since she had to work. Before he drove away, Lili ran back out and asked him to come into the lab. Morgan, one of the young technicians showed them the item they had retrieved from the tunnel. She said, "It's a brass button, but a very strange one. I've never seen anything like it. It looks like it was made from a spiral of brass rod."

"Can we get an expert from UMass to identify it?" asked Gil.

Lili said, "Since this probably isn't related to the crime being investigated, we could have Gil chase that down, right?" Morgan nodded and plopped it into Gil's hand.

"No problem. I'll head over to the campus."

Morgan started typing into her computer and said, "Hold on a minute." She searched with an expression of extreme focus. "It looks like the experts on colonial artifacts in this area would be from the UConn Department of Anthropology. Let me print you a list of faculty there."

• • • •

IT TOOK GIL LESS THAN an hour to drive down to the University of Connecticut. He had an appointment to meet with a Dr. Scrumm in Beach Hall. He found the Department of Anthropology and asked around, finding the lab where Dr. Scrumm could be found. There were several people in the lab, so he called Dr. Scrumm's name. A woman raised her hand while looking at a rusty piece of metal on her table. She had a large shock of frizzy red hair that was haphazardly scrunched in the middle.

"Hi Dr. Scrumm, I'm Gil Novak."

"Hi Gil, I'm Delilah. Please call me Dee. What have you got for me?" She spoke with a British accent.

Gil pulled out the evidence bag with the button in it and handed it to her.

Her eyes lit up. "An evidence bag from the Mass State Police?"

"I'm a consultant with the Police Department in Greenfield, Mass. We've been investigating some mysterious tunnels that have recently been excavated from people's cellars in Greenfield. I sent a robot down one of the tunnels, and we pulled out a lump of green metal. The State Police Crime Lab in Springfield soaked it in acid overnight and found this, which they think is a brass button."

"They are correct, it is a brass button. I've read about these, but I've never seen one. This is a homemade replacement button from someone's coat. It's made from a brass long pin. Long pins like this were used in the textile industry, mainly in the seventeenth century. Greenfield, you said?"

"Yes."

"The pin is crude and was probably made in the Jenks factory in Lynn, Mass, but it could have come over from England. What were these tunnels used for?"

"We have no idea. They don't really lead anywhere."

"Interesting! When you're done with the button, you may want to offer it to the Historic Deerfield Museum. I'll give you a signed summary of my findings so you can present it to the museum. What kind of robot did you use?"

"I built a remote-controlled robot from a tank-like chassis and added a camera and a collection arm, so far. I'm a retired robotics engineer."

"Ooh, can I get your contact info? We may want to engage your services at some point, if that's okay. Our engineering department is usually too busy for us."

• • • •

AS GIL WAS DRIVING back to Northampton, his phone rang on the dash. It was Kenny Tran, a reporter from the Greenfield Recorder. "Hi Kenny!"

"Hi Gil, how are you doing?"

"I'm great. How are you?"

"I'm good, too. I'd like to interview you about your pursuit of the mole people."

"The mole people? Oh brother. I'll have to ask Detective Tindall about that."

"I've already spoken with her. She'll okay it, so go ahead and ask. How about lunch on me?"

"Sure. If Karen says okay, how about 12:30. I'm driving up from Connecticut right now."

"Alright, so how about Bistro 63 in Amherst?"

"Since it's in Amherst, I can meet you at noon. See you there."

• • • •

GIL WALKED INTO THE restaurant and saw Kenny waving to him from a table in the back. Gil shook Kenny's hand and said, "You were right, Karen said I could talk to you about my part of the investigation."

A server came and took their drink orders. Gil ordered lemonade and Kenny ordered iced tea.

"How did you get involved in this investigation?"

"Detective Tindall called me and asked if I could make a robot to help them explore some mysterious tunnels. She asked because she knows that I am a retired robotics engineer."

"What kind of robot did you make?"

"I started with a commercially available chassis that has tank-like treads on it. Then I added a control system and a video-camera with a light. Later on, I added a robotic arm and a container for evidence collection. I'll show it to you after lunch. It's in my car."

The server brought their drinks and took their orders. Gil ordered the Thai chicken wrap and Kenny ordered the shrimp and avocado bowl.

"So far, I've collected a small, green lump of material which was sent to the Massachusetts State Crime Lab in Springfield. They x-rayed it, then cleaned it up, and it turned out to be an unusual-looking brass button with a spiral shape. I brought the button to the University of Connecticut's Department of Anthropology. They identified it as a homemade button made from a long pin made in the seventeenth century. The pin was likely made in Lynn. Here it is."

Kenny took a picture of it with his phone. He also snapped a picture of Gil. "So, what does this evidence tell you?"

"We don't consider this evidence related to the investigation. It was just a random finding from a town that was settled in the seventeenth century."

"What will happen to the brass button?"

"That's up to the police. I will recommend that it go to the museum at Old Deerfield."

"Anything else you want to add? I don't have any more questions."

"Nothing on that. Have you done any followup with Susan Rasmussen and Pam Leone from our last case?"

"Not yet. I have it in my calendar to inquire after a year from that ordeal. Have you talked to them?"

The server brought their meals and they started to eat. "I saw Pam the other day at a dinner party and she seemed happy. How are things going at the Recorder?"

"Things are good. I always thought that this gig would be a stepping-stone to a job with a bigger news outlet. But my wife and I are really happy living and working in this area. It's a great place to raise our kids."

After lunch, Gil set up his robot and Kenny took a few more pictures.

· · · ·

GIL SET UP AN APPOINTMENT to meet that afternoon with someone from the Historical Society of Greenfield. He walked into the small museum and introduced himself to a woman about his age, who was wearing a dark-green Victorian-era dress with a white bonnet. "Hello, I'm Veronica. Ned will be meeting with us in a minute."

"I'm Gil. You didn't have to dress up just to meet with me."

"Oh, I always dress like this." Gil scrutinized her, trying to tell if she was serious. Ned shuffled through the doorway, a puffy man with long, gray hair and denim overalls. "Gil, this is Ned. A police investigation, you said?"

"Yes. Have you heard about the mysterious tunnels recently found in Greenfield?"

"Oh, right, the mole people. How can we help with that?"

"I'm interested in any information you may have about the brooks that run through the town."

"Well, there's Cherry Rum Brook, over by Four Corners School," said Ned.

"Yes, I know about that one. I wonder why it's called Cherry Rum. But, I'm most interested in the brooks that are now buried under the town. I grew up in Greenfield, and when I was a kid, a sink hole opened up in the field behind the Junior High School. My teacher told our class about a brook that ran under the town called Graves Brook. He said that some men were killed by Indians there."

"Huh. Let me find some of our older maps," said Veronica. She pulled out a large box and started leafing through what looked like some very old maps.

Ned started leafing through an old book. "By the way, our Junior High School is now called the Middle School and our town is now a city."

"Oh right, sorry." Gil wandered around looking at an exhibit on transportation that showed street cars in the town. He'd never heard of that.

"Here we go," said Veronica. "Here's a map from 1871 that shows the brook you're talking about in great detail. I've never even heard of this. Unfortunately, this map doesn't label the brook at all." She rummaged around some more and said, "Here's one from 1830. It has your brook labeled as Gray Brook." Gil looked at the map, but it wasn't as detailed as the first.

"Let me do a computer search." She opened a laptop computer and got to work while Gil wandered around the museum.

"Jackpot!" said Ned. "I've found a passage that mentions your brook. It explains that it's called Graves Brook because three men killed by Indians in 1724 were buried where they fell, next to the brook. That would have been part of Dummer's War. It was named after a Massachusetts politician named William Dummer." Gil struggled not to make a crack about the name, as he hadn't yet detected any sense of humor.

Veronica said, "I've found a few newspaper articles. This one says it's called Graves Brook because a man named Graves was killed and buried there. That's kind of hard to believe. This article says it's been called Graves, Grave, and Grays Brook in various deeds in town, and that later it was called Maple Brook. Another article says that an unnamed stream by Lincoln Street combines with a stream fed by a large spring up in Highland Park to form Graves Brook. The spring at Highland Park is where the town got its water supply."

"Well, that's all good information. I think you've found enough for me, for now. Could I get a copy of that 1871 map that shows the brook in pretty good detail?"

"If you give me your email, I'll send you all of these things, and I'll see if I can find some more." said Veronica. "Now, could I interest you both in a cup of tea?"

NINETEEN

Gil picked Lili up from work. She had a grim look on her face. "Rough day?"

"I don't want to talk about it. Should we stop for dinner? How about Thai food?"

"How about something else? I had Thai for lunch."

"Then let's go to Johnny's Tavern in Amherst." Lili was texting on her phone. "Mayet is in town to see me, so I invited her to dinner. How was the Greenfield Historical Museum?"

"Well it definitely had a quaint vibe. I was met by Veronica and Ned. Veronica was wearing a Victorian dress and bonnet. I told her she shouldn't have dressed up just for me and she said she always dresses like that."

"That's unusual. What about Ned?"

"He was dressed like a farmer. They were both very helpful and gave me some good info about the brook that runs under Greenfield. It has several names, but I don't think most people in town even know it exists."

Lili put the radio on. It was an oldies station with music from the seventies and eighties. They listened to a series of songs by Paul McCartney and Wings. Gil parked in a public lot and they walked to the tavern. When they went in, a young woman waved to Lili and they went over to her table. "Gil, this is Special Agent Elsayed."

"Hi Gil, please call me Mayet. Dinner's on me tonight. Lili probably told you that her house and car were bugged." Gil's jaw dropped.

"Actually, I didn't get the chance to tell him yet because we were in his car. I didn't want any potential listeners to hear that we know about the bugs. The guys at work checked my phone and it's okay."

"Well, this is why I wanted to meet with you," said Mayet. There was also a tracking device in Lili's car. Rather than removing the listening and tracking devices, I'd like you to consider using them to set a trap for whoever is listening." A mischievous grin spread on Gil's face, but Lili looked concerned. "Gil, I would like permission to inspect your house, car, and phone for listening and tracking devices. I can check your car and phone before we leave here and have our Albany office check your house tomorrow."

A server stopped by and took their drink orders. Mayet and Lili ordered iced teas and Gil ordered a ginger ale.

"What kind of trap did you have in mind?" asked Gil.

• • • •

AFTER DINNER, LILI and Gil drove to Lili's house in Northampton. They went in and Lili said, "I'm so tired tonight.".

"Yeah, me too."

Lili's phone dinged. "Uh-oh, no rest for the weary. Rita texted me to see if I could get Martha's heart medicine tonight. Metoprolol. She ran out."

"What drug store?"

"The CVS on Main Street. It won't take long. I guess I'll go before I get settled. It looks like they're open till ten." Lili put a bulletproof vest on under her jacket and holstered her gun.

Lili drove to CVS. She went in and looked around, but didn't see anyone who looked suspicious. She walked over to the pharmacy counter and asked for Martha Eames' prescription. An FBI agent, posing as a pharmacy tech said, "This will take about ten minutes."

"I'll wait, thanks." Lili roamed around and picked up a few things she needed.

After a few minutes, an FBI agent called out "Martha Eames."

Lili paid and walked out of the pharmacy with her purchases, including a bottle of pills. She hadn't seen anyone suspicious in the store. As she drove out to a house on Lyman Road, the microphone in her ear said, "You've picked up a tail. It's a dark Kia Sorento." Lili turned into the driveway, parked, and approached the front door. Through the window, she could see Mayet sitting in the living room along with someone convincingly made up to look like Martha. Mayet opened the door and let Lili in. While they pretended to have a jovial chat, Mayet said, "The people following you drove past the house, turned around and parked within sight. I'm guessing that they'll wait until we're asleep to raid the house and kill Agent Ruhle. We have two more agents inside the house and four more outside."

"Please call me when it's done," said Lili. She left the house and drove home.

• • • •

LILI'S CELL PHONE BUZZED and lit up on her night stand. Both she and Gil sat up and she answered. "D'Amico."

"Lili, this is Mayet. Two men and a woman broke into the house. The woman opened fire and was killed. One of the men killed himself with a cyanide capsule. We have the other man in custody. He hasn't said anything, not even that he wants a lawyer. He seems to be foreign. There was no ID on any of them, so we're checking their prints."

Assuming someone might still be listening to the house, Lili simply said, "Thanks for the call."

"All is good with my people. Thanks for your help on this. We'll come and get the bugs from your house and car in the morning."

TWENTY

Gil and Karen met up with Special Agent Davis in Troy, New York. "Special Agent Davis, this is Detective Tindall," said Gil. Karen wasn't wearing her uniform, for a change.

Davis shook Karen's hand and said, "Your request to talk to Ms. Ryu's roommates was unexpected, but maybe they'll be more forthcoming with you." He knocked on the door of an off-campus row house.

A young man with bushy hair answered the door. "Hello Ira," said Davis.

Ira yelled into the house, "The Feds are here!" He led them into the living room and motioned for them to sit on the couch. The house was surprisingly clean for a college apartment, thought Gil. Another young man and a young woman came downstairs. Ira sat in the comfy chair while the others pulled over dining room chairs and sat down. Davis showed them his credentials, again. "This is Detective Karen Tindall from the Police Department in Greenfield, Massachusetts, and this is Gil Novak, a police consultant." Karen showed her badge. "Karen and Gil would like to ask you some more questions about Katrina Ryu, if that's okay."

"Could you give me your names, please?"

"I'm Ira Lapoff, this is Chenille Kenning, and this is Trey Fasig."

"Are you all architecture students?" asked Gil.

"I am," said Chenille. Ira's a double-E and Trey's a computer software engineer."

"Let me tell you a little about why we're interested in Katrina," said Karen. "In Greenfield, Massachusetts, we've discovered several mysterious tunnels that appear to have been created by people who unlawfully entered and modified the cellars of several residences. These tunnels were reinforced using unusual structures that were traced back to Katrina. The tunnels themselves are a minor matter, but we're hoping they will help us find Katrina."

"Are you talking about Roo's Slinkys?" asked Chenille.

Gil smiled and said, "Yes, they do look like very complex Slinkys. But the tunnels were dug using sophisticated machinery. Does Katrina have any friends who would have the equipment to dig those tunnels?"

"Roo doesn't really have friends," said Trey. She just sort of searches out people whose expertise she can use and connects with them."

"Internationally, even," said Chenille. "She's published papers that had collaborations from people in several different countries. Denmark, Chile, Australia, wherever the experts happened to be."

"Anything specifically about digging tunnels?" asked Gil, again. The sudents looked at each other and shrugged.

"Do any of you know where Katrina got her money?" asked Karen.

"I think she hit up her father for some money," said Ira. "She was depressed about it one day, so she was drinking alcohol, which I'd never seen her do before."

"Could we look at her room?" asked Karen. "Does she still have a room here?"

"I still get a check every month that pays her share of the rent," said Ira. "It's an auto-paid check from her bank."

Chenille led Karen, Gil, and Davis up to Katrina's room. There wasn't much in it. Some clothes, a lot of books, some miniature tunnel models, and a few posters and pictures of Roo, the cartoon character from *Winnie-The-Pooh*. "Did the FBI take anything from her room?" asked Karen.

"There was nothing of much interest to take, but we retrieved some dental floss from her waste basket to get her DNA, in case something bad happened," said Davis. Chenille stifled a moan.

"Did you access her emails and social media?" asked Karen.

"We looked at her public social media presence, which wasn't much. We didn't get a warrant to search anything else, because there isn't really evidence of any crime. It looks like she left of her own accord. It's strange that her father didn't tell us about funding her tunnel project. I'll have to revisit that."

"Our crime isn't sufficient to get a warrant, either," said Karen. "But that's what it'll take to find her, I think," said Karen. "At this point, I'm mostly interested in making sure Katrina is safe."

•   •   •   •

AFTER HAVING A NICE lunch at the Triangle Diner in Saratoga, Karen dropped Gil off back at his house. Fortunately, his house, car, and phone were not bugged. As she was leaving, she told Gil that she wanted to do a more thorough inspection of the tunnels, so Gil thought of some more gizmos he could add to his robot. He spent a couple of hours ordering parts online, after which he decided to head to the gym.

Gil went to Planet Fitness at the Wilton Mall. In Florida, he didn't go to a gym because he was active enough with walking, bike riding, and kayaking. He realized that he'd better take it easy getting back into his gym routine. He preferred to start with strength exercises, and he used the machines rather than the free weights. As a precaution, he decided to use lower weight settings than he'd used the year before.

After half an hour, he moved over to aerobics. He preferred to use an elliptical machine. Last year, he would typically do forty-five minutes, but today he'd start with half an hour. He put on his earbuds and listened to an eclectic mix of music from his phone while he was exercising. He also mindlessly watched the closed-caption televisions on the wall. He settled on a baking show where they were creating something called maamoul cookies, which he'd never heard of. He decided that he wasn't really interested in baking cookies.

By the time he was finished, he was dripping with sweat, but he definitely felt good.

TWENTY-ONE

L ili had been on edge all day at work. She'd thought that her work routine would have calmed her down, but it hadn't. If the people after Martha are professional soldiers, and are willing to die in their pursuit, how safe is Lili? They know where she lives, where she works, and what kind of car she drives. She went in to talk to her boss, Cherise Holmes. "I think I need to take some time off and disappear for a while. I'm really worried that these guys looking for Martha could come after me for information. They're hard-core soldier types, willing to die to get to her."

"Do you want to go into government protection?"

"Whoever is behind this has already compromised that system. They shot a US Marshal who was guarding Martha while she was in WITSEC. Martha's gone into hiding on her own. I think I need to disappear on my own for a while. If I'm not around, I'm hoping they'll forget about me."

"Okay, but if you need anything at all, call me. How about if we set up a process for you to let me know you're okay once a day. If you miss a day, I'll send the cavalry, if I know where to send them."

· · · ·

LILI PACKED HER SUITCASE and backpack. She then took a taxi to the Peter Pan bus terminal. She entered the terminal, went out the side door and found an ATM, where she withdrew a good amount of cash. She then walked over to the Academy of Music and boarded a regional bus to Springfield. After two bus changes and a few hours of travel, she arrived in Saratoga Springs. Gil picked her up in front of The Parting Glass Tavern.

Gil was worried about Lili's state of mind, as much as the risk of an attack. "I'm not sure how I can get you to relax."

"Feed me."

Gil smiled. "Well, I can certainly feed you." They went for dinner at the nearby Mouzon House restaurant. The server introduced himself as James and asked for their drink orders. Lili ordered a pinot grigio and Gil ordered cranberry juice with seltzer.

"I think I feel much better just leaving Northampton and coming here," said Lili. "Maybe I'm safer here. These people didn't bug your house or car. They haven't taken an interest in you so far, but they could. Gil, do you know how to use a gun?"

"I learned to use a twenty-two caliber rifle at Camp Apex when I was a kid," said Gil. "We shot at little paper targets, and I was a pretty good shot. I guess I've always relied on law-enforcement people to protect me and my family. I think there are too many guns around these days, especially with all of the nut-jobs that shouldn't have them. On the other hand, I think that a person who has a specific need to protect themselves should be allowed to do that. I don't like the idea, but I suppose that, right now, we're in one of those situations."

James brought their drinks and took their dinner orders. Lili ordered the étouffée, and Gil ordered the gumbo. "Camp Apex?" asked Lili.

"It was a little day camp run by the YMCA near Greenfield. We swam, did arts and crafts, archery, stuff like that. I only went one summer. I think it's still there."

"It sounds idyllic. I never went to a camp. I remember going to summer playgrounds where we did arts and crafts, used the swings and seesaws, and played dodge ball. I'm feeling better just talking to you. And drinking wine."

· · · ·

THE NEXT DAY, LILI brought Gil to Philbin's Gun Shop to buy a shotgun. The store was in a small prefab building in a gravel lot, with faux log-cabin siding. Gil was a little nervous as they walked in, but Lili was unfazed. She walked up to the counter and said "Hi. This guy would like to buy a shotgun for home protection."

The counter was staffed by a young woman who looked like a soccer mom. "Hi, I'm Rosie Philbin, and this is my shop. I see you're carrying a pistol, ma'am. Do you have a permit for that?"

"I'm an agent with the Massachusetts State Police."

Rosie smiled and asked, "Do you live in New York State, sir?"

"Yes, I live in Saratoga."

"Wonderful. Have you used a shotgun before?"

"No, only a twenty-two rifle, as a kid."

"Okay, no problem. You'll want a twelve-gauge for home protection. I have three good ones for you to choose from." She placed three, very similar-looking guns on the counter. "This is a Remington 870, our most popular model. This one's a Mossberg 500, and this one's a Winchester SXP. The Remington and the Mossberg are very similar, but the Mossberg holds six shells and the Remington holds five. The Winchester is a little lighter and less expensive. It also holds five shells."

Gil looked at Lili, confused. She said, "He'll take the Winchester, and two boxes of buckshot shells."

"Okay. It usually takes a few days to get cleared once you buy the gun, assuming you don't have a criminal record and the government's NICS system doesn't glitch out."

"No problem, right Gil?"

"Yep, no problem."

Rosie rang up the sale and said, "I'll call you when you can pick up the gun. If you don't hear from me in a week, please give me a call." She hesitated and then said, "I don't usually like to be nosy, but, well, that's not really true at all. I'm nosy as hell! So what's going on with you two, an armed agent from Massachusetts and a clean-cut guy from Saratoga buying a gun for protection?"

"Someone tried to kill a friend of mine in Florida, so I shot and killed him," said Lili. "My friend's gone into hiding. The bad guys think I know where she is, so they tried to kidnap me the other day. The FBI is working on it. I've decided to come hang out with my boyfriend for a while."

"Holy shit!" Rosie was stunned for a moment, then snapped out of it. "I'll get this background check started right away. Please let me know if you need anything else." As Lili and Gil turned to leave, Rosie said, "Wait a minute. It seems like Gil might need some training." Rosie handed Gil a card. "This guy teaches private courses for whatever you need. I'm sure he could combine a basic shotgun course with a defensive weapons course. He's a retired weapons instructor from the Marines."

• • • •

"ROCK-STEP, SIDE-CLOSE-side, side-close-side," repeated Lawrence, the dance instructor. "That's it, rock-step, side-close-side, side-close-side. You're doing great." Both Gil and Lili were laughing as they struggled with the unnatural movements, but they were keeping up. They held the rhythm as they continued awkwardly moving around in a slow circle. "That's it, keep it going everybody. Rock-step, side-close-side, side-close-side. "

Suddenly there was a loud "whoop" and a thump as a guy landed squarely on his posterior. "Everybody hold up. Hold up," said Lawrence as he stopped the music. He went over to the downed dancer and assessed his well being. After a minute, Lawrence helped the guy up and everybody clapped. "Okay, lets take five and have some water. We have to keep hydrated, people."

After practicing the basic swing-dancing steps some more, Lawrence demonstrated a faster variation of the same step called the jive. The couples practiced their steps a few times, then Lawrence put on the music. Gil and Lili were doing okay for a couple of minutes, but then they lost their rhythm and had to start over. Again, a few minutes later, they lost their rhythm. Just as they got back into it again, the music ended. "Okay let's take five, everybody." He walked over to Gil and Lily and said, "I was watching you when you lost it the last time. I think your problem is that you're both trying to lead. Lili, you have to let the man lead."

"Well I think that's generally what's wrong with this world!" She stormed off to get some water. Gil didn't know whether to laugh or be embarrassed.

TWENTY-TWO

The following morning, Gil drove Lili to the Walton Street parking garage in Saratoga Springs, and parked on the top floor. They looked out upon the surrounding area and didn't see anyone who looked like a tail. They walked around the block and entered the fortress-like post office. It was located right across the street from the city hall which housed the city's police station.

Lili had written a letter to Martha telling her what had transpired, and to emphasize that she should stay in hiding. She added that Martha should send messages to her addressed to the Massachusetts State Crime Lab in Springfield, since Lili was moving around a lot. She mailed the letter to a post office box in Jacksonville, Florida with no return address, and sent it "In care of office 44545," as she'd been instructed.

* * * *

GIL BROUGHT LILI BACK to his house and showed her how to use a Virtual Private Network for anonymity whenever she was online. Gil drove out to the Sucker Pond Shooting Range and met Lyle Chalcut. He looked more like a politician than a retired Marine, but he seemed to be in tip-top shape.

"Rosie told me that you and your girlfriend have some serious bad guys after you. Your girlfriend's a cop?"

"She's an agent with the Massachusetts State Police, but for many years she's been a supervisor at the Crime Lab in Springfield. She's winding down in her job, and went part-time this year. She still carries a weapon, though."

"Well, that's helpful. Okay, so let's get right to it. We'll start out with the basics. I'll show you all about a shotgun, how to use it and how to clean and maintain it. I'll show you the different types of ammunition. I'll train you on gun safety. Then I'll teach you how to shoot targets. We'll take a lunch break, then I'll show you how to use the gun defensively against assailants, with you on the move, them on the move, and both of you on the move. It'll be a long day, so if you don't think you can finish today, we can schedule you to finish another day."

· · · ·

LILI PULLED A STACK of paper out of Gil's printer and taped the sheets together to cover the dining room table. She proceeded to make a murder board of Martha's situation. She printed out a picture of Martha wearing her bathing suit at the pool in Florida. It made her smile as she taped it to her board. Assailant one attacked Martha and was killed by Lili. He was probably from El Salvador, based on his tattoos. She wrote on her board and taped down pictures as she thought of each aspect of the situation. There was an unknown assailant who killed Martha's neighbor, Barbara LeClerc. The next three assailants tried to attack Martha in a setup by the FBI. One was killed, and one committed suicide using cyanide. The third was in FBI custody, not talking.

Another unknown assailant team attacked Martha and her guard while she was in Witness Security, run by the US Marshals. Her guard was shot. Lili needed to call Special Agent Elsayed for an update on all of the assailants and the guard who was shot.

Possible motives. Martha is a retired middle-school English teacher. Probably no motive there. Her late husband had been a semiconductor scientist doing classified work. If the assailants were after any information, they would have ransacked her home, rather than pursue her all over the country. Maybe they think she knows something from her husband's time at work many years ago. That didn't sound very plausible.

Maybe Martha witnessed a crime recently. This is more plausible. It would have most likely happened near her home in New Hampshire, since they broke into her home after she traveled to Florida for the winter. That's why they entered her New Hampshire home. They had to find out where Martha went. The FBI needs to talk to other friends of hers to see if she mentioned witnessing anything out of the ordinary. Are there any unusual pictures on her phone? Lili will talk to Mayet about this theory.

Maybe Martha wasn't simply a retired teacher. Maybe she was somehow involved in illegal activities. But Mayet must have gone through her financial records and online activities. Again, her friends might know something relevant. Any other theories? Who would have the clout to infiltrate the US Marshals? Someone with federal access. A politician? Lili left a message for Special Agent Elsayed to call her.

· · · ·

GIL CAME HOME EXHAUSTED from his weapons class, so Lili suggested they get a pizza delivered. He went to take a shower while she ordered. Just after she hung up, she got a call from Mayet. "Have you made any progress on Martha's case?" asked Lili.

"A little. We confirmed that the guy who was killed in Florida was a gang member from El Salvador based on his tattoos, but we don't know his name yet. The woman we killed in Northampton was also a gang member from El Salvador named Silvia Algueta. The guy who killed himself was Russian and the guy who isn't talking is probably from the US or Canada based on the few words he said. We still have no motive."

"I've been thinking that Martha may have been targeted because, either she witnessed a crime and wasn't aware of it, or she's involved in a criminal activity of some sort. Have you looked at her finances? Have you examined her phone records?"

"I've been going with the theory that Martha witnessed a crime, without being aware of it. We have no probable cause to get a warrant for her financial or phone records. She isn't suspected of any wrongdoing, nor can I even imagine that scenario. Do you have a suspicion of something?"

"No, not at all. I just don't believe these guys were after anything she has. They seem to be intent on killing her. They tried to get her in Florida and in New Hampshire, which is bizarre. Do you have any other theories?"

"No. At this point I'm just following the evidence. The hit squads were almost certainly hired guns, but I'll try to find out how they were contacted and paid. Martha didn't seem to have any close friends other than her neighbor, just casual acquaintances. That makes it difficult to gain insight."

"Well, I'll try and get a discussion going with the girls from Florida. Maybe she mentioned something in passing that could help."

They said their goodbyes and Lili hung up. She wondered why the shower had been running for so long. She went upstairs to find Gil naked, fast asleep on the bed. She shook him awake and said, "You didn't even make it into the shower!"

He shook his head and said, "Thanks for waking me. I'll get in there now. Be down in a few minutes."

The doorbell rang as Lili was walking down the stairs. She could see a beat-up car in the driveway with a pizza sign on top. She grabbed her gun and wallet, and opened the door. The young pizza delivery guy's eyes went wide at the sight of the gun and he was turning to run. "Wait!" said Lili. He froze. "I'm a police officer. I won't hurt you." She put her gun in her holster. "I'm so sorry. I've put my gun away. Here's a tip for you." She handed him twenty dollars. "We've had some trouble lately." He handed her the pizza and hurried off.

While they were eating, Lili told Gil what happened with the pizza delivery guy. "I called the pizza place and apologized to the manager. He wasn't happy. He said it's hard for him to hold onto delivery guys."

"At least the guy didn't drop our pizza. Maybe we shouldn't get deliveries for a while."

"I talked to Mayet. She hasn't made much progress. They found what country the assailants were from. Two from El Salvador, one from Russia, one maybe from the US or Canada. She's trying to find friends to talk to, so I told her I'd get some discussion going with the Florida crowd. Maybe Martha mentioned something to someone. Mayet's been going with the theory that Martha witnessed a crime and wasn't aware of it. She doesn't think that Martha is involved with something criminal, and she has no cause to pursue that."

"Do you have any ideas?"

"Maybe I'll ask Martha for permission for the FBI to access her phone and financial records to see if anything suspicious is going on that she isn't aware of."

* * * *

AFTER WATCHING A COUPLE of shows on the television, Lili and Gil went up to bed. Gil was fast asleep while Lili tossed and turned. Martha's situation kept rolling around in her head. She must have finally dozed off because she woke with a start due to a thump. The clock read one twenty-six. Another thump that sounded like it came from the back porch. She shook Gil awake. "Someone's on the back porch. Get your gun."

Gil got up and slid the shotgun out from under the bed. Lili grabbed her pistol from the nightstand and they crept down the stairs. They heard some sliding, then the back doorknob was being jiggled. They heard nother thump followed by a wheeze. They looked out a window and could see a leg with a sneaker near the steps. The person was lying down. They looked out on the back porch and could see a person lying face down.

Gil flicked on the back porch light. Lili opened the inner door, while Gil aimed his shotgun. On the porch lay a man with an arrow sticking out of his back. Lili swept her gun left to right as she went out the door. Gil checked the backyard. Lili felt the man's neck. "He has a strong, rapid pulse. Sir, can you hear me?" No answer.

"I'll call 911," said Gil.

TWENTY-THREE

L ili and Gil quickly got into some proper clothes while the police combed the area for the shooter. The EMTs attempted to stabilize the injured man. Gil put on a pot of coffee for the responders. There was a knock on the back door and Lili let in two police officers in plain clothes. "I'm Detective John Varner, and this is Detective Greg Hurlburt. We're State Police."

"I'm Agent Lili D'Amico from the Massachusetts Crime Lab, and this is my friend Gil Novak. Let's go into the living room."

"You guys want coffee?" asked Gil. Both men were both eager for coffee and they negotiated cream and sugar.

The detectives sat down in the living room and Gil brought the coffee. "So, please describe what happened," said Varner. Lili and Gil described everything that happened up to the arrival of the police and EMTs. "Why bring weapons to respond to a noise on the porch?" asked Varner. Detective Hurlburt's phone rang, so he left the room.

"We've been involved in an unusual case that has us being extra careful. It started while we were in Florida for the winter. Our neighbor down there, Martha Eames, was attacked in her condo. I responded and ended up shooting the guy. He was strangling her and wouldn't stop, even when he knew I was going to shoot him. He died and was later identified as being from an El Salvador gang. I accompanied Martha back to her home in Portsmouth, New Hampshire because she needed assistance. Her neck was injured so severely that she needed emergency surgery, and couldn't speak. When we got to her house, she realized that someone had been in there, carefully searching for something. The FBI came and interviewed us. Police guarded her house until an alarm system was installed. At that point, I went home to Northampton, Mass."

"Just before I left, Martha's neighbor came over for a few minutes to drop off some food. When she left to go home, a sniper shot her dead on Martha's front porch. The neighbor looked a lot like Martha, so we think the shooter meant to kill Martha. The FBI put Martha into WITSEC. But whoever was after her found her and shot the US Marshal who was guarding her. Amazingly, Martha escaped on her own and went into hiding. Not bad for an eighty-one year old lady. The Marshal's okay. Since then, the FBI discovered that my house in Northampton was bugged, along with my car. They worked up a scheme to pretend I was bringing some medication to Martha. Three people were caught in the sting. One was shot and killed, one killed himself with a cyanide pill, and one is in custody, not talking. One from El Salvador, one Russian, and one from the US or Canada. The FBI has no idea what's going on. So, I decided to come here for a while until things cooled off."

Varner was silent for a moment, trying to make sense of the whole story. "I guess I understand why you were cautious when investigating the noise," said Varner. "Who's your FBI agent?"

"She's Special Agent Mayet Elsayed, out of Boston."

Hurlburt came back into the living room. "The guy with the arrow is Kevin Clarion, age twenty-one, from Queensbury, according to his ID. You know him?"

"It's a bolt," said Lili.

"Excuse me?"

"It's not an arrow. It's a bolt from a crossbow. Shorter and heavier than an arrow. But, no I don't know a Kevin Clarion."

"Oh right, you're Crime Lab," said Varner.

"I've never heard of him, either," said Gil.

"Mr. Novak, what do you do for work?"

"I'm retired. I was a robotics engineer."

"Is there anything else you guys can tell me about what happened here?" asked Varner. Lili and Gil shook their heads. "Well, this is definitely bizarre in so many ways. I'm sure we'll be in touch."

"I spoke to Ruth Clarion, the victim's mother," said Hurlburt. "She lives in Albany. She's on her way to Saratoga Hospital. Kevin's a student at UAlbany. She has no idea why he'd be in Saratoga or why he was shot."

Gil suddenly stood up. "Wait a minute! I'm working on a case that involves college students."

"What do you mean you're working on a case?" asked Varner.

Gil explained the case of the mole people, and why he was involved. "The Greenfield Police Department is working that case, but the FBI out of Albany is working the case of the missing student, Katrina Ryu. Special Agent Jameson Davis."

"I know Davis," said Varner. "I'll talk to him. The mole people case didn't seem to involve any violence. Do you know why Kevin Clarion would have been shot with a crossbow in your yard?"

"That sounds like a game of *Clue*," said Gil. "I have no idea. I'd like to find out what Kevin was working on."

"Could you give me the info for your contact at the Greenfield Police Department?" asked Varner.

• • • •

LILI WENT BACK TO SLEEP, but Gil couldn't. He made sure all the people working the scene had fresh coffee available. They left at about nine a.m., and Gil finally dozed off in his recliner. He woke half an hour later to the smell of bacon and eggs cooking. He was thrilled that Lili was cooking breakfast in his kitchen, but he was still very weary from lack of sleep.

Gil fell asleep again after breakfast. His phone rang and Lili quickly answered it before it woke him. "Ms. D'Amico, this is Detective Hurlburt. Is Mr. Novak there?"

"Please call me Lili. Gil's sleeping. Can I help you?"

"Oh well, okay. Mr. Novak wanted to know Kevin Clarion's major. His mother said he's a history major. The project he's working on is about Queen Anne's War. The doctors say he's going to pull through."

TWENTY-FOUR

Lili and Gil went to the ICU at Saratoga Hospital. A police officer checked their IDs and asked them to wait. The officer came out of Kevin's room with Ruth Clarion in tow. She looked like a strong woman who'd wilted.

"Mrs. Clarion, I'm Lili D'Amico, an agent with the Massachusetts State Police, and this is Gil Novak, a police consultant. Your son was found injured on Gil's back porch."

"Massachusetts?"

"Yes, we're investigating a case in Greenfield, Massachusetts that may be connected to the attack on your son, so we have a few questions for you. Would that be okay? We won't take up much of your time." Ruth gave a silent nod. "Let's go sit over here. Would you like some coffee?"

"No thanks. If I have any more coffee, I'll have a stroke."

They sat down and Gil said, "We're investigating the construction of several tunnels that were constructed under some streets in Greenfield, Massachusetts. We think some college students might be involved. One theory is that they were searching for historical artifacts."

"Well, historical artifacts are Kevin's thing. He likes learning about what this area was like before the Europeans came and when they first showed up. I don't know where he gets it. I'm a math teacher and his father was a sales rep for medical equipment. Gordon died a few years ago from lung cancer."

"I'm so sorry," said Gil. "Kevin goes to UAlbany?"

"Yes, he's supposed to graduate in May, but then he'll continue to work on his master's degree there. It's a very good school for American history."

"I think Kevin was coming to see me because I was involved in the investigation. I have no idea why someone would try to hurt him, though. What did Kevin do during his summers?"

Lili's mind zoned out for a minute while they were talking. Down the corridor, she saw a nurse smiling and talking to the guard in front of the ICU. Flirting maybe? She snapped out of it and listened to Ruth.

"Last summer Kevin worked at Fort William Henry, up in Lake George, as an intern curator. He also volunteered at an archaeological dig over in Hudson Falls. They found all sorts of artifacts, you know, pipes, belt buckles, arrowheads, those sorts of things. He loved that."

"Do you know any of his college friends?"

"I'm sorry, I really don't. He lived in off-campus housing for the past couple of years, and never brought any friends around."

"Has he ever been to Western Massachusetts for his studies or for work?"

"Not that I know of."

"I'm sorry, we should have asked earlier, how is Kevin doing?" asked Lili.

"He's stable. His surgery went well and the bleeding from his liver has slowed. He's in a medically-induced coma and they hope to bring him out of that in the next few days."

Lili looked down the corridor again and saw the nurse exit the ICU. Something seemed off about her. Her movements seemed unnatural and her eyes were darting around.

"Thank you so much for talking to us," said Lili. "We're pulling for Kevin."

"Here are our names and numbers, if you or Kevin would like to get a hold of us," said Gil. I think Kevin might have been trying to tell us something."

"STOP!" yelled Lili. She bolted toward the nurse. The nurse backed away, knocking a tray to the floor. The police officer stood up and put his hand on his gun. "That nurse did something!" Lili ran to the nurses station. "Get a doctor in here! Kevin Clarion's in trouble!"

The officer pulled his gun and pointed it at the nurse. She raised her hands, dropped a syringe, and continued to back away. She tripped and fell, arms shaking. "They have my daughter! They have my daughter!" she cried. The officer holstered his gun and began to handcuff the nurse.

Lili ran to the fallen nurse. "What did you give him?" she yelled.

"Heparin, it's heparin."

"Doctor! We need a doctor!" yelled Lili.

TWENTY-FIVE

A police cruiser dropped Lili off at Gil's house, an hour after he got home. She said, "Kevin's still alive, but it's touch and go. That nurse injected heparin into his IV. It's a strong blood thinner, and it caused a big increase of internal bleeding from his arrow wounds. The doctors gave him something to help his blood to clot, but they may have to take him back into surgery. They had to sedate poor Ruth."

"What about the nurse?"

"I don't know. The police took her away. Agent Davis from the FBI called me from his car. The nurse kept saying that someone has her daughter. Can you imagine? Apparently, she was given the choice of killing someone else's son or having someone kill her daughter." Lili's phone bleeped. "Davis wants me to meet him at the police station. Okay if I take your car?"

"Sure. Call me if you need me."

· · · ·

GIL CALLED KAREN TINDALL at the Greenfield Police Department and told her about Kevin Clarion. After ending the call, he settled into his computer chair and began researching the history of Greenfield, Massachusetts. It hurt his back to sit at the computer for long periods of time, but maybe he'd find a lead. The first thing he found was that Greenfield had been a part of the neighboring village of Deerfield until 1753. He remembered learning in elementary school about an infamous American Indian raid on Deerfield. The Indians attacked the village, killed some of the people, and took a large number of them, on foot, all the way to Canada. For the settlers, it was a horrific event. When Gil was a child, schools didn't teach much of the background concerning the Indigenous

Americans' point of view, and why they attacked. The book was mostly about the experiences of the captive colonists. Gil discovered that the Deerfield raid occurred in 1704. It was part of Queen Anne's War, at a time when England, France, and Spain were jockeying for territory in North America. The captives were marched up the Green River in the area that would become Greenfield. It was difficult for Gil to imagine being marched on foot all the way to Canada in February, back in 1704. Many of the captives didn't make it, but some did and a few eventually made their way home, years later. That raid didn't seem to have much to do with the Greenfield area though, so he didn't think it was relevant. But, Queen Anne's War was Kevin Clarion's main interest.

Gil searched for information about Graves Brook, which he learned about at the Greenfield Historical Society. He remembered that the graves were supposedly those of white men killed in something called Dummer's War. Online, he found that they would have been killed in 1724, in a series of raids led by a Woronoco Sachem, or Chief, called Gray Lock. That war was between the English Colonists and Indians who were urged to fight by French colonial leaders. These raids could possibly be of interest in the mole people case because they had to do with a brook in Greenfield.

The next article Gil found online described Captain Turner's infamous massacre on an American Indian village in what is now Gill, Massachusetts. This happened much earlier during King Philip's War in 1676. King Philip was the English honorary title for a Wampanoag Sachem called Metacomet. The English colonists attacked and killed mostly Indian women and children at a seasonal fishing encampment called Peskeompskut. After the massacre, a large number of fierce Indian warriors went after Captain Turner's men. The warriors killed many of the colonist soldiers as they tried to retreat toward the Green River in Greenfield. Captain Turner was among the soldiers who were killed. So, this event could be related to the tunnels because the area between the massacre site and the Green River is in present-day Greenfield.

Gil had had enough of online research for the day. About an hour and a half was all he could take before he got antsy. He settled into his recliner for a nap. A few minutes later, Lili returned from the police station. Gil opened his eyes and said, "Julia texted me and invited us to dinner. I haven't answered yet. Would we be putting their lives in danger?"

"Hmm. Some really bad guys went after Martha and now a new really bad guy has attacked Kevin Clarion. We have no idea why, but they haven't come after either of us. They've done surveillance on me to get to Martha. It's possible that they could kidnap me to find Martha, but I can't imagine they'd try to get me while we're visiting the kids. They'd want me alone. My gut says that we're okay visiting the kids, and I'd really like to."

• • • •

LILI WAS SITTING ON the family room floor, drawing and coloring with Ziggy and Dez. Lili said, "All you guys draw are rainbows, unicorns, and turtles. Let's draw something else."

"We don't know anything else," said Dez.

"Do you know how to draw monsters?"

"I do!" said Ziggy.

"I don't," said Dez, pouting.

"I'll show you. You can draw them however you want. I'll draw one with one huge eye and big ears. A little body with three arms, three legs, and big feet that are just a big toe. I'll give it purple hair coming out of its knees and elbows." Dez giggled.

"Mine has a big head with lots of eyes and a big nose," said Ziggy.

Gil was talking with Julia and Mike in the kitchen. "So some guy gets shot with an arrow on your porch, then a nurse tries to kill him in the hospital." said Mike. "And you think that has to do with tunnels in Greenfield?"

"Yes, the mole people. I think this young guy, Kevin, is searching for something that has to do with the Indian wars in the 1600s or early 1700s. He's a history major."

"You're saying that someone is trying to kill this Kevin guy because of something that happened hundreds of years ago?" asked Mike. "It makes no sense."

"No, it doesn't," said Gil. "But that's where we are, so far."

"And Lili is here because she was being followed in Northampton by assassins who want to kill an elderly woman named Martha?" asked Julia.

"Yes, but also because she likes coming here."

"Dad, I thought you retired so you could improve your health," said Julia. "Getting shot could be detrimental, don't you think? Are we in danger here because you're visiting?"

"We don't think so. These people aren't after Lili or me. They're after Martha and Kevin."

"Is Kevin related to Martha?" asked Mike.

"I doubt it. These are separate, unrelated cases. What's for supper? It smells good."

"Lasagna."

TWENTY-SIX

"**I** didn't get much sleep," said Lili. "I'm all wound up. It's hard for me to be involved in a case but not be able to go into work and make progress on it. I have all this pent up energy. It's kind of like a doctor becoming the patient."

"I slept okay," said Gil. "Would you like some scrambled eggs?"

"No thanks. Yogurt for me today."

"Karen texted me. She wants to know when I can come back and do some more tunnel inspections."

"This is all so messed up," said Lili. "We left Northampton because of a case in Florida. Then things go nuts in Saratoga due to a case in Greenfield. Maybe I can help with the Greenfield case. Can we stay in a hotel?"

"Of course we can. After breakfast, I'm going to work in my shop for a while. I'm building a new robot with even more gizmos."

"I'm going to mail a letter to Martha. I'm going to ask for her permission to have the FBI access her phone and financial records to see if anything is amiss. She'll send her response to the Crime Lab, as we had arranged."

· · · ·

KAREN RETURNED TO THE Greenfield Police Department after spending an hour at the courthouse testifying at an assault trial. A young woman was beaten up by her boyfriend who then threatened to kill her if she testified against him. The woman's roommate was in the next room with the emergency dispatcher on the phone. The dispatch call recorded the boyfriend making the threat. An easy case.

The officer at the front desk nudged his head in the direction of the seating area and said, "A little girl came in and wants to talk to you."

Karen saw a small Asian girl in pigtails holding a Paw Patrol backpack on her lap. She walked over and said, "Hello, I'm Detective Tindall. You asked to speak with me?"

"I'm Katrina Ryu. I wish to turn myself in." Katrina seemed very nervous.

Karen was stunned. She looked closely at the girl's face and realized that she was a young woman rather than a young girl. A very small woman, cleverly disguised as a child. "I'm so happy to meet you, Miss Ryu. "Please follow me."

Karen brought Katrina to an interview room and asked her if she wanted something to drink.

"Do you have grape or orange soda?"

Karen brought Katrina a ginger ale, and Katrina quickly gulped half of it down. "Thank you. I came here because my friend and I are being stalked. We decided to split up and seek refuge with the police."

"What's your friend's name?"

"Kevin. Kevin Clarion. He went to seek help from your consultant Gil Novak in Saratoga Springs, and I came here."

"Well, I'm glad you did. Kevin's been shot. He's in rough shape."

Katrina looked shocked. She thought for a moment and said, "I have another friend who was working with us in Greenfield. I can't get a hold of him. His name is Evan Melsty."

"Where does Mr. Melsty live?"

"He's a student at Virginia Tech. His hometown is somewhere around here.

I'll be back in a few minutes. I'll start a search for Mr. Melsty."

Karen went over to the office of Chief Reyes. He was talking to a civilian she didn't know, so she knocked and entered. "Chief, we have a situation."

Reyes excused himself from his office and asked, "What's up?"

Karen explained, and said she was going to assign some officers to track down Evan Melsty.

The Chief smiled. "The plot thickens! Keep me posted." He went back into his office.

Karen went over to Officer Sam Quirion and told him what she needed. Sam said, "I'll find Evan Melsty. There's probably not a lot of Evan Melstys in Massachusetts."

Back in the interview room, Karen turned on a recording device, and read Katrina her rights. "Do you wish to have an attorney present?"

"No. I'll tell you what I know."

"First of all, did you create the tunnels in Greenfield?"

"Yes. Kevin hired me to help create the tunnels so he could find some artifacts from colonial times. He's a history major. He was searching for some Asian gold statues, or something like that."

"Kevin Clarion hired you?"

"Yes, well, sort of. I borrowed $30,000 from my father for Kevin's venture. Kevin said the artifacts would be worth at least a million dollars. So far, I spent about $2,500 to build the tunnel structures. Kevin hired Evan to dig the tunnels, which spent almost half of the remaining money."

"Evan is Evan Melsty?"

"Yes."

"How did Kevin know Evan Melsty?"

"I searched for a student with the right skills and recommended Evan to Kevin."

"Why did you turn yourself in to me?"

"Back at my apartment in Troy, New York, I noticed someone watching my building. When I went to get some groceries, I kept an eye out and saw that this guy was following me about fifty yards behind. When I came out of the Fourth Street Market, I didn't see him. I decided to go home a different way and I didn't see the guy following. When I got back to my building, the front door had been jimmied, so I called the police. I saw the guy dive out of my window onto the fire escape. He ran down so quickly that the police couldn't catch him. This guy was in my apartment! I took off because I didn't want to talk to the police. The next day, Kevin called me and said he was being followed. I told him about my intruder. We decided to turn ourselves into the police and seek protection."

"Why did you leave school without notice and cease contact with your mother? Are you aware that you've been declared a missing person?"

"I assumed that the police might be looking for me. I rented a new apartment. I needed some time to decide what to do next with my life. I found school to be slowing me down in my career more than it was helping me. My mother's influence causes me to act more risk averse than I want. I'm sorry for the trouble I've caused."

"Kevin Clarion was shot with an arrow in Saratoga Springs two days ago. He was seriously injured. While he was in the hospital, a nurse tried to kill him by injecting him with heparin. The nurse said that someone had kidnapped her daughter. The kidnapper said that unless she killed Mr. Clarion, she would never see her daughter again. The people who are stalking you, Kevin Clarion, and possibly Evan Melsty are very dangerous. We're trying to locate Mr. Melsty. Ms. Ryu, at this time I am charging you with trespassing and malicious destruction of property due to your participation in the tunnel construction case. We will be holding you in a jail cell here until your arraignment, which may be as early as this afternoon. I recommend you find yourself a defense attorney. If you cannot afford one, we will assign one to you. Do you understand these charges?"

"Yes I do. I would like to call my mother, please."

TWENTY-SEVEN

Although it was a late April morning, fat snowflakes were falling as Gil and Lili drove over the Green Mountains of Vermont. Route 9 had been heavily salted, so there was no accumulation on the road. Gil was curious about Lili's state of mind, so he thought he'd probe. "Well, our lives are a little more exciting than we expected lately. I'm not sure if it's better or worse than having a much quieter life, at this stage. What do you think?"

"I was just thinking about that, too. I guess I kind of like acting as a detective or a consultant. It's more interesting than processing DNA backlogs, even though the DNA results may be more helpful. I really don't like people spying on me and bugging my house. That really creeps me out. I think it might be fun if we worked together on cases."

"I'd like that too, and I think we could steer things more in that direction. Are you thinking about retiring altogether?"

Lili thought for a moment and replied, "I guess I am. I'm curious to see how things work out for us, as a couple. I think it's great right now. What do you think?"

"I think we're great as a couple! I definitely love you as a best friend, and not just romantically. Maybe we need to think about if we should live together, and where. We were together in Florida for the winter and I really enjoyed that. Except for that minor shooting incident. Up here, you live in Northampton, I live in Saratoga, and I seem to be working a lot around Greenfield."

"I don't have a problem living somewhere besides Northampton. But your grand-kids are in Saratoga. I'm a little surprised that you would consider moving away from them."

"I don't know. I guess I'd be okay moving away from Saratoga. I've lived there for a very long time. I love the grand-kids, but I don't really babysit for them much. Mike's mom does that. Maybe I wouldn't mind living in Greenfield, but I'm not sure. We'll have to think about it and keep talking. Look, some deer!" Gil slowed down as a doe and fawn crossed the road in front of them.

Lili's phone beeped a few times, so she looked at it and chuckled. "It's the Florida girls answering my text message about Martha possibly having witnessed a crime." She read the responses to Gil.

"She witnessed adultery on *General Hospital!*" said Beryl.

"During a walk, she saw some kids spray-painting a bridge near her house," said Ellen.

"She talked about a guy in her neighborhood who doesn't pick up his dog's poop," said Francine.

"Is he good looking?" asked Beryl.

"Oh brother," said Ellen.

"Who'd want a guy who doesn't pick up after his dog?" asked Francine.

"At this stage of my life. I'd take just about any guy who can fog a mirror," said Beryl.

"She told me that somebody she knows cheats at mahjong," said Deb.

"How do you cheat at mahjong?" asked Francine.

"She explained it to me once, but I don't remember," said Deb.

Gil sighed. "I don't think any of that is fertile ground."

"But, it makes me happy to hear from those girls again," said Lili.

· · · ·

GIL WAS BACK IN GREENFIELD, slowly steering his new robot down through the tunnel opening in the woods on Oak Street. He and Lili were sitting in beach chairs, by a small folding table that held the remote controller. When Karen came to unlock the tunnel hatch, she discovered that the police lock had been removed and a new combination lock installed. Karen cut the lock off with bolt cutters and bagged it as evidence. Gil was taking a while to get set up, so Karen left them to it.

"I made the robot as big as possible so I could install a ground-penetrating radar unit that I bought used on eBay. It also has two arms, one for moving dirt around with a shovel and the other to grab samples. This robot isn't radio-controlled, though. It has a tether for power and control. That way, I could keep the batteries up here and make the robot lighter."

"At the State Police, my people were considered the nerds," said Lili. "But you could definitely out-nerd us all. What are these crescent shapes on the screen telling you?"

"These are probably rocks of various sizes and at different depths. This is what a fish finder screen looks like when it displays fish, unless the fish finder is put in the mode where little fish symbols show up. This down here is a change in density of the soil. Maybe the dirt they used to build up this area many years ago covered the original clay layer. We're looking for something closer to the surface. Can you explain why Karen is having us search the tunnels when Katrina Ryu already told us that Kevin was just looking for some artifacts?"

"Karen's hoping we can find the artifacts before back-filling the tunnels so people don't dig them up again," said Lili. "It's a long-shot. Whoa, what's that big thing near the top?"

"I don't know. Let's take a look." Gil backed up the robot to where the new signal started. He angled the camera so it was looking at the spot in question. Then he took the shoveling arm and clumsily wiped it back and forth to move the surface dirt around. "There's something. I don't know what it is." He moved it with the shovel.

"It's an ear!" said Lili. They looked at each other. "We'd better stop."

"I got a shiver up my spine, but somehow it doesn't gross me out too much since we're looking at it on a screen."

· · · ·

POLICE OFFICERS TAPED off the tunnel entrance areas on both ends. Lili's co-workers showed up to investigate the crime scene. The city engineer, Rona Polo, determined that the tunnel could not be made safe enough for the crime scene techs to enter, so they decided to haul the body out with the help of Gil's robot. Gil worked with his robot for over three hours to free the body enough to move it. The only way he could put a strap on the body was to loop it around one shoulder. He used the robot to attach a winch hook to the strap. A police officer used the winch on the bumper of his cruiser to carefully pull the body up toward the tunnel access. When it was close enough, they used a couple of hoes to pull the body up to the manhole. The body belonged to a guy with a reddish-brown beard that none of them recognized. Lili stayed with Gil and the other crime-scene techs while the robot was used to examine the tunnel for evidence in the area where the body had been buried.

Later that afternoon, Karen met with Katrina Ryu and her lawyer. The lawyer's name was Shaina Klein, from Springfield. Karen knew Shaina as a reasonable and competent criminal defense attorney.

Karen began recording and reminded Katrina of her rights. "Ms. Ryu, have you been inside all of the tunnel structures in Greenfield that you designed and manufactured?"

Ms. Klein nodded to Katrina, and she responded, "Yes."

"How many tunnels were constructed?"

"There were three main tunnels, but they also had some smaller side tunnels. I don't remember exactly how many."

"When was the last time you were in any of these tunnels?"

"Um, last fall, around October, I think. I don't know the exact day."

"When was the last time either Kevin Clarion or Evan Melsty had been in these tunnels?"

"I don't know."

"Did Mr. Clarion and Mr. Melsty ever discuss with you their activities related to the search for artifacts that you previously described to me?"

Ms. Klein gestured for Katrina to stop talking. She said, "Detective Tindall, you've been beating around the bush long enough. Please tell us what this line of questioning is all about, before we proceed."

"Very well. Earlier today, the police were searching one of the tunnels for evidence. A body was discovered." Katrina's eyes went wide and she looked at her lawyer. Karen showed them a picture of the deceased man, taken after his body was rinsed off at the Crime Lab. "Katrina, do you recognize this man?"

"No. I definitely don't know that man or anything about a dead body!" A tear ran down her cheek.

TWENTY-EIGHT

The next morning, Lili and Gil were searching the Lincoln Street tunnel from Cheryl Needham's basement. Lili's phone warbled. When she hung up, she said, "That was Cherise, from the Crime Lab. She said that the tunnel victim was killed by a twenty-two caliber bullet to the brain. He died a couple of days ago. No ID yet, but they're working on it."

"I found something here. It's small and I'm trying to dig it out. There, let's take a look." Gil zoomed the camera in. "It's just a little old tractor toy."

Lili smiled. "Well, maybe that's the artifact they're after."

"Well, it might be worth something."

Lili's phone rang again. After she hung up, she said, "That was Jeanie Peridot, the genealogist. She says she has some interesting results from Martha's DNA search. I told her we could meet for dinner in Northampton. Fitzwilly's at six."

The most interesting find from the Lincoln Street tunnel seemed to be a musket. It was very rusty and the wood was almost all gone. Lili bagged it as evidence. "I don't think this was the murder weapon."

· · · ·

LILI AND GIL STOPPED by the Greenfield Police Station so Karen could book the musket and the toy tractor into evidence. "Not as interesting as yesterday's find," said Karen. "AFIS shows that our murder victim was a guy named Paul Combs. A suspected hit-man. He's got a couple of violent crime convictions. He was a white supremacist out of northern New Hampshire."

"I guess we won't be sending flowers," said Gil. Lili chuckled.

"I doubt that Katrina Ryu knew the victim. He was killed around the time Katrina turned herself in. We're looking for her other partner in crime, Evan Melsty. He's a college student with no online presence at all, which is very unusual. No license, no credit card, no social security number. Probably a false name. He doesn't answer his phone."

"Did you get a warrant to track his phone location and get his phone data?" asked Lili.

"Working on it."

"We're planning to inspect the last tunnel tomorrow," said Gil. "Will there be anything else you need from us?"

"Not that I can think of, right now. We might need your robot again later, though. Now that this is a murder investigation, I can't close up the tunnels for a while." Karen's phone rang and she answered it as Lili and Gil started to leave. She held up a finger so they would wait, and then ended the call. "That was Special Agent Davis. Kevin Clarion died today." She paused to let that news sink in. "But, there's some good news. The daughter of the nurse who killed Kevin was released. She's being checked out at the hospital, but she appears to be okay, physically anyway. The FBI is trying to find out where she was held, and by whom."

• • • •

JEANIE PERIDOT HAD taken a table for them at Fitzwilly's, and had spread her papers out for their discussion. Gil found her extreme attactiveness distracting, and it made him uncomfortable. They ordered drinks, nachos, and pot-stickers, to start.

"Okay. I shared Martha's DNA results with the other major testing companies and I got some very interesting results. Here are the main ones." She showed them a basic chart.

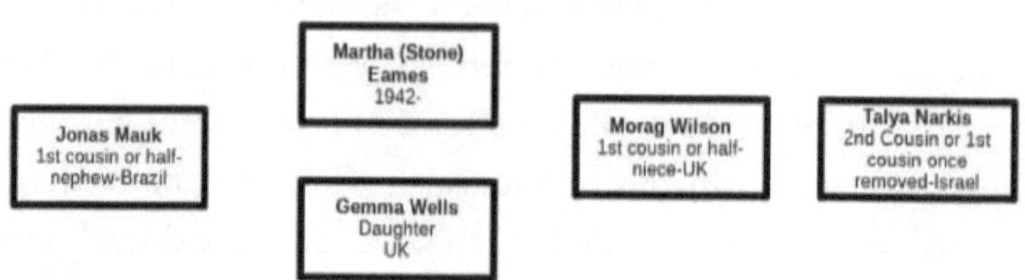

"We have a woman named Morag Wilson in Scotland, who may be a first cousin or a half niece. We have a Jonas Mauk in Brazil who may be a first cousin or a half nephew. We also have a Talya Narkis in Israel who may be a second cousin or a first cousin once removed."

"What's a cousin once removed?" asked Gil.

"That's the child of a cousin or the parent of a cousin. It's one generation apart from the cousin," said Jeanie.

"Why do you say they *may be* this or *may be* that?" asked Lili.

"Once you get into the realm of the children of half-siblings or cousins, it gets harder to distinguish the exact type of relationship. It's very complicated, and has to do with the amount of overlap between the DNA of two related people. That's why it's necessary to delve into the family tree and genealogical records of these people to figure out the actual relationships. But Lili, there's a real ho-hum-crasher in all of this data. Martha has a daughter."

Lili almost choked on her pot-sticker and yelped. "What? No way!"

"Yes way. There's a woman named Gemma Wells who lives in England with her husband Stephen. Gemma's profile says that she grew up knowing she was adopted, and she's been looking for her biological family. Because of this search, she now knows about Martha and is probably trying to get in touch with her."

"Oh jeez," said Lili. "She can't get in touch because Martha's off the grid."

The three of them ordered light dinners. "We've been lucky with the amount of family tree information these people have posted online. We've got these relatives in the UK, Brazil, and Israel, and I think we're starting to get a picture of what happened. I think Martha was born in Europe during World War II. One parent was Jewish and the other was a non-Jewish German. Both of Martha's parents had children from other partners, some in the UK, some in Brazil. Her Jewish parent also had at least one sibling who survived the war and ended up in Israel. I bet that Martha was born, or at least conceived, in continental Europe before moving to the UK."

"If Martha was the child of a Non-Jewish German and a Jewish parent, that would not have been kosher during World War II," said Gil.

"Definitely not kosher, and very dangerous. There could be several scenarios for that situation, some of which are very bad. It could end up being similar to what many African-American people find. A lot of us, including me, have at least one ancestor who was a white slave owner that had a child with one of his slaves. It's very strange to think about, but one of my ancestors was a slave owner and maybe a rapist. Or, maybe not a rapist." She paused to let them consider that. "Anyway, I'll need to do more document research on Martha's family. I'd like to keep working on this because we need to get more information so Martha will know who she'll be contacting. And besides, it's very intriguing."

"Will people know you're researching this? We can't let Martha be exposed."

"No, they won't see what I'm doing, since I'm only gathering information that's openly available. But some of them may be trying to contact Martha. Are you sure she's off the grid?"

"I hope so," said Lili. "I'd better confirm it. I'd like you to keep going on this. We should get a more complete picture before we try to connect with Martha. I don't even know when it'll ever be safe enough to connect with her."

• • • •

THAT EVENING, LILI and Gil met up with Gil's old friends Micky and Jane Tindall, as well as Eddie Locke at the Hawks and Reed Performing Arts Center in Greenfield. Eddie's girlfriend Pam was appearing there with her band, Soundslip. They set the tone for the evening with a haunting alternative rock song called *6 Underground*, originally by the Sneaker Pimps. Definitely not country & western that evening.

When the band took a break, Eddie said, "I've heard more live music in the past year than I had in my entire life before. I like their music, but I don't think it's helping my hearing."

"Does Pam wear hearing protection?" asked Jane.

"She does. She has custom earplugs that block out a lot of the volume, but allows her to hear the music, her own singing, and a metronome sound."

"Maybe you should get some earplugs," said Jane.

"Every year I have to do more things to try and keep myself healthy, but I still have more and more health problems anyway," said Eddie. "So many parts of me hurt that it's hard to keep track of."

"Just think, when all the pain suddenly goes away, you'll know you're dead!" said Micky.

TWENTY-NINE

G il and Lili inspected the third tunnel on Pond Street. All they found was a muffler and a lot of old, empty bottles. Karen arrived as they were finishing up. "I guess we're done with you guys for now. We're just blocking the tunnel entrances, for now. We'll fill in the tunnels when the case is closed. I'm still trying to track down this Evan Melsty guy. I think it's an alias."

"We'll be heading back to New York today," said Gil. "Call us if you need us."

Lili's phone rang and she answered it. She chatted for a few minutes, laughing. When she hung up, she said, "That was Cherise. She says that she got a letter for me with no postmark. She asked if they should check it for anthrax. It's got to be a letter from Martha, so I'd like to swing by there on the way home."

"Okay," Gil grumbled. "But I really don't like riding home on the Turnpike. For some reason, the back roads make me happy and the highways seem like drudgery."

"I don't see the difference," said Lili. "The Turnpike's just as scenic, and it's faster."

After stopping at the Crime Lab, they got back on the highway. Lili read Martha's letter and laughed. "Martha says she's doing great and her life is like a vacation. She says I need to solve her case before she has to lock in her condo rental in Florida. She has until mid-October." Lili made a call on her phone and said, "Hi Mayet, this is Agent Lili D'Amico. I'm calling because I just got a letter back from Martha Eames. She has given the FBI permission to access her phone and financial records. Yes, I'm on the road right now, but I'll send you a copy of the letter when I get to where I'm going, in a couple of hours. Yes, she says she doing great and having a wonderful time. Okay, you too."

• • • •

THE NEXT DAY, GIL AND Lili drove up to Lake George Village to visit Fort William Henry. They paid and entered, and began to look around. The curators were dressed in colonial garb. There were plaques describing the fort's construction in 1755. There was a lot of historical background about the French and Indian war. The French laid siege upon the fort until the British surrendered. The American-Indian allies of the French army misunderstood the terms of surrender, so they attacked the British soldiers as they were marching away. Many of the soldiers were killed, and their women and children taken captive. The French burned the fort.

"Well, that's a pleasant story," said Lili.

"Yes, doesn't it seem like history was mostly taught to us in terms of wars?"

"There were plagues and beheadings, too!" said Lili.

They found many great exhibits about what it was like to live in the fort during colonial times. At one point, Gil saw someone who looked like he was in charge. Gil introduced himself and Lili. "I'm John Fontaine. I'm the museum director."

"Did you know a Kevin Clarion who worked here as an intern last summer?"

"Sure, I know Kevin. He's an energetic kind of guy. Very knowledgeable about colonial history. He didn't return this season, though."

"I'm sorry to say that he died recently."

John blinked. "Really? I thought he seemed very healthy."

"He was murdered."

Fontaine seemed shocked. "Maybe we should talk somewhere more private." He led them to an area that was for authorized personnel only. "You're from the Massachusetts State Police?"

"Yes, we believe Kevin's death had to do with a minor crime he was involved in that occurred in Massachusetts. We think he was searching for some Indian artifacts," said Lili.

"Wow. How was he killed?"

"With an arrow."

"Really? That must be very out of the ordinary. This is horrible! He was a really nice guy. How can I help?"

"Well, we're wondering if there's anything here that has to do with historical events in Greenfield, Massachusetts."

"Greenfield, that's in western Massachusetts. I don't think so. Not specifically, anyway. Certainly, in general terms, the Greenfield area would probably have been involved in the French and Indian wars. Kevin was mainly interested in our written archives. Most of the interns are interested in artifacts, but some are more interested in the role playing of colonial Americans. Kevin seemed to gravitate toward the written records and the English language used back then. I suppose he could have found something in our archives, but I don't know how to find out what specifically he would have been reading. Let me ask around and see if anyone has a clue. Feel free to look around some more, and I'll find you."

They followed Fontaine out of the office. He turned and walked away with intent. Lili and Gil continued to wander around. As they were looking at one of the exhibits, Gil said, "This might be something. This powder horn has an inscription. I can't read much of it, but it was transcribed onto a small plaque over here. It talks about a Captain Turner, the Green River, and Hatfield."

1676 *I followed old Cap^n Turner north from Hatfield through the ruin^t settlement of Deerfield. God failed those people. At the Great Falls, I kill^t 2 savages sneaking a* *sack to they^r mishoon. The sack held gold gods and juelree from the orient. Savages poured from the woods like bees in anger. I ran upstream in a brook that flowed belowe the red cliffs, praying to God that he would guide me to*

safety. Many of ours were kill^t, Cap^n Turner among them. I could not run with a sack so burdened. I berried it under

a small stream fill^t with green turtle stones, 20 paces up, as my trail had become block^t with bramble.

Samuel Stagg

William Stagg

Gideon Palmer

"It mentions gold artifacts," said Lili. She took a picture of the powder horn and the plaque, using her cellphone.

Gil was really excited. "This must be it! Holy moly!"

John Fontaine found them by the exhibit. "My staff are devastated by the news of Kevin's death. Nobody seems to know what he might have found that could be related to Greenfield. Sorry."

"We found something," said Gil. "I think this powder horn inscription is talking about Greenfield."

John read it and said, "I'm not an expert on Massachusetts, but we have someone who is. Let me get Shawn." He came back with a young woman. "This is Shawn Delaney." Lili and Gil introduced themselves. "Shawn, what do you make of this inscription?"

"Let's see, I remember something about a Captain Turner. A mishoon is a dugout canoe. I'm not familiar with the other references, but I can do a little digging on the internet if you'd like to come to my office." Lili and Gil followed Shawn. She had one guest chair and brought in another. She clicked and clacked on her keyboard, squinting at her monitor through large cranberry-framed glasses. "Here we are. I think you're right, Mr. Novak. Captain Turner was a notable character in the Massachusetts militia. He was jailed in Boston for being a Baptist and speaking against the Puritans. He was released from jail on the condition that he lead a large militia contingent against an Indian encampment called Peskeompskut, which the English referred to as the Great Falls on the Connecticut River. This was an action of reprisal in King Philip's war. King Philip was the English title given to a Wampanoag sachem named Metacomet. The militia assembled for the attack in a town called Hatfield."

"It's still the town of Hatfield," said Lili.

"Cool. The encampment was mostly women, children, and old men. They were fishing the spring salmon and shad run at the falls. Captain Turner was killed in this battle. But I don't know where the Green River is."

"I do. It's in Greenfield," said Gil.

"Cool. Okay, if there are in fact gold Asian figurines from the 17th century Indigenous Americans in Greenfield, that would be a very significant find. As far as we know, there was no trade between Asia and the Indigenous Americans, at that time."

"Do we know who these three men were?"

Shawn did some more typing on her keyboard and said, "Bingo! Gideon Palmer was here in 1757. When the fort was surrendered to the French, Palmer was killed in an Indian attack when the fort's occupants were retreating to Fort Edward. His powder horn was discovered very recently in a dig nearby. Samuel and William Stagg would have been his forebears. Based on the order of the names, Samuel Stagg would have been the inscriber of this powder horn. I may be able to find him, since he was in the British militia, but it will take a little digging. I'll make you a deal, I'll call you when I find information on the Staggs, if you call me when you find out more about these artifacts. It would be a great plaque for our exhibit!"

"It's a deal," said Lili. "Here's my card."

"Hold on a second." Shawn typed some more. "Green turtle stone is the state gemstone of Michigan. Hmm...I'm not sure that helps."

• • • •

WHEN LILI AND GIL GOT back to Gil's house, Gil sat down at his computer to research Captain Turner's attack at the Great Falls. 1676 was less than sixty years after the English Pilgrims first settled in Massachusetts. It was a hundred years before the Declaration of Independence. There were less than 40,000 English people in Massachusetts, at that time. In 1620, when the Pilgrims arrived, there were about 60,000 Indigenous Americans in New England. By 1676, there were only about 10,000 Indigenous Americans, mainly due to epidemics caused by European diseases, for which they had little immunity.

Gil had assumed that, as the population of the Massachusetts Bay colony grew, villages expanded west from the Plymouth area. An old map that he found online showed that he was mistaken. The English population of western Massachusetts had spread north from Long Island Sound, along the Connecticut River. The Dutch settlers were similarly establishing settlements north from the Sound, along the Hudson River. Deerfield, the closest village to what would become Greenfield, was settled in 1673, only two years before King Philip's War. It was one of the most northern settlements on the Connecticut River. At first, it was called Pocumtuc, after the Indian tribe that inhabited the area.

King Philip's War evolved from friction between the Massachusetts Bay Colony and the Wampanoag tribe. The English settlers repeatedly violated previously negotiated treaties with the Indigenous Americans. Their cattle grazed beyond established borders, they prosecuted and hung Indians according to English laws, they attempted to get the Indians to turn in European weapons they'd acquired, and they tried to convert the Indians to their religion. King Philip encouraged his tribe and neighboring tribes to increasingly harass and raid the English settlements.

The English declared war in 1675 and its intensity increased rapidly. By the end of the war in 1678, the Wampanoag tribe and the neighboring Narragansett tribe had essentially been wiped out, and other tribes were severely impacted. Thousands of Indigenous Americans who survived and surrendered were sold into the harsh conditions of slavery in the Caribbean islands. As Gil researched this period of history, he would take breaks and discuss what he learned with Lili.

Lili said, "I have about four percent Native American DNA."

"Really?"

"I did a DNA test a few years ago. I never bothered researching my family tree to find out where I got that DNA. Maybe I'll get Jeanie to do it for me someday."

"You are a warrior!"

"Oh brother. Don't get too excited. Well, maybe go ahead and get excited."

Everything Gil learned about from his historical research was new to him, surprising, and horrifying. He wondered what it had been like to be an Indigenous American in New England during that time. It kept rolling around in his mind as he tried to fall asleep.

THIRTY

April 20, 1676

Sequankoon walked silently along a forested hill above Peskeompskut. Her name meant spring snow, a name given to her by her mother twelve springs ago. Peskeompskut was the site of the northeastern tribal people's spring fishing encampment, below the Great Falls on the Connecticut River. She paused on an outcropping of rock to look down upon the temporary village. It was early morning, but she could already see many people beginning their daily activities among the wetu huts. The older men and young boys were fishing for the plentiful salmon that gathered below the falls. In the surrounding forests and fields, younger men would be teaching the older boys the skills they would need for hunting. The women were cleaning and smoking strips of fish and game on racks. A few warriors were staying at the encampment for protection, in case the Mohawks attacked again. Other warriors camped separately at the two islands south of Peskeompskut, and some distance away at several other camps surrounding the falls. The warriors' mission was to protect the encampment from attacks from anyone, in any direction.

Sequankoon felt happy in this idyllic place that was far away from the evil white men. Her moment of happiness faded toward hopelessness as she recalled the loss of her family and her village. Two years ago, her mother and younger sister had died within days of each other from the white man's fever. Most of the people from her village had died from the fever. Last summer, white men had attacked and destroyed her village. Her father was killed, and her older brother taken captive. She was from the Nipmuc tribe, and her village had been located southeast of Peskeompskut. Sequankoon and her younger brother Mooi Anequs, fled north with the few remaining people of their village. They joined a larger group of

Nipmuc at Wachuset. There were other Nipmuc and Wampanoag there who had been displaced from their own villages. She and her brother were taken in by a Nipmuc woman named Sukkikesuk, who had recently lost her children to the fever.

The encampment at Peskeompskut included many people from the Wampanoag, Narragansett, Pocumtuc, and Nipmuc tribes, among others. Some of the village women were frustrated with Sequankoon's behavior. Instead of helping to clean and dry the fish and game, cook meals, mend clothes, and watch the small children, she hunted. But she knew there were other women hunters-warriors, and she wondered if they had also received the rebukes of the other women. She'd been told of her father's grandmother Wompohtuck, who was a hunter and became a sachem of her people. Perhaps she carried the spirit of Wompohtuck. She had grown faster than other boys and girls her age. She'd made her own bow, arrows, quiver, and knives. She'd often been cautioned to stay away and not disturb the warriors while they were hunting.

Sequankoon continued to walk quietly along the hills, parallel to the Fall River. The Fall River ended at the base of the Great Falls at Peskeompskut. She caught a glimpse of movement on the side of the hill below her. She crouched down and watched, notching an arrow onto her bowstring. There! A large hare was sniffing a sprouting plant. The hare still had small patches of white winter fur, making it more visible. Silently, Sequankoon crept closer. When she was close enough, she drew back her arrow and let it fly. The hare squealed as it collapsed and rolled down the hill a few feet and laid still. Sequankoon carefully approached the hare when she suddenly became aware of two people standing in front of her.

One was a boy, a little older than her, called Nish N'keke, and the other was a warrior whom she did not know. The boy rudely said, "Go back with the other women, little girl. Leave my hare alone." Sequankoon looked at the boy incredulously, since she was significantly taller than he.

The warrior walked over and pulled an arrow out of the ground just up the hill from the hare. He said, "Nish N'keke, here is your arrow. The hare belongs to the girl." The boy snorted with disgust, grabbed his arrow from the man, and walked away. "What is your name, little hunter?"

"Sequankoon."

"My name is Tuspaquin. You have hunted well, but you must go back to the camp now. You must not disturb the hunting warriors." He spoke in a different dialect of the Algonquian language than was used by her Nipmuc tribe, but she understood. She made a subservient gesture to indicate compliance. The man quietly walked away and disappeared into the forest.

With her knife, Sequankoon removed the entrails from her hare. She began walking back toward the encampment with a feeling of great pride. She'd have to watch out for Nish N'keke, who might seek retribution for his embarrassment. She decided to leave for her hunt before dawn the next morning.

· · · ·

METACOMET WAS SACHEM of the Wampanoag tribal confederacy, around the area that the white men called the Massachusetts Bay Colony. For years, the Wampanoag sought ways to live in harmony with the white men. The English even bestowed upon Metacomet the title of King Philip to show him respect during their negotiations. But many more Englishmen kept arriving by boats from the sea, and their leaders sought to subjugate the Indians to their laws. During the past year, Metacomet had formed an alliance among nearby Indian tribes, and together they began harassing and attacking the white men's villages, hoping to drive the settlers out of the land.

Metacomet held a council fire with sachems and warrior leaders from the Wampanoag, Narragansett, Pawtucket, Nipmuc, Pocumtuc, Pequot, and Micmac tribes. They spoke of the continuing toll of the white man's sickness. Fewer died from the disease this year, but they'd already lost most of their people. They needed to carefully plan their battles to effectively use their remaining warrior forces. They spoke of battles won and battles lost.

Metacomet gave examples of the difficulty that the English leaders were having trying to control the actions of their rapidly growing population. Weetamoo, sachem of the Pocasset Wampanoag, spoke of new strategies. She noted that whenever new English arrive, they seek to trade for gold, which, she explained, is a soft, yellow metal similar to lead. This gold was used for adornment rather than for making musket balls. The other sachems said that they too had been approached to trade gold, but their tribes have no knowledge about this yellow lead. Weetamoo recalled that one of the English merchants told her that the Spanish were getting this gold from Indians who lived in lands far beyond the mouth of the Connecticut River, in a place where the air is always hot. Metacomet remarked that if they could trade for some of this gold, maybe it could be used to cause competition and betrayal among some of the English leaders. Sagamore John, sachem of the Pawtucket tribe, offered to trade guns for some gold. Such a trade could be made with the tribes that live along a great river that is far away in the direction of the setting sun.

Metacomet said, "We don't need a great deal of gold, for it isn't the gold itself that is of value. It is the promise of more gold that will capture the minds of the English. We could tell them that the gold came from the land of the Mohawk. Then we will let the English poke at that bees' nest."

THIRTY-ONE

May 18, 1676

In the dark of night, a large company of soldiers stopped to water their horses at the edge of the Deerfield River. Samuel Stagg shivered from cold and fear, as thunder rumbled through the valley. He was regretting his agreement to join the militia and fight the Indians instead of spending another eight months in the Boston Gaol. He had been sentenced to a year in that hell-hole after he assaulted a shop owner to steal money from his till. He had only been pilloried for his first offense.

Samuel spread more mud on his face and neck and lit his tobacco pipe again, trying to ward off the incessant onslaught of mosquitoes and black flies. At least they gave him a horse to ride. He was one of a hundred fifty dragoons following old Captain Turner. They left from Hatfield early that morning. He felt miserable, having been drenched with cold rain for a few minutes every hour, all day long.

They made their way through the eerie ruins of the Deerfield Settlement, which the colonists had evacuated after a vicious attack by savages. Upon seeing the devastation, Samuel thought that God had certainly forsaken those poor settlers. They reached the shallows of the Deerfield River. The soldiers were told to pay attention to their surroundings so they would be able to find their way back to the Green River and Deerfield River fords after the battle. They were also told to be very quiet, because the savages might be watching the river fords. Samuel was pretty sure he would never find his way back on his own. The night was pitch black except for periodic flashes of lightning. If they retreated, he would just have to follow the others. Better yet, he could recognize the two guides they'd hired. He would follow them after the attack, if he was able.

After another two hours, the militia forded the Green River. They made very little noise while crossing, and the frequent thunder covered any noise from their horses. But Samuel still feared that savages would attack them at any moment. The men followed a brook upstream toward a swamp called White Ash. The formation came to a stop and the overall battle plan was explained. Three men would guard the horses at the Fall River ford. The rest would approach on foot over the nearby hill, and down to the Indian encampment on the Connecticut River. When given the signal, they would creep up to the huts and simultaneously fire directly into them. After hearing the plan, they were divided into small groups and given specific orders. Samuel Stagg and Eli Cass were ordered to cross to the west side of the Fall River's mouth. They were to kill any savages trying to get into their canoes and any that were hiding in the cliffs on the bank of the Connecticut River.

It took them the best part of an hour to get into position, but the men were ready just as dawn began to break. Samuel was shivering uncontrollably, and he didn't think he would be very accurate in his shooting. He tried hard not to make any noise even when the black flies flew up his nose and into his eyes. As the sky became lighter, he was amazed at how large the Indian encampment was. The falls were beautiful, but soon this would become a place of death.

ay 19, 1676

M   Before dawn, Sequankoon sneaked out of the wetu for her morning hunt. She gathered her bow and arrows which were hanging by the hut. As she headed toward the hill, the warrior, Tuspaquin, grabbed her from behind, his hand covering her mouth. Her instinct was to yell, but he signaled for her to be quiet. She saw that the boy Nish N'keke was standing behind him. It was then that she saw two other warriors launching their canoes. Tuspaquin half whispered and half gestured that many white men on horses were about to attack. "Both of you take one of the mishoons from below the falls, and get help from the warriors on the islands to the south. Tell them to ambush the English at the swamp with the white ash trees. Go as fast as you can!"

Sequankoon and Nish N'keke quickly forded the Fall River, then ran to the mishoons. Sequankoon climbed into the front of a mishoon, and Nish N'keke pushed it into the fast-moving current, and jumped in. They paddled furiously to steer the boat away from the rocky bank as it rounded a sharp bend in the river. It was difficult to see ahead in the dim light and early morning fog. They were both startled when they heard many guns firing at the encampment. Shouts, screams, and more gunshots echoed off the valley walls. They paddled as fast as they could, but worried that their mishoon would shoot, uncontrolled, past the warrior encampment. As they approached the first island at high speed, Sequankoon pointed to a large eddy that had formed downstream of the island. They paddled with all their might, making it into the calmer water. They slammed into several other mishoons and came to an abrupt stop. They crawled out and over the other canoes, climbing onto the rocky shore.

They found the warriors running out of their huts, awakened by the gunfire. Sequankoon and Nish N'keke excitedly explained what was happening and where Tuspaquin said to go. The warriors sprung into action, fording a narrow stream of water from the island onto the western bank of the river. Sequankoon and Nish N'keke followed the large band of warriors to the north. Sequankoon noticed at least ten women among the warriors. The group arrived at the swamp with the white ash trees, but no one was there yet. They heard a continuous barrage of gunfire in the distance, and they smelled smoke.

Warriors were deployed to several different locations around the swamp, and a group was sent to the Green River ford, to where the English were expected to withdraw. Some of the warriors wanted to proceed to the encampment, but they were told to wait until the white men retreated. Nish N'keke was told to follow one of the warriors. Sequankoon was instructed to climb to the top of the nearby wooded hill and report back if some of the English soldiers tried to escape through the forest. Sequankoon thought of her little brother, but suppressed her urge to cry as she ran up the hill and into the forest.

The soldiers were heard coming toward the swamp where the Indian warriors waited in ambush. Instead of an orderly column, the soldiers came in small groups being chased by other warriors. Some of the English fell silently when shot, while others went down screaming. Some fell with their wounded horses. The Indians were able to reload their French flintlock muskets much faster than the English could reload their old fowling guns. Many of the soldiers got through and were being chased as they tried to ride or run haphazardly back toward the Green River ford. They howled in fear and agony as the Indian warriors set upon them.

Sequankoon crouched in a thicket and watched for escaping soldiers. A chill ran up her spine as she heard blood-curdling screams from the swamp. She slowed her breathing when she heard footsteps approaching through the forest. She saw two soldiers running along the crest of the hill, carrying a heavy sack. She heard no others, so she followed them.

THIRTY-THREE

May 19, 1676

Samuel Stagg and Eli Cass found more than a few savages hiding among the rock cliffs. After shooting each of them, the soldiers took a few minutes to reload their guns. Most of their victims were children, but they felt no remorse. They didn't view savages as people. They viewed them as dangerous pests that needed to be eradicated. Samuel saw two old Indian men struggling to carry a heavy sack toward a canoe on the river bank. Samuel shot one of them and the other dropped the sack and jumped into the fast-moving river. He and Eli ran over and looked into the sack. Gold! The sack held a number of figurines and pieces of jewelry. "Let's take this and head back to Boston!" said Samuel.

As they started to haul the sack up the hill, they heard gunshots nearby. Samuel felt a musket ball fly right by his head. They retreated back down to the rocky bank of the river, struggling to carry their heavy load. Eli looked back and saw two warriors running toward them. He dropped his end of the sack, turned, and fired his gun at one of them. That warrior fell, but the other came running at them shrieking and wielding a war club. He leapt at Eli, but Samuel hit him in the head with the butt of his rifle. Eli grabbed the warrior's club and hit him in the head again. The warrior stopped moving.

Samuel and Eli grabbed the sack and ran down the riverbank until they came to another path that veered upward toward the hilltop. They struggled to drag the awkward load up the hill. Luckily, the sack was made of tough deer hide with strong stitching, and it remained intact. They continued along the hilltop until they could see the White Ash Swamp, down below. They saw small groups of soldiers being chased by warriors in the direction of the Green River ford. The warriors were coming from the south, the same direction in which Samuel and Eli were heading. Many of the retreating soldiers died in a barrage of gunfire from the savages. Those still running were screaming as they were set upon.

Samuel and Eli quickly shuffled along the hilltop path until they could see that no more Indians were approaching from the south. Tired of stumbling over tree roots, they turned and followed another path that led them down to the plain below. They trudgeded along the base of a small mountain with exposed cliffs of red rock. Suddenly, Eli screamed and fell, an arrow in his back. Samuel dropped the sack and saw a young Indian girl drawing an arrow. He realized that he hadn't taken the time to reload his gun. He dove at the ground and rolled as she shot toward him. The arrow missed. He picked up his gun and ran at the girl as she drew another arrow out of her quiver. He barreled into her, knocking her down, then he thumped her in the head with his gun. She stopped moving. He ran over and checked on Eli, but he wasn't breathing. This time, he took the time to reload, fumbling while watching for more savages. He continued to move along the base of the mountain, on a small path by a brook, dragging the heavy sack.

Samuel reached an area of impassable bramble, so he decided to head up a narrow rivulet that was flowing down the mountain. He continued to hear the voices of men in the distance, screaming as though they were being burned alive. He feared that he would die a painful death if he didn't abandon the sack. At the mouth of the rivulet, he saw what looked like green stones shimmering in the flowing water. He thought he would be able to find that spot again. He measured twenty paces up the hill and dug down into the bed of the flowing stream with his knife and his hands. He pulled out rocks and clay, forming a hole deep enough to hold the sack. He pushed the sack under the water and into the hole, covering it with rocks until it was no longer visible. Then he ran.

THIRTY-FOUR

Sequankoon woke with a start, as something brushed her face. It was the nose of a horse. The left side of her head was so painful, she could hardly move. Her fingers probed her head, finding her hair matted with sticky blood. She rose slowly to her feet and felt dizzy. She was startled to see a white man laying on the ground, her arrow in his back. He wasn't moving, but she couldn't be sure he was dead. She decided not to risk touching him. She could hear men shouting and screaming in the distance. She had shot a man. She was a warrior. She felt as though she shared the soul of her father's grandmother, Wompohtuck.

The white men had been carrying a sack. She walked over to the horse and saw a white man's saddle on it. She patted the horse's face to see that it was friendly, then quickly mounted it. She rode the horse along the bank of the brook. The brush was getting too thick along her path, so she found another path further from the brook, headed in the same direction.

After a few minutes, Sequankoon reached a field that led to the bank of an unfamiliar river, smaller than the Connecticut. As she approached the river, she saw the other white man climbing out of the far bank. He had swum across, but he had no sack. He looked back at her, then turned and ran. He was too far for her to shoot, and it seemed that the river was too deep to cross there with a horse. Sequankoon wasn't very experienced at riding a horse. She decided to search for the sack. She could see the path where the white man came out of the brush. She tied the horse to a tree and walked back along that path. Around her neck she wore a necklace of sweet grass that kept most of the biting flies away. After a while, she reached the fallen white man, but she still hadn't found the sack.

Sequankoon rode the horse back toward Peskeompskut. Her head throbbed fiercely, and she felt like she had a fever. She dismounted and led the horse toward a hill that overlooked the encampment. All was quiet. Looking down, she saw utter devastation. She could smell burnt flesh and gunpowder. She walked to the path that led down the hill, where she was stopped by an old warrior. "I am Mawtamps. What is your name?"

"I am Sequankoon."

"Sequankoon, down there is a place of death. You are up here, with the living. You must not go down there."

"I need to find my brother."

"Your brother is not there. No one is there. Come with me and tell me how it is that you survived."

As they walked, Sequankoon told Mawtamps that she woke before light to go hunting. When she set out, she and the boy Nish N'keke were sent by Tuspaquin to take a mishoon and rouse the warriors on the islands and have them go to the swamp with the white ash trees. She and Nish N'keke joined the warriors as they headed to the swamp. She was told to be a lookout on the hill, and it was there that she saw two white men escaping with a heavy sack. She chased them and shot one, and she thought he was dead. The other escaped across a deep river, but when he left the water, she saw no sack. She searched, but could not find the sack.

"That sack is important. We were bringing it to Metacomet. It contains the totems of another tribe from far away. You will lead me to where you last saw the sack, and where you last saw the white men." Mawtamps summoned two warriors and told them to join them. They took horses and followed Sequankoon as she rode to the body of the man she had shot. One of the warriors dismounted and checked the white man, declaring that he was dead. The warrior took the dead man's gun, knife, powder horn, and musket balls. Sequankoon showed them where the other white man crossed the river. They searched the area between the river and the dead man, but found nothing.

Mawtamps said, "He may have put the sack in the river." The warriors dove into the cool waters of the Deerfield River and searched. After a few minutes, they said that it was not there. As they headed back, Mawtamps stopped near a small stream where the soil had been disturbed. They dug in the area and found nothing. He told them to search the bottom of the small stream.

They found the sack. Mawtamps inspected the items in the sack and took a few out. He said, "Put these back in the stream and bury them. If the white man returns, he will find some of the gold and he will leave this place. If he finds nothing, he will bring his friends and come after us."

Mawtamps looked at Sequankoon and said, "You are no longer a little girl. You deserve the name of a warrior. From now on, you will be called Wappenaugh." She was now named after the small animal that hunts, the marten. "You will ride with the warriors as we go upstream to the great river bend, where we will meet with those who survived."

· · · ·

THE NEXT DAY, WAPPENAUGH rode her horse with the other warriors into the temporary camp set up by those who survived the massacre at Peskeompskut. Nish N'keke rode with the warriors, as well. Wappenaugh tied her horse to a tree and wandered through the village, asking if anyone had seen her little brother Mooi Anequs as well as her new mother Sukkikesuk. She was pleased to see that quite a few survived, but a great pall of death hung over the camp. Hundreds had been killed. Many of the older women were loudly mourning their losses. She saw a girl that she knew. The girl was crying, but when she was asked about Mooi Anequs, the girl just shook her head and cried some more. Wappenaugh wandered through the camp and realized that her brother was not there. She suppressed her urge to cry. She was a warrior.

Mₐy 4, 2023

Gil was so excited by the powder horn finding, that he and Lili drove right back to Greenfield the next morning. They met up with Detective Karen Tindall at the Greenfield Police Station. Karen said, "Katrina Ryu was taken into protective custody by Special Agent Davis from the Albany FBI. At this point, she isn't a likely suspect for the killing of Paul Combs. The Crime Lab says she was probably in custody while he was being interred. She didn't have any gunpowder residue on her hands or clothing, and her story about being pursued in New York checked out. The FBI is still looking for her cohort, Evan Melsty, who doesn't seem to exist."

Gil smiled and said, "I think I figured out what Kevin Clarion was searching for. Lili and I went to Fort William Henry at Lake George, where Kevin worked last summer. They have a powder horn at the fort's museum. Its inscription describes a sack with gold figurines and jewelry from the Orient buried under a brook in Greenfield." He showed Karen pictures of the powder horn and plaque. "It was dated from 1676, during Captain Turner's massacre of the Indians at Turners Falls. The way it's described, I think the sack might be buried in the area where Sergeant Phillips spotted someone searching, near Highland Pond. I'd like to take the robot and search in that area. The museum expert said that the artifacts would be an important historical find, and I think that could be why Kevin was searching for it. They also would be very valuable."

"Wow. That certainly would be something, but I don't think we could pay you to search for that. It isn't really evidence for the mole-people case."

Gil smiled. "Well, it was stolen from murdered Indians back in 1676, which, I think is definitely a crime. But, it doesn't matter if you pay me. I'll just go and search for it, anyway. It's on town property."

"City property. We're a city now," said Karen.

"Whatever," shrugged Gil.

• • • •

AS THEY LEFT THE STATION, Gil said to Lili, "I'd like to go down to UMass to find out more about turtle stones, before I start searching."

"Okay. Maybe I'll go with you so I can stop by my house and pick up a few things. I'll drive." They got to the UMass campus and found the Morrill Science Center. An administrative assistant there found them a geologist to speak with."

"Hi, I'm Kerry Izzo."

"I'm Gil Novak and this is Lili D'Amico. Lili is an agent with the State Police and I'm a consultant for the Greenfield Police Department." Lili showed her ID. "We're researching an inscription on a powder horn from colonial times," said Gil. "It mentions a brook in Greenfield that has 'green turtle stones' under the water. I'm trying to figure out what they may be, so I can find this brook. It's connected to some unsolved crimes." Lili showed Kerry a picture of the powder horn and plaque.

"Well, that all sounds very intriguing. There are several kinds of rocks called turtle stones. Kerry quickly typed on her keyboard and turned the monitor toward Gil and Lili. This type of rock looks like a turtle shell. It's found in this area near water, with many types of stones. The turtle shell pattern is created when water erodes away what were veins of minerals that were more soluble than the surrounding strata. The rocks are usually gray in color, but I suppose you could have rocks that have a greenish tinge to them in your brook."

She typed some more. "This is green turtle stone, the state gem of Michigan. Its a mineral called chlorastrolite. As you can see, it's very green and has a turtle shell pattern. But, as far as I know, it's only been found in Michigan, Canada, and the Isle of Skye in the UK." She began typing again. "This here is called septaria, or turtle rock. It's similar to the gray turtle stones I showed you, but the washed out veins have been filled with some colorful mineral deposits making the rocks look like turtle shells. These are sometimes found on the banks of rivers in New York State, but I haven't heard of any around here."

Kerry thought for a minute and typed some more. "This might be it. There's a mineral called prehnite that's found around here. It comes in a variety of forms, but one form is very rounded and could look like a small turtle under water. It's also usually green in color. I actually have some samples in here." She walked over to a cabinet, searched through several drawers, and pulled out a clear plastic box. She showed Gil and Lili some prehnite samples and, with a little imagination, they could look like the little jade turtles found in gift shops. "I think this could be what you're looking for. You can find them around some of the rocky hills in western Massachusetts." Gil thanked Kerry for her help.

• • • •

THEY GOT TO LILI'S house and went in. It was cool inside because Lili had turned down the thermostat before leaving. Lili went upstairs to pack a bag with some more clothing. Gil looked around the living room. There were quite a few framed pictures of Lili's family and friends. He realized that he didn't know much about any of them. He hadn't spent much time there. There was an electric piano with a book of sheet music. Gil had never heard her play. There was a lot he didn't know about her. Living together in Florida removed each of them from their normal lives. What would their living room look like if they shared a house?

The doorbell rang. Gil opened the inner door and saw a couple of young women with clipboards. He opened the storm door and said, "Hello, can I help you?"

One of the women said, "We're wondering if you'd sign a petition. It's about increasing transparency in the city council. We're concerned that..."

Gil interrupted and said, "Sorry, I don't live in Northampton. Let me get my girlfriend. Please come in." He went to the bottom of the stairs and called, "Lili, you have a petition to sign."

"Coming!"

Gil turned around and ZAP! A stun gun was pressed to the side of his rib cage. He collapsed, shaking, and his mind was scattered. He couldn't speak. Lili came down the stairs and, as she turned at the bottom stair, ZAP! The stun gun was pushed into her neck. She went down shaking. A needle was plunged into her neck, sinking her into unconsciousness.

· · · ·

GRADUALLY, GIL REGAINED awareness of his surroundings. He was lying on the floor. He had severe pain in his side where he had been stunned. He was shaking uncontrollably. Tears filled his eyes.

He looked around and realized he was in Lili's house. "Uhh," he croaked. "L-L-L-Lili! Lili!" His phone was in his pocket. He fumbled trying to hit the emergency call button, and then, 9-1-1.

"Northampton Emergency Dispatch. Do you need police, fire, or medical?"

"Police! Girlfriend...missing! I, uh, I was tased."

"What is your location, sir?" He struggled to say the address. "I have police on the way. Are you hurt, sir?"

"Uh, Hurts all over. Hard to breathe. Lying on floor."

"I have an ambulance on the way. What is your name, sir?"

"G-G-Gil. Novak."

"Okay Gil. I show that you are in a house owned by Lili D'Amico. Is that your girlfriend who is missing?"

"Yes. She's police. State police.."

"You're saying she is a state police officer? Is that correct, sir?"

"Yes. Hear siren."

"Is your door unlocked?"

"I think so."

"Are the perpetrators still in the house?"

"I, I don't know."

"Are you armed, Gil? Do you have any weapons."

"No. Lili does. Police are here."

THIRTY-SIX

Gil was lying in a bed in the emergency room at Cooley Dickinson Hospital. The doctor had given him an anti-anxiety medication. Within a few minutes, Gil stopped shaking, and it was easier for him to breath. An ECG showed that his heart was okay. A man and a woman approached. "Mr. Novak?" Gil nodded. "I'm Detective Chris Varney and this is Cherise Holmes from the Crime Lab." Varney showed his badge.

"Lili's boss."

"Yes, Gil. I've heard so much about you."

"Do you know who took Lili?" asked Varney.

"It's probably related to the Martha Eames case," said Gil.

"The woman from Florida?" asked Cherise. Gil nodded. Cherise and Gil told Detective Varney about that case and the related attack in Northampton the month before. Gil also mentioned the related murder of Barbara LeClerc in Portsmouth. Cherise said, "We've got Crime Scene techs at Lili's house."

Gil suddenly sat up. "Wait! She has a tracker!" He took his phone out of his pocket and fumbled around for a minute. "Look, the app says she's on I-95 near New Haven!"

"How do I get that on my phone?" asked Varney. Gil showed him what app to install and how to track Lili's tag, along with his own tag. The detective turned to leave.

"Wait!" called Gil. "One more thing. Call Special Agent Mayet Elsayed from the FBI. This is her case. I have her number here." The detective took the number and ran out the door."

"You may have just saved Lili!" said Cherise. "Hopefully she still has it on her,"

"We got them after finding out her house was bugged. We put them in these little useless pockets in our jeans."

"How are you feeling, Gil?" asked Cherise.

"My muscles are sore all over. They gave me some ibuprofen for that. I couldn't stop shaking, so they gave me some anti-anxiety medication and it calmed me down. I'm afraid that when it wears off, I'll be frantic about Lili."

* * * *

SPECIAL AGENT ELSAYED'S helicopter was en route from Boston to New York City, where the FBI were gathering to intercept the kidnappers. Agents from the Bridgeport, Connecticut FBI office were coordinating with the Connecticut State Police to catch up with the car.

Mayet was receiving constant updates through her headset. A State Police helicopter was following a black Tesla sedan from which the tracker signal was being transmitted. Mayet was concerned that the kidnappers could have found the tracker device and placed it into a random car.

Suddenly, an agent out of New York told Bridgeport Police to stand down. The tracking device was a ruse. Mayet demanded to know who had provided that information. She was told that it came out of headquarters in D.C. Mayet told New York and Bridgeport to disregard the directive out of D.C. and to intercept the tracked vehicle. New York argued with her, but she explained that the people behind the kidnapping had reecently infiltrated the Federal Government and shot a US Marshal who had been guarding someone in WITSEC.

Bridgeport reported that the subject vehicle left I-95 at exit 29. State police were in pursuit. Mayet told New York to track down where precisely in D.C. headquarters the direction to stand down originated. The police were still eight minutes out of Bridgeport, but their helicopter had eyes on the tracked car. "The subject vehicle is entering a marina. Steelpointe Marina. Bridgeport Police have been directed to the marina, as well."

As Mayet's helicopter approached Bridgeport, the New York office said that D.C. headquarters were adamant that they stand down. "Do not stand down. Continue to apprehend," directed Mayet. "We are rescuing a kidnapped police officer!"

"The subjects have boarded a dark cigarette boat. We observed two subjects forcing a third onto the boat. The victim tried to jump off the dock, but was thrown onto the boat. There is another subject driving the boat. Police are converging on the scene. The boat has left the marina!"

"Get the Coast Guard on it!" yelled Mayet. She watched as the boat sped out of the harbor. "The boat is turning southwest, heading toward New York City."

"The Coast Guard has deployed a fast boat out of Easton's Neck, Long Island," a voice reported. "They have also deployed a helicopter."

"The boat has turned around and is now headed northeast! I repeat, the subject boat is now headed northeast!" shouted Mayet. The cigarette boat was faster than the Coast Guard vessel. "The subject boat is passing New Haven harbor!"

"A second Coast Guard boat is being deployed from New Haven."

Mayet could see a Coast Guard crew running toward their dock. "The subject boat has turned into New Haven harbor, along the east shore!" She said. The boat sped into the harbor, seemingly heading straight toward the second Coast Guard boat which was just pulling away from its dock. Suddenly, the boat veered toward a little bay. She looked at the map on her cellphone. "They're heading into Morris Cove, toward a dock!" She zoomed in on her map. "They're heading to the New Haven Yacht Club. I'll get the police on it."

Mayet's helicopter hovered over the yacht club. She saw four people get off the boat, one of them apparently Lili, who was being forced along. She didn't appear to be injured. A silver van pulled out of a parking spot and intercepted the group from the boat. Lili was shoved into the van and the kidnappers piled in after her. "New Haven police, this is Special Agent Elsayed with the FBI, we are in pursuit of at least four kidnappers and their victim who are in a silver van currently pulling out of the New Haven yacht club. I am observing from an FBI helicopter. The subjects are headed east on Cove Street. You are requested to intercept and apprehend. They should be considered armed and dangerous. The kidnap victim is an agent with the Massachusetts State Police."

"Subjects have turned north on Lighthouse Road." Mayet could see two cruisers speeding from the north and one from the south, lights flashing. "Subject vehicle is continuing northeast on the Morris Causeway. Wait, subject vehicle has exited Morris Causeway onto a dirt road. They're headed toward the fence at Tweed Airport. A fence gate is open! They're now on airport property near the south end of runway 2. A dark-colored private jet is turning onto runway 2." The police cruisers changed direction and headed to the airport. The helicopter pilot radioed the airport and directed them to hold all traffic. "The van has rendezvoused with the aircraft and the subjects are entering the cabin now! We're losing them, people!" Mayet was losing hope.

She called FBI headquarters in New York City and quickly explained the situation. She was told that their only option at this time was to track the jet and intercept them at their destination. The New York office would initiate those actions. The jet powered down the runway, took off, and headed north.

• • • •

GIL WAS GETTING READY to leave the hospital when his phone rang. "Hi Gil, this is Special Agent Elsayed. How are you feeling?"

"I'm okay. Where is Lili?"

"I'm afraid the kidnappers got away with her. They are on a jet, currently heading north over Quebec."

Gil collapsed onto the floor. A nurse heard the noise and rushed into the room. The nurse rang the call button and another nurse came in. Mayet was yelling on the phone, "Gil? Gil? Are you there?

THIRTY-SEVEN

A foggy image formed in Lili's mind that she couldn't quite grasp. The fog suddenly dissipated, and an unfamiliar room appeared. She was reclining in what seemed like a dentist's chair. An IV containing clear fluid dripped into her right arm. Her wrists and ankles were fastened to the chair with blue cable ties. The tray table held several surgical instruments. It looked like the typical torture setup she'd seen in spy movies.

Lili frantically tried to free her hands. The cable tie on her right arm was a bit loose, presumably to enable good flow from the IV. She moved her hand around and the bottom edge of the chair's arm seemed to be slightly sharp. She aggressively moved her wrist back and forth, trying to saw the cable tie. A sudden wave of nausea hit her and she forcefully vomited off the side of the chair. When she recovered, she continued to saw her cable tie.

Snap! The cable tie flew off Lili's wrist. She heard footsteps coming. She snatched a scalpel from the tray and hid it under her wrist on the arm of the chair. A disheveled woman with a mop of frizzy dark hair and large glasses entered the room. "Ach, you were sick. I'll get something to clean it up." She spoke with a strong foreign accent of some sort.

As the woman left the room, Lili grasped the scalpel and furiously cut at the cable tie holding her left arm. Snap! It was free. Next, she freed her left leg. She feared that the woman would find the cut ties as she cleaned up the floor. She heard the footsteps returning, but hadn't finished cutting the tie holding her right leg. She hid the scalpel under her right wrist again, and sat back as if she were still bound.

The frizzy-haired woman entered the room pushing a large metal bucket with a mop. The woman stopped and said, "Lili D'Amico, you are going to die today. My job is simply to get you to tell me how to find Martha Eames. If you just tell me, I will not have to torture you. You will die quickly and painlessly. Think about that." The woman pushed the bucket around to the right side of her chair. Lili grabbed the woman's hair, pulled back her head, and stabbed her in the eye, as hard as she could. The woman grabbed Lili's arm and collapsed, shrieking. Lili was pulled over the arm of the chair awkwardly, with her right leg still tied to the chair. The woman released Lili's arm and scrambled backward, crab-walking. Lili grabbed a long, metal tool from the tray and pried the cable tie on her right leg until it snapped.

The IV stand and instrument tray crashed to the floor as Lili scrambled out of the chair. Lili pulled the IV out of her arm. She ran to the door, set the door lock, and pulled the door shut as she left. The woman had come from the right, so she ran to the left, down a hallway. She heard people running to the interrogation room. They were yelling in what sounded like Russian. Lili kept running until she reached what appeared to be an exit door. She stepped out of the building cautiously and saw no one around. She heard a vehicle approach the building on the other side. Reinforcements.

Peering around the corner of the building, Lili saw a fence surrounding the building. The fence had only one gate, but it was open. Her bladder was about to burst, so she pulled down her pants, crouched, and urinated for what seemed like a very long time. When she finished, she ran for the gate as fast as she'd ever run in her life. There was a small paved road beyond the gate. It appeared to be a rural area, but there were very few trees, and not many leaves had appeared on the bare branches. Turning to the right, she ran along the open road, eventually veering off into a small grove of trees. She looked in all directions and she saw no place to hide. She tried to calm herself. She'd been running on instinct, fight, flight, or die. Now she had to stop and think. She had been at an abandoned airport. In one direction, it looked like there was a town in the distance. In the opposite direction were farm fields offering little cover. The town would offer more opportunities for concealment, disguise, and help. She ran, staying just off the road and heading for cover wherever she could find it. When two cars suddenly sped out from the airport, she dove into a grassy ditch.

....

GIL PULLED INTO JULIA'S driveway. He paused, mustering up his courage to discuss Lili's situation. He'd already told her on the phone that Lili had been kidnapped, but hadn't yet updated her on new information he'd received. He got out of the car and saw five-year-old Dez jumping up and down in the window. He couldn't help but smile at her.

When he entered the house, Julia and Dez gave him hugs. Ziggy gave him a fist-bump. "Will you color with me?" asked Dez. "Where's Lili?"

"Grampy will color with you after supper," said Julia. "Go wash your hands. You too, Zig."

"Lili isn't in Saratoga today. She had something else she had to do," said Gil, forcing a smile.

As the kids went to wash up, Julia asked, "Any word?"

"I do have an update. We'll talk after dinner."

During dinner, Gil was distracted. He was comforted by Julia's wonderful lasagna along with the normal family conversation. He was doing his best to hide his anxiety, fear, and feeling of helplessness. He kept smiling. Jazz seemed unusually cheerful. "Jazz, it's good to see you so happy. Do you have a boyfriend?" he teased.

Her face and neck turned crimson. She looked at her parents with a panicked expression. Julia smiled at her and said, "No way!" Jazz ran upstairs and slammed the door to her bedroom. Julia went up after her.

"How can a ten-year-old have a boyfriend?" asked Mike. He seemed upset.

"At ten, I'm sure it's just a boy who is her friend. It's too soon to ask if he has a good job with benefits."

"How come you see Jazz for only twenty minutes and you can tell she has a boyfriend, and Julia and I had no idea?" asked Mike.

"Maybe I'm just gifted at reading people. Or maybe it was obvious."

"Can I be done?" asked Ziggy.

"Me too?" asked Dez.

"Okay Zig, bring your dishes to the kitchen. Dez, you take four more bites." Dez ate four more bites and left the table.

Julia came down the stairs. "I guess we could have handled that better."

"I'm sorry I was so abrupt," said Gil. "I shouldn't have said anything."

"She's alright. She's friendly with a boy from her class named Rory. He kissed her twice, on her cheek. He's nine years old."

"Is he rich?" asked Mike. Julia punched him in the shoulder.

"So tell us about Lili, Dad."

Gil took a deep breath. "You know how I told you that she has a tracking tag? Well, she was flown to a sort-of country called Transnistria." His voice was shaking.

"Where is that? What do you mean, a sort-of country?" asked Mike.

"Transnistria is an unrecognized country on a strip of land between Moldova and Ukraine. It's basically the city of Tiraspol and its surrounding area. Officially, it's part of Moldova, but they have declared their own government, and have suspicious ties to Russia. It's one of those areas like Crimea and Eastern Ukraine where Russia sets up a puppet state until they invade the area and declare the area part of Russia."

"So, she's kidnapped by unknown people to a non-country with Russian ties, near Ukraine which is at war with Russia?" asked Mike. "Could she be in any more danger? Holy shit!"

Julia looked up Transnistria on her phone. "She's very far from any country that looks safe."

"There's more," said Gil. She was initially flown to a defunct military air base, but now she seems to be wandering around the surrounding area. The FBI thinks she may have escaped and is on the run."

"Seriously?" asked Julia. "I can't even imagine that. I doubt anyone within three hundred miles speaks English."

"This all sounds like a movie plot." said Mike.

"The FBI says they're working on getting her out of there," said Gil. "I'm going nuts because there's nothing I can do about it. Lili's a trained police officer, so if anyone could escape, she could. Plus she's a warrior! She's part Native American."

"Really?" asked Julia. Gil nodded.

"I am so glad I came here for dinner. It was so nice to be with you guys, and it took my mind away from fretting about Lili's situation, for a little while. Even just talking to you about it has helped me." Gil was tearing up.

"Oh, Dad. This is so horrible. Tomorrow you should do a workout of some sort. Exercise helps with stress."

"I think I'll head back to Greenfield tomorrow and use my robot to search for clues in the tunnels again. That will keep my mind occupied. Please keep this situation between us."

THIRTY-EIGHT

Lili made it to a residential area. She knelt behind a bush and watched a small house for half an hour. There didn't seem to be anyone in the house. Lili felt tired, thirsty, hungry, and filthy. She had no idea where she was, but it seemed to be an industrial city surrounded by farms. The landscape was flat. She moved cautiously from the brush to the side of the house. She opened the hose spigot and cringed when it squealed, but no one appeared. She drank eagerly to quench her thirst, then she rinsed her face and hair with the cold water. She darted quickly back into the brush.

Lili reached a highway that ran east-west, based on the direction of the sunrise. She knew she was in Eastern Europe, as all the signs were written using the Cyrillic alphabet. Maybe Russia. She decided to head west, since Western Europe seemed more friendly than Eastern Europe, from the little she knew. She continued to use brush for concealment. She'd seen several drones flying around, which she presumed were looking for her. Whenever a dog barked, she assumed they were tracking her. As she continued on, she smelled something like rotting flesh, then a horrendous noise made her dive to the ground. She looked up and saw a huge black boar rooting for food, only twenty feet away. She got up and ran away as fast as she could. She felt as feral as that pig.

Lili kept moving, darting from cover to cover until it began to get dark. She was running on empty. She sneaked over to a garden shed, but it was locked. She heard people talking nearby, so she crawled into a narrow space under the shed. She began to shiver, so she dug a depression in the dirt, laid down, and pulled dried leaves over her body for warmth. Within a few minutes, she was asleep.

• • • •

SOPHIE POSTAN WAS THE operations chief at the American Embassy in Chisinau, Moldova. She was young to hold such a senior position, only twenty-seven. She was primarily an analyst, based on her prior experience working at CIA headquarters in Langley, Virginia. She was given operational training before being deployed to her parents' home country. She took a call about Lili D'Amico's predicament, and was provided with the method for tracking her.

Sophie walked to the communications room and spoke to the operator on duty. One of their contacts in Transnistria was an elderly man named Bogdan whose hobby was operating a ham radio. The embassy's communications operator sent Bogdan a ciphered message using Morse code.

That evening, when he returned to his home, Bogdan checked his signal-recording software for prior radio traffic. He returned several calls he'd received from his radio friends. Then he discovered the ciphered message from the Americans. He decoded the message and called his granddaughter Amina. He told her to call in sick to work, and get her brother Marius to do the same. They were instructed to go out early in the morning to find the woman code-named Parjoale, which meant meatball. Parjaole was located a few kilometers from the Dnister River, which she would have to cross into undisputed Moldovan territory. He told Amina that drones would be searching for the woman along the river, perhaps with thermal imaging. Amina was instructed to use special code words to get the woman's attention, but that she wouldn't be expecting them and will be frightened.

· · · ·

AT DAYBREAK, SOPHIE took a dark blue RAV4 from the carpool and headed toward the town of Bender. It would take her over an hour to get there via the R2 highway. Before going on the road, she stopped at a market and bought some meat pies, bottled water, and chocolate for her guest. She also had some money for her Transnistrian assets.

At dawn, Lili crawled out from under the shed and ran. She continued west alongside a raised railroad bed that had plenty of shrubs for cover. She moved along the edge of a large farm field growing a sea of bright yellow flowers. In the distance she could hear barking dogs and shouting men. If they were following her trail, they were gaining ground. She tried to run faster, but her energy level was low. She passed the field and entered another residential area with paved streets and single-family houses. She crossed over the rail bed several times, seeking as much cover as possible.

As she continued to dart among the shrubs, Lili could hear that one of the search dogs was about to overtake her. She grabbed a large stick from the ground and waited for the confrontation. Suddenly, she found herself face-to-face with a young woman who held her finger to her mouth, indicating that she should stay quiet. She said, "Mayet says hi." The dog raced toward them, and the woman threw some chunks of meat several yards away. The dog whipped around and ran to the unexpected meal. A drone zipped overhead to the dog's location. The young woman grabbed Lili's arm and pulled her down, under some bushes. A gunshot rang out and the shattered drone fell to the ground.

Lili's shaking hands covered her face in disbelief. The woman pointed to herself and said, "Amina." She indicated for her brother to come over. "Marius." Marius took a small stick and drew a map in the dirt. "Dnister," he said, indicating a river. He made a sound like a train indicating the railroad track and showed where it crossed the river. Then he showed where the highway crossed the river, adjacent to the railroad. He indicated that there were drones flying above, searching along the river, and pointed one out as it zoomed by at a distance. He gestured that they would need to swim across the river under the railroad bridge. Amina gestured that it would be cold. Lili nodded.

The three of them ran. When a drone approached, Amina signaled for them to stop. She ran back the way they came, and the drone followed. Marius shot the drone out of the sky. They continued to run toward the river. As they approached the railroad bridge, they stopped and watched the border guards, who maintained a lookout on and around the highway bridge, just two hundred feet away. There seemed to be a rhythm to their patrol, so Marius timed their own movements to avoid them. The three of them ran under the railroad bridge to the river bank. Marius hid his shotgun among the metal beams of the bridge, then quickly led them into the water. The cold took Lili's breath away. She was shivering uncontrollably, but began to swim with all her might. All three were strong swimmers, but the current took them downstream from the railroad bridge toward the highway bridge. When they were halfway across, they could hear shouting from above. Machine gun fire erupted, and they dove underwater. When they finally popped up to get some air, the gunfire had stopped. They were now directly under the highway bridge. They swam as fast as they could toward the western shore of the Dnister.

Lili was freezing as they made their way up the bank. The border guards did not pursue them. Marius led them to a nearby war memorial. A woman was waiting for them. "Lili, I am Sophie, from the American Embassy." Sophie gave them blankets.

"W-w-what e-e-embassy? Where?" asked Lili.

"Welcome to Moldova!" Sophie laid out a spread of food and drinks. Lili drank an entire bottle of apple juice without stopping. Then she ate ravenously. As they finished their meal, Sophie announced, "We should get going." She handed Amina an envelope full of cash and some bus tickets to get them back across the border. Sophie thanked them, and Lili gave them each a hug.

THIRTY-NINE

Gil was back in Greenfield, struggling to steer his ground-penetrating radar machine along Graves Brook. There were a lot of trees and brush along the brook near its source at Highland Pond. So far, he'd found an old wooden tennis racket and a hockey skate. He was glad that his bug repellent was working and that he was wearing knee-high rubber boots. He heard a car drive up and stop behind him. The car door opened and shut.

"Hey Gil," said Karen.

"Hello, Detective."

"Are you and Lili up for dinner tonight?"

Gil took a deep breath and climbed out onto the road. "I asked you to come out here because there's something I have to tell you. Lili's been kidnapped." Gil explained everything that had happened to Lili. He struggled to keep from crying. "I'm here to try and keep from going nuts."

Karen gave Gil a hug. "Oh my God, why didn't you tell me?"

"I just told you. I wanted to tell you in person. We have to keep this quiet to prevent it from becoming a worse nightmare in the international arena. And anyway, there's nothing you and I can do about it right now."

"Unbelievable. Now I'm going to go nuts. Do you need any help right now?"

"No, I'm okay. It's just a pain getting through this brush, but I'll manage. I'll cut through the brush, if I have to. Anything new with the mole people?"

"There is, as a matter of fact. Special Agent Davis called yesterday and told me that Katrina Ryu remembered something. She told the US Marshals that while she was working on the tunnels, Evan Melsty asked her to look at some plans for an underground network of tunnels and rooms that his father was working on. He asked for any ideas she might have to improve his design. He told her that it was going to be built in this area. He paid her three thousand dollars for her input. Katrina didn't remember the town's name. We still haven't figured out who this Evan guy is."

"You know, Evan Melsty sounds like a made-up name, maybe an anagram. You know, where the letters are mixed up to form different words."

"Huh. I'll go work on that idea." Karen went over to her car and used the back of a piece of scrap paper. She talked to herself while she scribbled. After a few minutes, she ran back over to Gil and said, "I think I've got it! Steve Manly."

"Let me see." Gil looked at all the rearrangements she'd tried and said, "Maybe, but it doesn't look quite right to me. I think the name Manly would normally have an e before the y. You could also try Lyman. Steve Lyman, how about that?"

"I like that. I know that there are Lymans around here. I'll work more on this anagram theory. I gotta go. Please keep me up to date on Lili."

· · · ·

GIL CONTINUED TO SCAN the bank of the brook with his radar unit. He was searching for smaller brooks that flowed from the adjacent hillside and had turtle stones under the water. It looked like this brook, and the pond from which it flowed, were fed by springwater flowing off the mountain. There was a dirt road between the hillside and the brook that must have changed the flow pattern from what it had been in the seventeenth century.

As he continued to search, Gil encountered what looked like intermittent areas of underground water flow. They were only about a foot or two wide and didn't seem to flow in continual streams. He looked up toward the dirt road and saw that the streams were flowing out of small culverts, only about a foot in diameter. He steered his robot across the mouth of one of the streams, and several rocks appeared on his video screen. He steered the robot toward the next stream and, just before it got there, his screen showed a strange pattern, about three feet underground. It looked like bubble-wrap.

Gil took his shovel, stepped into the deeper brook, and dug into the bank. It was awkward, and he couldn't see a thing as the hole filled with muddy water. At about three feet in depth, he encountered a rocky layer. He dug out a piece of the rock and rinsed it off. The rock was stained, but there were definitely rounded green minerals embedded in dull brown rock. Prehnite! He dug deeper to uncover more of the rocky layer, but water was flowing over it. He tried to clean the rocky layer with his hands, but couldn't see anything. They might have felt like little turtles.

Gil washed his muddy hands off in the brook, and attempted to dry them on his wet and muddy pants. He took out his phone and looked up the powder horn's inscription. It said the sack was buried twenty paces up. With his shovel, he walked across the road and up the hill until he'd counted twenty paces. There was no stream there, but he stuck the shovel into the ground to mark the location. He went back to get his robot and his water bottle. There were a lot of small trees on the hillside, but there was enough room to maneuver his robot.

Gil steered his radar machine in a search pattern and found what looked like flowing water underground. He searched a few yards up and down the hill but didn't see anything interesting. When he searched farther down the hill, he saw what looked like a rock ledge. The ledge caused the stream's flow to shift sharply to the left. So, the stream he had found was probably the one that fed the next culvert down the road. The stream he was after might be a few yards farther to the right.

Gil guided the robot to the right along the ledge and found another underground stream. He steered the robot uphill, along the stream, and he saw something unusual on his radar display. Gil cleared layers of decaying leaves out of the way and dug down through the soil. When he was down a couple of feet, the bottom of the hole filled up with muddy water. He kept digging, but the mud on his shovel oozed back into the water before he could move it out. It was a losing battle.

He left his shovel by the hole, but packed up his robot and put it in his car. He drove to the nearest big-box hardware store and bought a battery-powered water pump and some batteries. When he got back, he placed the pump in the water and turned it on. It wasn't strong enough to pump the hole dry, but it lowered the water level sufficiently to enable digging. Gil dug down another two feet and his shovel clunked against something hard.

He used his bare hands to search through the mud and he pulled something up. He rinsed it off and saw that it was a small gold statuette. He was so excited, he couldn't catch his breath. He set it to the side and searched some more. He found another gold statuette. He went to his car and got his wand-style metal detector. He probed around the bottom of the hole, but didn't find anything else. According to the powder horn, there should be some jewelry. Gil went back to the car and got his bigger, more powerful metal detector. He searched inside the hole and in the surrounding area, but he didn't find anything else.

Gil looked at his clothes and confirmed that he was a complete muddy mess. By this time, he was shaking both because of chill and anxiety. He was excited that he'd found the gold statuettes, but Lili's life was in grave danger, and there was nothing he could do. He slumped to the ground and cried.

When he regained his composure, he wiped off his hands as best he could and took out his phone to call Karen. Before he could dial, his phone rang. "Gil, this is Special Agent Elsayed. We have Lili. She's okay. She's good."

Gil's heart was racing. "Where is she?"

"She's at the American Embassy in Chisinau, Moldova. She's safe."

"Moldova? Is she hurt?"

"She's not physically hurt, not at all. But, she's obviously been through a major ordeal. Our doctor gave her a sedative and she's sleeping."

"What should I do?"

"Tomorrow, we plan to fly her to our London office for a debrief. Then we'll fly her home."

"Can I meet her in London? I have an idea about the people who are after her and Martha."

"Where are you now, Gil? I'd like to hear your theory, but not over the phone."

"I'm in Greenfield, Mass."

"Tell me where you're staying and I'll meet you there at about four o'clock."

Back at the hotel, Gil showered and dressed. He cleaned the dirt off of the gold statuettes and brought them to the Greenfield Police Station. Karen was on the phone at her desk, so he stood behind her, reached around, and put one of the figures on her desk. She jumped out of her seat. "I'm sorry, I have to call you back. Something's come up." She ended her call and said, "Oh my God, you found it!"

Gil said, "Karen, Lili escaped. She's safe."

Karen yelped and gave Gil a long hug. "What happened?"

"I don't have the whole story yet. She's at the American Embassy in Moldova."

"Moldova?"

He shrugged. "She's not injured. I'm meeting with Special Agent Elsayed at the hotel in an hour."

Gil placed the other figurine on her desk. One was about ten inches tall, and looked like a chubby guy without a shirt, wearing jewelry and a huge headdress. He had a dour expression. The other was a a couple of inches shorter. It was a slim guy, no shirt, with the head of a bird and a smaller headdress. Both figurines were somewhat heavy, but they were probably hollow. "The powder horn inscription said they were from the Orient, but I'd say these are from Central or South America. I bet they're worth a lot of money, but I think the real value is their historical significance. Can you imagine how the Indians in New England got their hands on gold figurines from South America? I wonder why they had them."

"I was expecting more treasure," said Karen. "Didn't the powder horn say there was jewelry?"

"It did. I was expecting more also, and I thought I'd find remnants of the sack. But I didn't."

"Hmm. My gut tells me to book the figurines into evidence, although they really aren't evidence of a crime. Well, maybe a theft from four hundred years ago. Let me go get the Chief."

Chief Reyes came to Karen's desk and looked down at the statuettes. He picked one up to see how heavy it was. "Unbelievable. Your robot really works! Let's book them into evidence for the time being. We should lock them in the heavy-duty safe in the evidence locker. What do you think we should do with them, Gil?"

"I'd give them back to the Indians."

Chief Reyes nodded. "I think that would be the right thing to do. Why don't you figure out who specifically we would give them to? Karen, let me know what the DA has to say about this."

● ● ● ●

GIL PACED BACK AND forth in the lobby of his hotel. Special Agent Elsayed walked in a few minutes after four o'clock. She walked right over to Gil and asked, "Is there somewhere we can talk privately?"

"Follow me. There's a little business center room over here. Would you like some coffee?" Mayet poured herself a cup of coffee from the urn in the lobby and put a creamer in it. Gil poured himself a decaf and added two creamers and a packet of sugar. After they sat down at the meeting table, Gil asked, "Is there any more news on Lili?"

"No. I'm sure she's still sleeping. There's a seven hour time difference, so she'll probably leave for London while you're sleeping tonight. So, what's this theory of yours?"

"Before Martha went into hiding, she asked Lili to help her look into the results of a DNA test she had done to find out about her ancestry. She was adopted as a child and doesn't know anything about her background. Since this whole situation seems to be international, I'm thinking maybe it has to do with her ancestry testing."

"What do you know about her ancestry?"

"What I'm telling you is private, but I suppose if it could put a stop to an attempted murder, it's all right. Jeanie Peridot is a genealogist Lili hired to look into Martha's family history. She said that Martha has close relatives in the UK, Israel, and South America. She also discovered that Martha has a daughter living in the UK, who Martha apparently doesn't know about. But, I don't have a theory of how any of this information could endanger her life."

"I don't know either, but it's a theory worth looking into. There are definitely well-connected people in the UK, Israel and South America that might be able to get information from the high levels of our Federal government, like the US Marshals. I've been trying to find out how Martha's location was compromised in the witness protection program. Knowing I could search for an international connection could be helpful. How is it possible that Martha doesn't know she has a daughter?"

"Martha said that she and her husband had a baby in England, but they were told it was stillborn. Apparently, the baby was stolen from them." Gil stood up and started pacing. "I want to fly to London to meet Lili."

"Do you have your passport?"

"It's back in New York."

"Let me see if I can get you an expedited one today in Boston. I'll make some calls." Mayet used her phone while Gil drank the rest of his decaf. "It's all set. You have a high-level security clearance."

"I do. It's from my work before I retired. I thought it would have lapsed by now."

"I'll drive you to Boston while you book your flight. You can catch the red-eye."

• • • •

IT WAS NINE-THIRTY a.m. when Gil stepped up to the passport control window at Heathrow. The agent scanned his passport, looked at his computer monitor and gave a wave to his supervisor. They conferred for a few seconds and the supervisor waved to someone behind her. Gil was sent through the gate where a young woman intercepted him. "Gil Novak, I'm Special Agent Adams with the FBI. I'm here to take you to the US Embassy. Do you have checked luggage?"

"No, just my carry-on." Gil looked very weary.

Adams led him to a kiosk and bought them each a coffee. Gil had his usual decaf. She led Gil to her car, a black Tesla Model Y. She drove expertly and they reached the Embassy in less than an hour. It was a jarringly futuristic-looking building, to Gil's eye. A guard checked their IDs at the gate and let them through. Adams drove into an underground parking garage and brought Gil up in an elevator. They walked along the corridor until Adams stopped, knocked on a door, and stuck her head in. She entered and motioned for Gil to enter. Lili jumped out of her seat and ran to him. She hugged him hard, put her head on his chest, and burst into tears. The agent in the room motioned for Adams to follow her out, and they left Gil and Lili alone.

A few minutes later, Adams returned and said, "We've booked a room for you in a nearby building with good security. You can rest up, but I'd like you to stay in your room until I come this afternoon. You can order room service. We've scheduled a video-conference with Special Agent Elsayed at one thirty."

· · · ·

"LILI, I'M SO GLAD YOU made it out of Transnistria," said Mayet. "This whole situation was terrifying, but also very intriguing. Gil has a theory that the threats against Martha might have something to do with her genealogical research. Based on this idea,

I was able to get a warrant for Martha Eames's genealogical information. I'm also trying to figure out how her underground railroad involvement could be a motive, but I haven't come up with anything yet. I'd like you to work with Special Agent Adams to contact some of Martha's closest DNA matches in the UK, if you think you're up to it. What do you think?"

Lili smiled. "I'd like to do that. Gil, what do you think?"

"How much danger is Lili in, here?" Gil asked.

"I think she's probably safer here than in Massachusetts, for now. Even if whoever is behind this has been able to infiltrate the FBI, it would take them a while to find Lili. I don't think either of you will be in any one place for very long. Also, Special Agent Adams will be in charge of your protection."

"I guess that makes sense. I'm in," said Gil.

"I'll need the contact information for the genealogist."

"I don't have my phone, so we'll need to search online," said Lili.

FORTY-ONE

Karen drove slowly down the long, dirt road leading to the Belinski farm in Colrain, Mass. She parked and walked up to the front door of a dirty white farmhouse that was showing its age. There was a mist in the morning air, and the heady smell of damp grass and cow manure. A dog was barking over by the barns. Cows were mooing. A middle-aged woman answered the door. "Hi, Mrs. Belinski?" The woman nodded. "I'm Detective Tindall with the Greenfield Police Department." Karen showed her badge. "I'm wondering if I could ask you and your husband a few questions about some construction around this area."

"Come on in. My name's Carol. I don't know anything about any construction, but let me get Stan." She texted on her phone for a few seconds and said, "Stan will be here in a few minutes. Coffee?"

"No thanks, I just had some." Karen looked around and saw framed pictures everywhere. A very furry gray cat sidled up to Karen's ankle.

"That's Angel. She won't hurt you." Karen smiled.

The back door opened and a lanky man entered the mud room and pulled off his knee-high rubber boots. "Hi, I'm Stan. What's this about?"

"I'm Detective Tindall from the Greenfield Police Department. I'm trying to track down a farmer around here who's building some kind of underground tunnel system. Somebody raised a concern about that project, and whether it's related to some unexplained tunnels that were found in Greenfield. They didn't know where exactly this tunnel system was being built. I couldn't find any kind of building permit for construction like that. So, now I'm knocking on doors, trying to find information. I figure that you farmers probably know everything that's going on around here."

Stan chuckled. "Well, maybe we do know more about other people's business than we should. You'd be surprised what goes on with people on these farms. I don't know about any tunnels being built, but if there were, I wouldn't expect anyone around here to bother with a building permit. I do remember that Randy Heisler rented out his mini-excavator to someone over in Shelburne a few months ago. He's got a nice Wallemac. You also could ask the concrete suppliers around here if they did any pours for something like that."

"Do you know who the concrete suppliers are?"

"I'm sure there are a few around. The last time I used one, which was years ago, I used an outfit out of Chicopee. Chicopee Concrete, or something clever like that."

"Well, you've been a big help, Stan. I appreciate it. Here's my card if you think of anything else that could help."

· · · ·

KAREN PULLED OFF A dirt road into the paved driveway of a recently built ranch-style house with a three-car garage. Behind it was a compound of several recently constructed barns and outbuildings. The rain had stopped. As Karen got out of the car, a good-looking, middle-aged man pulled up on his four-wheeler. A small shepherd dog sat on the back-rack. "Can I help you, Officer?"

"Hi, I'm Detective Tindall with the Greenfield Police Department." She showed her badge. "Are you Randy Heisler?"

"Yes Detective, I'm State Representative Randy Heisler. How can I help?"

"Oh excuse me, Representative Heisler. I'm looking for someone around here who's building a tunnel complex. This inquiry is possibly related to some unauthorized tunnels that were recently found in Greenfield."

"The mole people?"

"Yes, that's the case. Earlier I spoke with Stan Belinski, and he mentioned that you recently rented out your mini-excavator."

He thought for a few seconds. "I guess I never asked what the guy was using it for. Tunnels?" He shrugged. "I suppose it could be."

"Who are we talking about?"

"Keith Lyman, from Shelburne." Karen's ears perked up. She'd been searching for farmers named Lyman, Manly, and Melsty around there, but was coming up empty. "He rented my Wallemac for a couple of weeks. I needed it to dig a culvert, but when I called him to get it back, he asked if he could buy it off me. He offered me two thousand over what I paid for it, so I sold it to him and bought myself a new one."

"Is that unusual?"

"Well, I suppose."

"Could you show me what a mini-excavator looks like?"

She walked with Randy to a narrow dirt road that headed around the side of a hill. A chartreuse machine was sitting next to a freshly-dug trench. It looked like a miniature bulldozer combined with a backhoe. "You operate that yourself?"

"Sure. I'm a farmer first, Representative second."

"What do you know about Keith Lyman?"

"I don't really know him, and I don't know where his farm is. He struck me as being infatuated with camouflage. His truck was camo, and so were his pants and jacket. I'm not sure what that tells you about somebody, though."

"I don't know either," said Karen. "I think if he lives in a tunnel, he probably doesn't really need camo, does he?" Heisler laughed. "Well, here's my card, if you think of anything else. Thank you, Representative Heisler."

"You're welcome. And you can call me Randy." He winked.

"Then please call me Karen." She smiled. "See you later."

· · · ·

AS SHE DROVE AWAY, Karen's spidey senses were niggling at her. She decided not to show up at Keith Lyman's farm right away, plus she didn't know where it was. She would head back to her office and do some more research. Why didn't any of her searches come up with a Lyman farm in the area? If the farm isn't under his name, how would she find it? Time for some records research.

She stopped at the Town Clerk's office in Shelburne Falls. The town clerk introduced himself as Perry Narden, and Karen figured that he was well into his seventies. "Of course, I've heard the name Lyman over the years, but I'll have to look. There are Wymans too."

"Oh, look for both, if you would, please," said Karen. "Why don't you take your time, and give me a call when you find something." She handed him her card.

Karen headed back to the Greenfield Police Station and stopped into Chief Reyes's office. "Hey Chief, I want to brief you on the tunnel case." He motioned for her to sit in a chair. "First of all, I know that this is an FBI case, but I was thinking that we could make some headway by finding the farm with the tunnel complex being built. I decided to talk to the farmers in the area. I don't think the FBI is doing that."

"Karen, I've always given you free reign to look into anything. FBI involvement doesn't change that."

"And I appreciate it. So, I went to talk to a couple of farmers in Colrain who gave me a lead on a guy in Shelburne named Keith Lyman. By the way, one of the farmers I talked to is State Representative Randy Heisler."

"Did you bother him?"

"No, he was really nice and he gave me the name of this Lyman guy. It turns out that another Lyman, Steve, is an anagram of Evan Melsty, which is the name Katrina Ryu gave us as the other guy involved in the tunnel case."

Chief Reyes sat up. "An anagram? What the heck are you talking about?"

"When I told Gil Novak about this Evan Melsty guy, he told me that his named sounded more like an anagram than a real name. I scrambled the letters around for a while and came up with Steve Manly. Gil said Manly without an E was unusual, so he suggested Steve Lyman."

"This sounds like something out of an Agatha Christie novel."

"Anyway, Keith Lyman doesn't seem to exist in this area. No farm deed, no license, no tax record. The anagram guy, Steve Lyman, also doesn't seem to exist. I'm going to keep digging through records and I'm about to call Special Agent Davis, too."

"Any word from London yet?"

"Not yet, I'll let you know."

FORTY-TWO

"**M**r. and Mrs. Wells, I'm Chris Tomlins from MI-5. We spoke on the phone yesterday. I apologize for the crowd here today, but I'll explain. This is Special Agent Adams from the American FBI. This is Agent D'Amico from the Massachusetts State Police, and this is Gil Novak, a police consultant from Massachusetts. We're talking to you today because the woman who is your biological mother is currently under protection due to recent threats on her life. Agent D'Amico and Gil Novak are personal friends with this woman."

"Are we in danger?" asked Stephen Wells.

"We're evaluating that possibility," said Tomlins. "I'll defer to Agent D'Amico to fill you in."

"Gemma, your biological mother's name is Martha Eames, which you may already know from the results of your DNA testing. She lives in the United States, in Portsmouth, New Hampshire. She's eighty-one years old. She has no idea that she has a daughter. She's been in hiding since this information became available. When we met, she told me she had no family, but that she'd had a baby who was stillborn. Apparently, you were stolen from her when you were born."

Gemma paled and looked at her husband. "Can we please hold on a minute whilst we let that sink in?" asked Stephen. "I have tea ready." Stephen brought a tray of tea and biscuits and served the visitors, Gemma, and himself.

"Thank you, Mr. Wells."

"Oh, please just call me Stephen."

"Gil and I know Martha because she's our neighbor at the condominium complex in Florida where we spent our winter this year," said Lili. "While we were there, a man attacked Martha in her condo and tried to kill her. The perpetrator died in the incident and

Martha survived her injuries. Since then, there have been two more attempts on her life and now she's in hiding. My communications with her are minimal and tightly controlled. We're currently investigating if her DNA query may have led to this situation. We have no evidence that it did, or even a plausible theory for that. You're the first one we're interviewing to try and sort this out."

"So, as you can see," added Tomlins, "we have no evidence that you are or are not in any danger, but we're trying to find out one way or another." "Can you think of any reason why this DNA search would have led to Martha's situation?"

Gemma gave a quizzical look at her husband and said, "This is one of the most bizarre stories I've ever heard. You're saying that I was stolen from my mother nearly sixty years ago, she has no idea I exist, and somebody is trying to kill her? You couldn't even make this up! The only person I can think of who wouldn't want this to come to light is the person who stole me to begin with. That person would be over a hundred years old!"

"Well, that answers our main line of inquiry," said Tomlins."

"We have a few more questions about your genealogy research, if that's okay," said Gil.

"Very well," said Tomlins. "I'll work on setting up our next interview."

"So Gemma, what we understand is that your parents are Dennis and Clare Ableford," said Gil. "Where were you born?"

"I was born at Whipps Cross Hospital. As a child, I lived in Walthamstow, which isn't far from here. Mum still lives in the same house. Dad passed a few years ago."

"Oh, I'm sorry," said Gil. "Do you have any siblings?" Tomlins came back into the room.

"No, my parents adopted me and that was that. I had a lovely childhood. I was always told I'd been adopted as a baby. My parents couldn't have their own. And, based on what you've told me, I don't have any biological siblings, either. My DNA results show various cousins and such, but I don't know what to make of that."

"Do you know what agency handled your adoption?" asked Lili.

"No, but Mum might have some papers. I'll take a look."

"Here is my contact information," said Tomlins. "If you find anything, please get a copy to me and I'll share it with Scotland Yard."

"Gemma, could we take a look at your DNA results?" asked Lili. "We can try and help you build you a better picture. Hopefully, soon, we can get you together with your biological mother."

"My mum will have a tizz when she finds out I was stolen. This whole situation is making me nervous."

"We'll have a proper visit with Mum for that discussion, luv," said Stephen.

"What about my biological father? I haven't found anything in the DNA report about him."

"Oh, of course," said Lili. "Your father's name was George Eames. He was from England. He worked as a semiconductor scientist at Lincoln Labs in Boston, Massachusetts, until he retired. Unfortunately, he passed away three years ago."

"A scientist! I'm a scientist, too," said Gemma. I develop new molecules for pharma. I guess it's in my genes!"

"I'll see if I can get you some more information on your father from our genealogist."

• • • •

LILI LOOKED OVER AND smiled at Gil as Tomlins steered the van into the beautiful seaside town of Torquay. Gil was relieved to see Lili smiling again. They'd been having a wonderful time touring London and now, pursuing the intriguing mission that brought them to this place. Their busy schedule helped keep Lili's mind off the horror she had experienced during her kidnapping and escape.

Tomlins parked the van. They all got out and entered a beautiful Bed and Breakfast.

The desk clerk retrieved a middle-aged woman from the office. Tomlins introduced them all to Mrs. Wilson, who showed them to a large table in the empty dining room. "I'd say we've an hour in here till the lunch crowd starts to come in," she said. "If need be, we can move out to the garden later, but it's still a bit chilly this morning. Oh, and please call me Morag."

"As we discussed on the phone, we're here to talk about the DNA results of a relative of yours named Martha Eames," said Tomlins. "She is currently in hiding due to recent attempts on her life. We're trying to see if her genealogy query could have anything to do with the matter."

"Do I need to call my solicitor?"

"You're not suspected of anything at this time. We don't even have any idea if or how the genealogy query might be related to the crime. We're just exploring a remote possibility, and you're one of several newly discovered relatives we're talking to. But of course, you are free to call your solicitor."

"Well, I don't like solicitors. And I'm not trying to kill this Martha person. I don't even know who she is."

"Martha's DNA results indicate that you are either her first cousin or a half-niece," said Lili. "Let's see if we can figure out which is true."

"What's a half-niece?" asked Morag.

"A half-niece would be the daughter of a half-sister or half-brother," said Gil.

"So, either I'm the daughter of a half-sibling or the daughter of one of her parent's siblings? This is all very confusing."

"Well, you're right. Perhaps one of her parents had a sibling who was your parent, or one of her parents had a child who was your parent," said Lili. "How old are you, Morag?"

"I'm fifty-six. How old is Martha?"

"She's eighty-one. That makes it less likely that she's your first cousin, but it's not impossible. Did your DNA report show any Jewish ethnicity?"

"Yes, it did. Twenty-two percent. But I expected that. My grandmother was Jewish."

Lili's eyes lit up. "Would you please tell us what you know about your grandparents and your parents?" asked Lili. "This is very exciting. Your grandmother may be the key to figuring out your relationship with Martha." No one else in the room looked particularly excited. Gil and Special Agent Adams looked mildly interested. Tomlins went off to make another call.

"My grandparents on my mother's side were Stephen and Frieda Gillies. Neither them are still alive."

"I'm sorry," said Lili.

"Frieda was from Germany. During the Second World War, she spent time in Paris. As the situation became more dangerous for Jews, she escaped to Portugal and bought passage to England on a fishing boat. Then, she was advised to take a train to Glasgow where she was most likely to find work. She was seventeen years old, had very little money, and didn't speak any English. When she arrived in Glasgow, she went to a synagogue. They helped her to find work as a cook in the house of a rich Jewish family. The Jewish community there found people to help her learn English." Lili was furiously taking notes.

"How did she meet her husband?"

"I was told that she became known for being a really good cook. She was hired by the Gillies family, who owned a restaurant. I guess they met there."

"I imagine it must have caused a stir for their son to marry a Jewish immigrant."

"Love conquers all, well, except for my lousy marriage to my lousy ex-husband." Gil laughed and Lili and Special Agent Adams gave him a scornful look. "Anyway, my parents were Ian and Sarah Duncan. Sarah was Frieda's daughter."

"Do you have any siblings?" asked Lili.

"I have a sister, Emily Duncan. My mother also had a brother named Laith Gillies. So he would be Martha's half-sibling. Uncle Laith has children, as well. My cousins."

"Frieda is the key to all of this," said Lili. "I'm guessing that she gave birth to a baby before she even met your grandfather. Maybe she didn't intend to get pregnant in Germany during the war. It may have been a bad story. So, she probably gave the child up for adoption, either in Glasgow, or before she ever got there. Do you know Frieda's maiden name?"

"I think I have it on my genealogy chart on the computer. I'll look it up."

"Could you print out your chart for me?"

Morag came back with several pages of printout. "Sorry, my printer only prints A4-sized paper. Frieda's maiden name was Meyer. Frieda Meyer. So Martha is my mum's half-sister. Mum will be gobsmacked!"

"Do you consider yourself Jewish?" asked Lili.

"No. Just because I have a little bit of Jewish DNA, doesn't make me Jewish."

"Actually, according to Jewish law, being Jewish follows the maternal line," said Lili. "So, if your grandmother was Jewish, your mother is Jewish, then you and your sister are Jewish, too."

"Hah! I can't wait to tell them that!"

"One last question," said Lili. "Do you know what happened to your grandmother's family in Germany?"

"Grandmother said they were all taken to the concentration camps. She never saw them again. I think that's how she lost her parents and five or six brothers and sisters."

. . . .

GIL REGRETTED HAVING to leave Torquay so soon, especially as Tomlins drove them into metropolitan London. Gil always gravitated to towns or very small cities. Lili was carrying on an intense conversation on the phone with Jeanie, updating her on the latest genealogical information. Once Lili finished her call, Special Agent Adams said, "I've spoken with Special Agent Elsayed. We both agree that, so far, there is little information suggesting a motive to kill Martha. But we still think we should continue to pursue this line of investigation. As we understand things, the next two people to interview are located in Israel and Brazil. We recommend that you return home now, and include Special Agent Elsayed in your video-conferences."

FORTY-THREE

For the second day in a row, Detective Tindall drove around the winding dirt roads of Shelburne, Mass. She saw a sign saying 'Ly Farm.' She pulled up a long dirt driveway to a freshly painted white farmhouse set upon a landscape of freshly tilled fields. As she got out of her cruiser, Karen could hear the noise of farm machinery echoing off the surrounding hills. She knocked on the front door, and a very small, middle-aged woman answered. "Can I help you?"

"Hi, I'm Detective Tindall from the Greenfield Police Department." She showed her badge. "I'd like to ask you some questions about a farmer who is building a network of tunnels."

The woman's eyes lit up. "Finally! We've been complaining for months."

"Please, what is your name?"

"My name is Binh Ly." She pronounced her name Bin Lee.

A big old furry dog ambled over to Karen, sniffed the air near her, ambled back over to his spot on a braided rug, and he plopped down. "What have you been complaining about?" asked Karen.

Binh pointed toward a large window. "There's been construction going on, up on the hill every day for months. Even on weekends! This used to be a nice, quiet place. My husband, Hao, went up there to find out about it, but the guy up there had a gun and warned him not to come up there again."

"Did your husband see what was going on up there?"

"No, but a couple of weeks ago, when my son Ken was home from school, he snuck up there and spied on the guy. He said the guy is building a bomb shelter or something. The construction was underground and they were pouring concrete."

"Do you know the name of the farmer up there?"

"We don't know his name, and neither did the police. I don't even think he's a farmer. There's no farm up there. I'm not sure it's even his land. As far as I know, it's always been state land up there."

"How long have you lived here, Mrs. Ly?"

"Oh, about thirty-five years, ever since I got married. Hao's father bought this farm. He escaped from Vietnam. He was one of the boat people, like my parents. He's no longer alive." Something slammed into the back screen door causing Karen to jump. "Oh, it's just the goat. Hold on." Binh went out back and yelled at the goat for a moment. When she came back in she said, "He chewed through his rope again, but I tied him back up. We'll have to get a chain."

"Mrs. Ly, is there anything else you can tell me about the man on the hill?"

"I think he's some kind of survivalist or militia or something like that. He wears camo clothes and carries a gun."

"Well, you and your family should probably stay away from him. I'll investigate what's going on. Here is my card if you think of anything else you want to tell me."

• • • •

KAREN STOPPED BY THE Shelburne Town Clerk's office. Perry Narden said, "Hello Officer Tindall. You saved me a call. I didn't find a Keith Lyman, but I asked around and found out about a guy named Keith Wyman. He sold his farm in Leverett last year. I don't show him owning any land in Shelburne, though."

"Well, I talked to a woman named Binh Ly. She showed me a hill where someone was doing a lot of excavation work. Could you tell me who owns the land?"

Perry went over to a cabinet with wide drawers and pulled out several maps which he set on the counter. He pointed out the Ly farm and Karen showed him the hill where, according to Binh Ly, the excavation was taking place. He said, "This is state land. He would have to have a contract or a land-lease from the state to excavate there."

"Is there a way for you to find out?"

"I'll have to make some calls. I'll give you a call later today. I have your card."

· · · ·

TWO DAYS LATER, KAREN stood by her car and watched as State Troopers Nash and Freelander confronted the man on the hilltop. The man didn't point his gun at the troopers, and he placed it on the ground when directed. Officer Freelander put him in cuffs and Officer Nash asked him his name. He told them his name was Keith Wyman. Nash said, "Mr. Wyman, we are arresting you for unauthorized construction on state property. This warrant authorizes us to search this property for weapons and evidence related to the murder of Kevin Clarion." Wyman didn't say a word and Freelander put him in the back seat of their cruiser.

Karen accompanied Trooper Nash on a search of the property. The underground complex was four stories down, with quite a few tunnels and rooms. They found a cache of weapons, including two fully automatic assault rifles and guns with suppressors, which were illegal in Massachusetts. Another State Police cruiser showed up and another officer helped catalog and confiscate the weapons. There were several bows, crossbows, and many razor-tipped arrows. Karen told the troopers that one of the crossbows might be the murder weapon in a New York case, and a gun with a suppressor could be relevant to a murder case in Greenfield. Nash told Karen that Wyman and the weapons would be taken to the State Police barracks in Northampton.

· · · ·

KAREN WAS IN CHIEF Reyes's office explaining what she had found and laying out her strategies on what should happen next. His desk phone rang and he picked it up. His face turned red, and he stood up and started pacing. "What about the potential murder weapons?" he asked. "What a mess! How can we help?" He put the phone on hold and collapsed into his chair. "This is ADA Chen. She said that some fancy lawyer from Boston showed up in Northampton with proof that, as of six months ago, the state property that Wyman was excavating became federal land. He also had proof that Keith Wyman received a federal land-lease with permission to build. He told Chen that, since they had no jurisdiction to search that federal property, they must release Wyman and return his confiscated property. Chen said that they would probably have to release Wyman within the next few hours while they figure this out. Chen wants to know who the FBI agent on this case is."

Karen's face went pale. "It's Special Agent Jameson Davis, from Albany." Karen wrote his number on a note pad. "Holy crap." Chief Reyes started talking to ADA Chen again, so Karen left his office.

· · · ·

SPECIAL AGENT DAVIS called and asked Karen to attend a late-afternoon meeting at the FBI office in Springfield, Mass. Davis was the only person Karen knew in the room. He led the meeting, which included quite a few people by video-conference. Davis ran through the background of his missing persons case involving Katrina Ryu, and how that case intersected with the mole-people case being investigated by Officer Tindall. Ms. Ryu was now in Witness Protection with the US Marshals. There had been two murders: one victim was Kevin Clarion, a college student, in Saratoga Springs, New York, and the other was Paul Combs, a suspected hit-man, in Greenfield, Mass. Clarion was killed by a bolt from a crossbow, and Combs was killed by a twenty-two caliber rifle.

Davis showed pictures on the monitor of each person being discussed. "A person of interest in both of these cases is Keith Wyman. No criminal record. He seems to be a doomsday prepper. He's building an underground fortress of some kind on what was, until recently, state-owned land in Shelburne, Mass. Wyman was recently arrested for unlawful excavation of state land, and upon execution of a state search warrant, a cache of guns, ammo, bows, and arrows were confiscated. Among them were several fully-automatic guns and guns with suppressors. Shortly after his arrest, a lawyer from Boston showed up and provided evidence that, as of six months ago, the land was transferred by congressional legislation to be federally-owned, and Mr. Wyman was given a land-lease for a home construction project. The State Police released Mr. Wyman, but through some legal wrangling, I was able to obtain a federal warrant to retain some of the weapons for the murder investigations and to confiscate the illegal weapons. Massachusetts issued an arrest warrant for Kevin Wyman on a weapons charge. The FBI is working with the State Crime Lab to examine the guns and crossbows in relation to the murders."

"We're also looking for his son, Steven Wyman, aka Steve Lyman, aka Evan Melsty, as a person of interest. He is the third suspect in the mole people case, along with Katrina Ryu and the late Kevin Clarion. Steven Wyman's real name was only recently identified, so we may be able to track him down quickly. Although this is a complex case, the reason you are attending this meeting has to do with the broader picture. On the monitor is a picture of US Representative Borden Ritchie from Idaho. Over the past year, Ritchie's staff has inserted forty-one land transfers distributed over sixteen states into a variety of bills having nothing to do with land or land transfers. So far, our agents have inspected one in the

Adirondack mountains where another underground fortress is being constructed. I don't know if these people are preparing for war or an apocalypse, but whatever they're doing may not be consistent with appropriate use of federal lands. I'm enlisting your support to initiate an investigation."

FORTY-FOUR

Gil was sipping a cup of decaf in the breakfast area of The Hampton Inn & Suites in Greenfield. Lili was already standing and putting on her jacket. "I can't believe you're going into work," said Gil. "I can hardly even move with this jet lag."

"I feel fine, maybe because I drink real coffee. Anyway, Karen asked me to help expedite processing some of the evidence in the tunnel murder. But, I'm only planning to work a half day. This afternoon, you and I have a meeting with Jeanie to talk with more of Martha's DNA relatives. Mayet's coming, too."

"That may put me back to sleep, unless something really interesting pops up. Good luck with the guns."

After finishing his coffee, Gil decided to take a walk. It was a warm and sunny spring morning. He walked along the broad sidewalks of Main Street, where some of the shops were opening up for the day. Most of the proprietors were cheerful and greeted him as he walked by. He heard a car beep from the other side of the street. Micky Tindall, Gil's old high school friend, stopped his car and yelled, "Coffee at Brad's?" Gil waved and nodded.

Micky was Detective Karen Tindall's father-in-law. He and Gil sat at the counter on old-fashioned chrome stools, upholstered in red. "The town's all abuzz about the Indian treasures you found," said Micky. "Unbelievable! Karen says you want to give them back to the Indians?"

"Well, I don't know if they're mine to give, but that's what I recommended to Chief Reyes. It's impossible to right the wrongs of the past, but it would be a nice gesture. Have you ever read about the massacre at Turners Falls? It was horrible."

"I don't really know much about it. I don't think anyone around here does. Can you send me something to read about it?"

"Sure. I think the Indian side of that history wasn't taught in schools here because, until recently, most of the local people didn't question the story that our ancestors fought a righteous war. Did you know that many of the Indian people in New England that we didn't kill, we sold into slavery to work in the Caribbean sugar plantations?"

"Well, it isn't really 'we.' I didn't have any ancestors here until the late eighteen hundreds. Did you?"

"No. Mine came over in the early nineteen hundreds. But it's still a 'we' from a white man's perspective, and you and me are definitely a couple of old white guys. The American Indian wars are a part of our history now. It seems to be part of the unchanging story of humanity. Invade, conquer, and subjugate. Based on today's war in Ukraine, people haven't changed. The Turners Falls massacre can't be erased, but it could at least be understood and acknowledged. I'm sure there's a lot more that could be done to help the Indigenous Americans, but I definitely don't know very much about the subject."

"Maybe you could team up with a local Indian and help give a talk about it at the local schools. More coffee?"

"No thanks. Two decafs a day is my limit or it will affect my sleep."

"What can you tell me about Lili's kidnapping?"

"Not a lot. We still don't know who's behind it. She's physically okay, but I'm worried about her having PTSD or something. She went to work today to help with Karen's investigation."

• • • •

LILI PHONED KAREN. "I've matched the murder weapon on Paul Combs, the tunnel guy. It's a twenty-two caliber rifle with a suppressor. One subject's DNA appears on all of the confiscated weapons, presumably from the owner, Keith Wyman. However, most of the DNA on the murder weapon is from a son of Keith

Wyman. I still need DNA samples from Wyman and his son to compare."

"Keith Wyman only has one son, as far as we know." said Karen. "His name is Steven Wyman. His mother was raped and murdered in Dorchester when Steven was a young child. That may have something to do with Keith Wyman's state of mind. I already have a BOLO on Steven. The guy that was killed, Paul Combs, was a known bad guy. So, Steven may actually have killed him to prevent him from killing someone else, like his father or Katrina Ryu. I gotta go. Thanks so much for expediting this."

. . . .

LILI MET UP WITH GIL, Jeanie, and Mayet at the Main Street Bar & Grill in Greenfield. They had lunch while Lili and Gil went over what they had learned from their meetings in the UK. "Gemma Wells knew she was adopted, but she had no information on her biological parents," said Lili. Apparently, she was stolen from them right after she was born. Martha was told that the baby was stillborn. Morag Wilson is the daughter of Martha's half-sister Sarah, and her husband, Ian Duncan. Sarah was one of Frieda's three children. Neither Morag nor Sarah had any knowledge of Martha's existence."

"I expanded Martha's family tree based on the information from Gemma and Morag," said Jeanie.

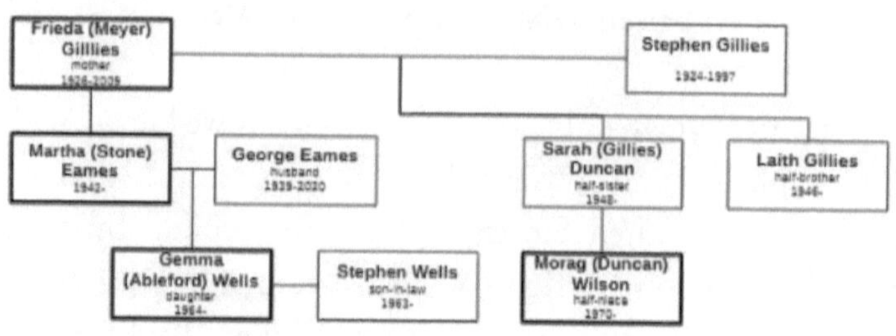

. . . .

"I HOPE WE GET TO SHOW this to Martha soon."

"What kind of a name is Morag?" asked Gil. "It sounds Hungarian or something."

"It's a Scottish girl's name," said Jeanie. "It isn't uncommon. Morag Wilson grew up in Glasgow. Morag also happens to be a girl's name in Israel. I've reserved a conference room at the library. Today we'll be talking with Jonas Mauk, who lives in a city called Niterói in Brazil. It's across the bay from Rio de Janeiro. Jonas may be the son of a half-sibling of Martha's. It's two hours later in Niterói."

Mayet said, "We still don't know the identity of your kidnappers, Lili, but we're getting close to identifying the woman who was preparing to torture you. She's known to Interpol by several different names. We don't yet have any identification on who is behind the attempts on Martha's life. We are, however, closer to finding the leak that compromised Martha's security in WITSEC."

. . . .

A MIDDLE-AGED MAN APPEARED on the video monitor, along with an elderly woman. "Hello, Senhor Mauk? This is Jeanie Peridot."

"Yes, I am Jonas Mauk and this is my mother Liesl Mauk. Is Martha Eames there?"

"No, I'm sorry Jonas. This is Agent Lili D'Amico from the Massachusetts State Police. We are calling on behalf of Martha. She is currently being protected because someone has tried to kill her, several times. We are trying to find out if anything in her past could be related to these attempts on her life. In addition to Jeanie and me, we also have Gil Novak, a police consultant, and Special Agent Elsayed from the Federal Bureau of Investigation. Jeanie is the genealogist who is helping Martha build her family tree."

Jonas translated what was said into German for his mother. She looked quite alarmed. She spoke to Jonas in German. "My mother asks how Martha is related to us."

"We think Martha is your mother's half-sister," said Jeanie. We think Martha's father and your mother's father were the same person."

Jonas translated. Liesl smiled and asked something in German. Jonas looked shocked. "My mother asks if Martha is Jewish. Does this make sense?"

"Yes, Martha's mother was Jewish," said Jeanie. "Martha didn't know this until she took the DNA test."

Jonas interpreted and his mother started to speak at length in German. Jonas listened with wonder and drank a lot of water. After a few minutes, he said, "I wish I had something stronger to drink. My mother's father was named Horst Weber and he was from Germany. This I knew. I knew my grandfather. But in Germany, his name was Horst Konig. My grandmother's name was Helga Konig in Germany. I didn't know they changed their names." Jeanie was taking notes.

Jonas asked his mother some questions before continuing. "She says that she thinks Martha's mother must be a woman named Frieda Meyer. Frieda was the nanny for my Uncle Wolfe and my Aunt Elsa who were very young children in Germany. My mother wasn't yet born. She was born in Brazil." Liesl talked some more, and Jonas translated. "My grandfather was an officer in the German Army.

He was stationed in Paris during the Second World War. When it became too dangerous to be in France, my grandfather sent my grandmother back to Germany with my Aunt Elsa and Uncle Wolfe. They couldn't send their nanny Frieda back because she was Jewish. She would have been killed." Jonas asked some more questions in German. "My mother says that Frieda and my grandfather had a child together whom they named Rebecca. My grandfather smuggled Frieda and Rebecca out of France to a ship in Lisbon. He was supposed to find them later in Rio, but he never found them again. He later smuggled my grandmother, aunt, and uncle to Rio to be with him. He had deserted the German army and changed his name to Weber so they wouldn't be able to find him."

"How does your mother know this?" asked Gil.

Jonas asked his mother. "She says that, when Uncle Wolfe was grown, my grandfather told him the story and asked him to help find Frieda and Rebecca. After my grandparents died, my uncle told his sisters. I think maybe that is why I received this DNA test as a gift for my birthday."

Jeanie said, "This is a remarkable story. Martha doesn't know any of this. She was adopted as a baby in England by a family named Stone. Frieda must have gone to England somehow instead of Brazil, and given Rebecca up for adoption. After that, she ended up in Glasgow, Scotland. She married and had two more children."

Everyone was looking at each other, not knowing what else to say. Special Agent Elsayed asked, "Senhor Mauk, do you have any idea why anyone would be trying to kill Martha?"

Jonas spoke to his mother. "We both say absolutely no. We would love to meet her! She is like a mystery to our family."

Lili said, "Well, I think we've all learned everything we can from this discussion. You and your mother have been very helpful. Hopefully, we will arrange a meeting between you and Martha, once it is safe. If you have any more questions, please contact Jeanie."

"Thank you so much for arranging this meeting," said Jonas. "I wish you luck in solving your mystery."

· · · ·

IN THE WANING DAYLIGHT, Carrick set up his equipment in the London flat he had rented. It was across the street from Gemma Wells's corner townhouse. From the flat, he could see directly into her kitchen. Carrick watched Gemma arrive home from work. He had carried out surveillance over the past two days by walking around the neighborhood and watching video from the webcam he had set up in his flat. Her children would already be home, but he didn't expect Gemma's husband home for another hour or so. He waited half an hour more, when darkness fell. He set up his rifle's bipod stand on the windowsill and aimed the gun toward the kitchen window.

Suddenly, a whining sound filled the air and a small drone came down from above and shined a bright light directly into his scope. The door behind him crashed open, and he found himself surrounded by tactical police officers. He raised his hands and let his rifle clatter to the floor. Although he'd agreed to take a cyanide capsule in the event of capture, he never had any intention of doing so. Instead, he intended to escape from prison, again.

FORTY-FIVE

Paris, France February 1942

Frieda Meyer was preparing beef bourguignon, while little Wolfe and Elsa played tag around her in the kitchen. Frieda could hear Herr Major and Frau Konig arguing in the sitting room of their large apartment. She couldn't quite hear what they were discussing. She decided to wait until things calmed down before setting the dining room table.

After the dinner table was set, Frau Konig instructed Frieda to bring the children to the table and serve dinner. Frieda helped the children wash their hands and faces, then brought them into the dining room. She served dinner while Herr Major asked the children about their day. Frau Konig' face was flushed and she could not disguise her anxiety.

Once the children were excused, Frieda had them wash up again and sent them to their shared bedroom to get into their nightclothes. She brought them in to give their parents a goodnight kiss, then she took them into the bedroom to tuck them in for the night.

When she came back downstairs, Frau Konig asked Frieda to join them in the sitting room for a few minutes.

Major Konig said, "We have some difficult things we must discuss with you." Frieda stiffened, expecting to be let go. "The war is getting more dangerous in France, now that the United States has joined the fight. My logistics command has started to prepare for a potential allied invasion on the French coast. Because of this, Frau Konig and I have agreed that she and the children will return to Berlin."

Frieda was trying hard not to burst into tears. With a quivering voice, she asked, "Will I be returning with them, Herr Major?"

"No, I'm afraid not. You see, it isn't safe for you in Berlin anymore. The German High Command has been increasing its efforts to remove all Jews from Germany, as well as from the new German territories."

"But my parents... I haven't received any letters from them in more than two months."

"Frau Konig will inquire about your parents when she gets to Berlin. They may no longer be allowed to use the mail service. Or, maybe they are traveling out of Germany. We'll try to find out."

"But what will I do? Where will I go?"

"Don't worry. You will remain here and continue to cook for me and keep house, if that's agreeable to you. I'll pay you the same wage."

Frieda felt uneasy about the whole situation, but what other choice did she have? A sixteen year-old girl couldn't just live on her own in a foreign country. She didn't even speak any French. "I will continue to keep house here, Herr Major. Thank you."

FORTY-SIX

P*aris France, March 1942*

Frieda reflected upon her situation while dusting the living room. She felt safe there with Herr Major for now, but he had already sent his family back to Berlin for their safety. How long would she be safe in Paris? It was not safe for her to return to Berlin. It was terribly boring for her in Paris. She had no friends, no one to talk to. In the last last letter she received from her parents, her father wrote that the German military was now an enemy of the Jewish people, and so she must try to leave the Konigs and find different work. In Germany, the government no longer allowed Jews to work at all, and he was fired from the bank that he had managed for many years. She thought that perhaps she could go to the south of France, because the Germans had not occupied it. But she had little money. She would be sleeping on the streets. How would she defend herself from bad men? What would she do if she got to southern France?

Crash! She heard glass breaking, a commotion outside. She looked down at the street from the third-floor window. She saw a group of French policemen pulling people from a building across the street. The people were wearing yellow stars on their clothing. Jews. The Jews were shouting at the police. The police were shouting at the Jews. A policeman picked up a young girl and threw her into the back of their truck like a sack of potatoes. They tried to pull a woman into the truck, but she fought back and wouldn't leave her young children who were screaming in fear. A policeman hit the woman on her head so hard that Frieda could hear the sickening crack from her window. The woman collapsed to the ground and two policemen picked her up and threw her into the truck. Then they grabbed her screaming children and threw them into the truck, too.

Frieda wanted to turn away, but she was transfixed. The police dragged a teenaged boy out of the building, but he was resisting with all his might. The policemen beat him with their sticks, but he fought back. Another policeman ran over and, bang! He shot the boy in the head. The boy collapsed, dead. Frieda screamed and rushed away from the window. She ran to her bed and fell into it, sobbing.

CRASH! The building shook. The police were coming into Frieda's building! They were banging on the doors of the ground floor apartments. They were breaking down doors. Herr Major had told Frieda not to wear a star on her clothes, but her identification papers identified her as a Jew. She ran into Herr Major's room and climbed into the back of his armoire, hiding behind his hanging uniforms. She buried herself among blankets that were stored there. She could hear the police shouting as they entered the homes on the second floor. There was a lot of yelling and crashing. Frieda shook uncontrollably as she heard footsteps coming up to the third floor. She didn't dare to breathe.

Frieda heard loud yelling in the hallway. She heard the front door open, and the footsteps of a soldier searching the house. She forgot to lock the bedroom door! She buried her head in a blanket to quiet her sobs. Moments later, the bedroom door opened. Suddenly, the armoire doors were pulled open. "Frieda, the police are gone," said Horst. "You can come out now." He helped her out and held her while she cried.

• • • •

A FEW DAYS LATER, HORST came home with meat, eggs, and vegetables for Frieda to cook. Horst was a logistics officer, so he was able to obtain all the food he wanted. As she turned to put the food away, Horst asked Frieda to come into the sitting room. He poured them both a shot of schnapps. "Sit down and drink this. I have some bad news."

Horst downed his shot while Frieda took a sip of hers. "Helga found out what she could about your family and it's not good news. Frieda took a bigger sip and felt the warmth in her stomach. Your parents and your younger brother were deported to a place called Theresienstadt, in Czechoslovakia. People are told that this is a resettlement village, a resort. But Helga's friend told her that the Jews sent there are either put into forced labor or sent on to Auschwitz. Auschwitz is a place in Poland from where no one returns." Frieda began shaking uncontrollably as Horst went on. "Your older brothers and sisters, and their families, have disappeared, so we assume they were also deported." Frieda fainted.

Frieda woke with a start a few minutes later in Horst's arms. She started to wail and, as her cries weakened, she curled up into his lap and fell back to sleep. Frieda woke up in the middle of the night. She was still in Horst's lap and he was asleep. She crept off to her bed, but her mind was racing and she could not sleep.

FORTY-SEVEN

Paris, France—April, 1943

Horst came home late, as he had for several weeks. His clothes were disheveled. He headed for a bottle of schnapps, which had become his routine. "I'll get your dinner from the oven," said Frieda. She put little Rebecca down on a blanket with her stuffed rabbit toy. She felt nothing toward the baby. She'd come to think Horst was pathetic. But, most of all, she'd come to hate herself. What had she become, just to be safe? She was going through the motions, pretending to be Horst's ersatz wife. Maybe she would be better off deported.

Frieda had already eaten, but she sat at the table so Horst could vent out loud while he ate. "Most of the shipments I arranged for defense of the coast never arrived. The General blames the Resistance, but it's as though someone in our own Army is deliberately stopping my orders or rerouting the trains. The Allies will take North Africa within a matter of weeks. Once that happens, they will invade the continent, maybe Italy, maybe France, maybe both. The Americans are an unstoppable force, and they will eventually take Germany. I must get you and Rebecca out of Europe."

Frieda was shocked out of her disinterest. "Out of Europe? Where out of Europe?"

"I'm not sure yet. Maybe South Africa, maybe South America. Somewhere not involved in this damn war."

· · · ·

HORST DROVE THROUGH the night while Frieda and Rebecca slept in the back of the car. He had to shout at the guards to let him through the border, into Spain. They soon deferred to his rank and his orders which showed he was in charge of shipments coming from Spain into France. It was cloudy and windy when they reached the docks at Bilbao. Horst found that he was able to communicate in Spain by speaking French and using exaggerated gestures. This enabled him to find the correct dock.

Horst bought some pintxos from a street vendor. These were little slices of bread, each with a slice of fish, and topped with a vegetable sauce. Frieda wondered what it would have been like if she were just a tourist exploring the city. Horst handed Frieda two tickets. "Here are your tickets to Lisbon for that ship over there. He handed her two more tickets. These are your tickets from Lisbon to Rio de Janeiro aboard the ship Serpa Pinto. Once you reach Lisbon, you should be safe from the SS, but be careful. You'll be able to find German-speaking people at the port. You should find a bank here and change your Deutchmarks to escudos. You'll have to change your money again when you reach Brazil."

Frieda looked sad and tired, with dark circles under her eyes. "What will I do in Rio de Janieiro?"

"I want you to go to the town of Marica, on the coast. There is a large German community in that town. You'll be able to find work there. It's small enough I will find you again, but it might be another year until I can come. I love you, my dear." Horst hugged and kissed Frieda and Rebecca, then he walked away. He did not look back.

Frieda asked around, mainly by using gestures, and she was able to find a nearby bank. She exchanged her Deutchmarks for escudos. Then, carrying Rebecca, her valise, and her handbag, she made her way to the fishing port and searched for someone who spoke German. She was guided to the Harbour Master's hut, where she found a short, rough-looking man who spoke some German. "I want to sail to England. Any kind of boat. I have escudos."

The man looked her up and down and asked, "Jew?" Frieda froze, but then slowly nodded. The man gestured for her to follow. Walking along the dock, they made their way to a very rusty fishing vessel. The man indicated for her to wait, and he walked up the gangplank and into the wheelhouse. When he returned, he said, "Thirty thousand escudos."

Frieda shook her head and acted as though she was going to cry. The man looked her in the eye and said, "Fifteen thousand." She sighed with relief, nodded, and turned around to take out her money, unseen. When she started to hand it to him, he shook his head. "Go there."

Trying hard to keep her balance, Frieda struggled up the gangplank. She went to the door of the wheelhouse, and held out her money. A middle-aged man nodded and politely took her money. He gestured for her to follow. The man carried her valise down the hatch and she carefully followed down the ladder with her baby and handbag. The man spoke to a young deckhand and handed her off. The deckhand led her down a series of passageways, and gestured for her to stop. He knocked on the side of the passageway, *knock, knock-knock*. Then he pulled on some brass fittings and a section of the wall came away. He gestured for her to climb in.

There were two young men and a young woman in a small compartment. It smelled of cold dampness, oil, and sweat. The deckhand secured the hatch. Fortunately, there was an electric light in the space. The woman motioned for Frieda to sit next to her, on the deck. As she was sitting down, the boat swayed a little and she fell forward, jostling Rebecca who started to cry. The woman took the baby while Frieda got settled. The young men passed down Frieda's valise and bag.

"Do you speak English?" asked the woman. She handed the baby back to Frieda.

"Nein, nur Deutche."

"Papieren, bitte?" asked the woman. Frieda handed the woman her identity paper.

"Ah, a Jew," said the woman in English. "Well Frieda, you'd better start learning English. That's what you'll need starting tomorrow." The woman put her hand on her chest and said, "My name is Phyllis. What's your baby's name?"

"Rebecca."

Using gestures, Phyllis said, "Frieda, this is Alwyn and this is Danny. They are British fliers who were shot down." Frieda nodded an understanding.

Rebecca started to fuss, so Frieda prepared to breastfeed her. The wide-eyed young men shyly looked away and Phyllis laughed. "That's what they're there for, lads. Remember that!"

The boat's engines started up, and a strong vibration filled the boat.

• • • •

ONCE THE BOAT GOT FARTHER out to sea, it began to pitch and roll dramatically. Danny ran to a bucket just in time, and vomited. The smell was overpowering in the small compartment. When the baby finished nursing, she gave a great burp and fell right to sleep. Frieda fell asleep soon after.

Some time later, Rebecca's cries woke Frieda. The others were asleep. Frieda relieved herself in one of the buckets, then nursed Rebecca. She could hear men shouting to each other and winches operating, up on the main deck. She heard hatches opening and what she assumed were fish being loaded into the hold. The ship's rolling motions were more consistent and, after a while, she found it relaxing, along with the vibration of the engines.

One of the fliers woke up and used his bucket as privately as possible. When he was done he turned to Frieda and asked, "Where are you from?"

Frieda thought she understood, so she said, "Berlin. She gestured for him to say where he was from."

"I'm from Wales."

Frieda repeated the word," but her W sounded like a V, "Vales."

Alwyn chuckled and said, "Wales," emphasizing the W sound.

Frieda tried again and said, "Oo-ales," and they both laughed. Suddenly, they heard a lot of loud radio chatter from above. There was shouting, then a very loud *woop, woop* sound. The boat slowed. Alwyn roused Danny and Frieda gently shook Phyllis.

Alwyn said, "I think we've got company."

Phyllis looked at Frieda and put her finger to her lips to gesture quiet, then she pointed to Rebecca who was still sleeping. There were loud footsteps on the deck. Then in the passageways. There was shouting in German as the boat was searched. Rebecca started to cry, so Frieda put her coat over both their heads.

The hidden passengers were sweating with fear and trying not to breathe too loudly. The hold hatches on the main deck were winched open and closed. The Germans were shouting louder, trying to communicate with the boat's captain, but he didn't understand them. After about twenty minutes, which seemed like an eternity to the hidden passengers, they heard the Germans leaving the fishing boat. Their boat motored away. Everyone sagged with relief.

FORTY-EIGHT

B*ristol, UK—April, 1943*
After a day-and-a-half at sea, a deckhand removed the hatch to their hidden compartment. He winced at the horrible smell. He said, "We're pulling into Bristol Harbour. You can come up on deck now. How about you blokes bring up the buckets and empty them overboard."

Phyllis explained to Frieda that they were sailing along the River Avon and coming into the port of Bristol, in England. She told her that she would help her to find out where to go. The passengers stood on deck, breathing fresh air, and watching their boat dock in the bustling harbour. Frieda walked off the boat with her baby, toward freedom and uncertainty. A deckhand carried her valise down to the dock. During their long walk to the Immigration Hall, Phyllis found a street vendor selling Cornish pasties, which Phyllis described as hand-held meat pies. Phyllis bought one for Frieda, since she had some British currency. Frieda found her pasty to be so delicious that she started to feel hopeful. When they arrived at the Immigration Hall, Phyllis sat Frieda down while she went to make some inquiries.

Frieda watched the people coming and going in the great hall wondering who they were and what they were all up to. After about half an hour, Phyllis returned and told Frieda to follow her. They went down a hallway into a large room filled with immigration clerks and hopeful immigrants. Phyllis brought Frieda right to the desk of the head clerk, where she was asked for her identity papers. There was some discussion between Phyllis and the clerk. The clerk gave Frieda back her papers, and asked her to fill out two additional forms, one for Frieda and one for her baby. Phyllis helped her with the forms. As they left the office, Phyllis said in German, "You've been given a visa to stay in Great Britain as a domestic worker."

Phyllis walked with Frieda to a nearby bank to exchange her currency. They then took a taxi to the Temple Meads train station. As they rode along, they saw some areas that had been heavily bombed in air raids. Phyllis said, "I'm going to put you on a train to Glasgow, which is in Scotland. I was told that there are too many refugees coming into London and Manchester these days. Glasgow will be more welcoming and it will be easier for you to find work there." They arrived at the train station and Phyllis bought Frieda two tickets. She pointed to one of the tickets and said, "This is the number of your train from here, and it leaves from track seven. You'll have to change trains in Birmingham to this train, here," pointing to the other ticket. "Here, I've gotten you a map of Glasgow. I've circled the train station where you'll arrive and this here is the Garnet Hill Synagogue. If you go there, you will find Jewish people who speak German and will help you get settled. I'm sure you'll get extra help because you're really only a child yourself. I've written my name, Phyllis Hahn, and my telephone number here on your map. Please call me if you need help."

Frieda hugged Phyllis tightly. "Thank you so much. Phyllis, why were you on that boat?"

"Oh, it's my job, dear. I'm a spy." Frieda's eyes went wide.

It was evening by the time Frieda's train arrived at the Central Train Station in Glasgow. Once outside, she checked her map and the nearby road signs, and got her bearings. Carrying her baby, her valise, and her handbag, she headed toward the synagogue. She passed a church along the way, looked all around, and saw no one. She quietly entered the church and carefully placed Rebecca inside the doorway, wrapped up in her blanket, asleep. Then, she quietly left and did not look back.

FORTY-NINE

G*reenfield, Massachusetts—April, 2023*
Karen knocked on the Chief's door. He grunted in acknowledgment, and she walked in. "Yesterday, Steve Wyman was spotted by campus security at Virginia Tech. They tried to chase him on foot, but they lost him. The Blacksburg police got involved, but they couldn't find him or his car. They've alerted the Virginia Staties."

Chief Reyes's phone rang and he answered it, holding up his finger for Karen to wait a moment. He said, "Cuff him" and hung up the phone. "Steven Wyman is out front. Wants to turn himself in."

Karen spun around and quickly walked out to the front desk. "Steven Wyman, I'm arresting you on suspicion for the murder of Paul Combs." She cuffed him, read him his rights, and escorted him into an interview room. "Can you afford an attorney?"

"I don't need one."

"Yes, you do. This is a murder charge. Can you afford an attorney? Can you call your father and have him get an attorney down here?"

"I definitely don't want any lawyer my father sends. This is all his fault. I can't afford a lawyer, I'm just a college student."

"You will be assigned an attorney." She had an officer escort Steven to the lockup, while she called for a public defender.

• • • •

KAREN CARRIED OUT THE interview alone. The Chief didn't want it to appear as though they were intimidating the young man. Chief Reyes and ADA Chen observed from behind the one-way mirror. Karen re-read Steven his rights while being recorded, and acknowledged the presence of the public defender, Cicily Barnes.

Mr. Wyman, you are here because you are suspected of killing Paul Combs and burying him in a tunnel."

Steven looked at his lawyer and she nodded. He said, "I admit that I killed a guy and buried him in the tunnel. I killed him because he was about to kill Katrina Ryu. If I hadn't killed him, Katrina would be dead."

"Please tell me everything that happened, leading up to your killing of Paul Combs."

"I was home from school for a long weekend, staying with my father in Shelburne. I overheard a conversation there implying that someone was being sent to Greenfield to kill Katrina. They expected her to be going to the police station there. I grabbed a rifle from my father's gun safe and drove to Greenfield. I parked at the High Street end of Stone Farm Lane. I walked up the Poet's Seat Mountain trail to a spot where I could look down on the police station, on High Street."

Steven took a few gulps of his Mountain Dew. "I could see Roo walking up High Street on the other side of the street from the police station."

"By Roo, you are referring to Katrina Ryu?"

"Yes, Katrina Ryu. I don't think there's a sidewalk on the side with the police station. I saw leaves shaking in the bushes in front of the far side of the police station parking lot. I looked through my rifle scope and could see a guy aiming his rifle at Katrina, so I shot him."

"How many times did you shoot?" asked Karen.

"Once. Just one shot to his head."

"Why didn't you report the incident to the police right then and there?"

"I probably should have. I wasn't thinking clearly. I had just killed a man!"

"Why did you turn yourself in today?"

"After I shot the guy, I waited till dark and pulled the guy out of the bushes and into my car. I was right in the police station parking lot! I was really stressed out. I drove to the tunnel access on Oak Street. I dragged him into the tunnel and buried him with my bare hands. Then, I took off and drove to school."

"That's Virginia Tech in Blacksburg, Virginia?"

"Yes. When I got there, I saw that the police were after me. They chased me. I realized that if I can't go to school, and I can't live my life, what's the point? I didn't do anything wrong. I need to clear my name."

"Who was involved in the conversation you heard that implied that Katrina Ryu would be killed in Greenfield?"

Steve hesitated and looked at his lawyer. She shook her head. "No comment," he replied.

"Mr. Wyman, the person who is behind the attempt on Katrina Ryu's life is not in custody, and therefore, they are in a position to try again. Maybe they'll succeed the next time," said Karen. "Just like you said, if Ms. Ryu can't go to school and can't live her life, what's the point?"

"No comment."

"Did you participate in the construction of unauthorized tunnels in Greenfield?"

"Um, yes, I did." Steven hung his head.

• • • •

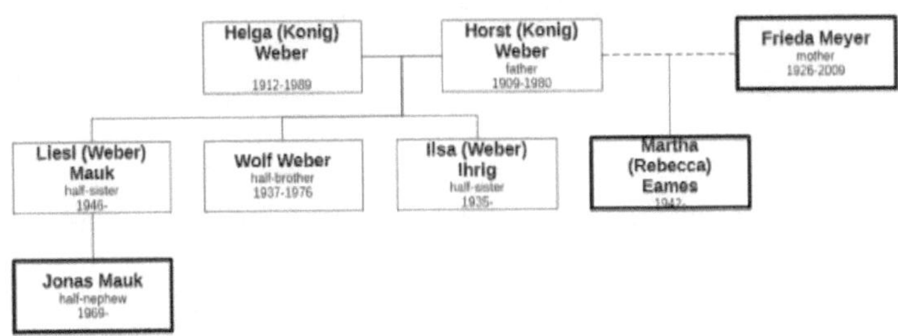

LILI SHOWED GIL THE latest family tree chart she had received from Jeanie. "This is so intriguing," said Lili. "I'm anxious to see what Martha's whole family tree looks like."

Lili, Gil, Karen, and Karen's husband Jeff went to dinner at The Farm Table restaurant in Bernardston, Mass. "Here's to solving the case of the mole people!" said Karen. They all clinked glasses. "That was one of the strangest cases I've ever worked."

"What about Kevin Clarion's murder?" asked Gil.

"There's an arrest warrant on Keith Wyman for murder and conspiracy to commit murder, but he's in the wind," said Karen. "We think that he was trying to kill his son's friends because they knew too much about the prepper tunnel he was building. Special Agent Davis said that, when they catch him, Wyman might be eligible for less than a life sentence if he testifies about whatever scheme was being been cooked up by Representative Borden Ritchie. That's still under investigation, and it's bound to be big news sometime over the next few weeks. Oh, and there's some bad news for you, Gil. The Chief says that, since you found the gold artifacts as a police consultant on state land, the state owns the artifacts. However the good news is, since the items were stolen from the Indigenous Americans, it's been agreed that the items should be returned to them."

"I think that's very good news," said Gil. "That's exactly what I recommended to Chief Reyes."

"I think there will be some sort of ceremony," said Karen.

FIFTY

"Hello, am I speaking to Talya Narkis?" asked Jeanie. Jeanie had initiated a video-conference with the Israeli branch of Martha's family tree.

"Yes, I am Talya, and I am with my sister Leah Ganz. Who is this, please? Is this Martha?"

"My name is Jeanie Peridot. I am a genealogist working on behalf of Martha Eames. This is Agent Lili D'Amico with the Massachusetts State Police, Gil Novak, a police consultant, and Special Agent Mayet Elsayed with the Federal Bureau of Investigation. We are calling from Greenfield, Massachusetts."

"Police? FBI? What is going on, please?" asked Talya.

Lili said, "There have been some attempts to kill Martha Eames, so she is in hiding. We are trying to find out who might be after her. One possibility is that it could be related to her DNA search, but we really don't know."

Talya and Leah had an animated discussion in Hebrew. "We don't know who would try to kill Martha. We do know that our father did not want us to contact her. He said that her side of the family is considered dead to our side of the family. If Martha is who we think she is, she is the daughter of my grandfather's sister and a Nazi soldier. Is this true?"

Lili has a brief side discussion with the others and they all nodded. "We found out that Martha was born during World War II. She is the daughter of a German officer and a Jewish woman who was named Frieda Meyer. Based on what we know, Frieda Meyer was seventeen years old when Martha was born. Martha was named Rebecca when she was born. Another thing you should know is that Martha was adopted in England as a baby and doesn't know any of this, yet. She never knew her biological mother or anything about her family. Before she went into hiding, she had seen that her DNA report said she had a lot of Jewish ancestry, but she didn't understand how that could be. She hired me to find out more information."

Talya and Leah had another discussion in Hebrew. "Our grandfather's name was Fishel Meyer and our grandmother's name was Malka. Our grandfather was Frieda's brother. Their parents, three siblings, and their siblings' families were all killed in the concentration camps during the Holocaust. Our grandfather survived the camps. He later discovered that Frieda had a baby in Paris with a Nazi soldier, and that she had survived the war. He never tried to contact her, so she probably never knew he survived. Our grandfather settled in Israel after the war and helped to establish our kibbutz, Kibbutz Nevo."

Lili said, "We contacted the descendants of Martha's biological father. His name was Horst Konig. Apparently, he was a German officer and Frieda was the nanny for his children in Germany, and later in Paris when he was stationed there. When an allied invasion of France was expected, he sent his wife and children back to Germany, but he couldn't send Frieda back because she was Jewish. Apparently, Horst Konig and Frieda conceived a child soon after that. Horst's son told us that Horst helped to smuggle Frieda to Portugal and bought her a ticket to Brazil. However, for some reason, she boarded a boat to England instead. It appears that she gave her child up for adoption soon after she got to England. Horst Konig deserted the German Army and escaped with his wife and children to Brazil. He changed their name to Weber. For years, Horst and his son searched for Frieda in Brazil. But again, Martha doesn't know any of this, yet."

Talya and Leah had another animated conversation in Hebrew. Talya said, "This is such an amazing story!"

"There's more," continued Lili. "Frieda ended up in Glasgow, Scotland and married a man named Stephen Gillies. We spoke to her granddaughter, Morag Wilson, who lives in England. She was aware that her grandmother was Jewish, but she was unaware that, according to Jewish law, she and her sister are also Jewish, by descent. She was very surprised, to say the least." Talya and Leah laughed. "One more thing, Martha Eames has a daughter that she doesn't know about."

"How is this possible?" asked Talya.

"Martha had a baby with her husband, George Eames," said Lili. "At the hospital, they were told that the baby was stillborn, that it had died before birth. But now it appears that the baby was stolen from them and given up, or sold, for adoption. We met with Martha's daughter in London. Her name is Gemma Wells, and she knew she was adopted, but didn't know anything about her biological parents. It seems that she is Jewish, as well."

"I think that's the whole story," concluded Jeanie. "Talya, Leah, do you have any further information or questions for us?"

Talya and Leah had another discussion in Hebrew. "This is all very overwhelming," said Talya. When will we be able to meet with Martha?"

Special Agent Elsayed said, "You will be able to meet with Martha when the threats to her life are resolved. Do you know of any reason her life would be threatened?"

Talya and Leah looked at each other and shrugged. "No, we don't. We are very thankful to you for this discussion and we are anxious to meet Martha. Could we get a copy of her family tree? We will give you ours."

"Yes, of course," said Jeanie. "And you can call me with any further questions."

They signed off from the video-conference. Mayet said, "I didn't hear anything there that would possibly be a threat to Martha's life. There was some family animosity between people who are no longer alive, and Talya's father didn't want her to contact Martha, but that's far from being a motive for murder."

• • • •

A WEEK LATER, LILI was back at Gil's house in Saratoga. Jeanie called a video-conference with Mayet and Lili. Jeanie said, "A few days ago, I sent you the third family tree chart I have for Martha which includes the additional information we received from her relatives in Israel."

"Pretty soon I'll put them together as one all-inclusive chart, but it will be too big to show like that in a video presentation. In addition to the family tree information, I've been researching the people themselves, and I think I found some things that might interest you."

Jeanie posted a photograph of Horst Konig's family. "This is Horst Weber, aka Horst Konig, and these are his children. His wife Helga probably took this picture. This girl is Liesl, the mother of Jonas Mauk, with whom we spoke. What I discovered is that Horst Konig was a German officer and a member of the Nazi party. He was a logistics officer which means he was responsible for shipping people and materials. Specifically, he was responsible for making sure the German army had all the food and weapons they needed in France. Horst Konig was reported to be missing in action in August 1943."

"According to the manifest from the ship Serpa Pinto, Horst Weber arrived in Rio de Janeiro in August 1943. Weber was his mother's maiden name. In Brazil, he bought two small cargo ships and started a shipping company that became very successful. His children, and now some of his grandchildren, run the company. They are very wealthy. I didn't find anything that would be a reason for them to harm Martha."

Mayet said, "I also researched some of the people on the chart. I found that Wolfe Weber, Jonas's uncle, had many run-ins with the law. He was a playboy and a drunk. He died in a car wreck when he was thirty-nine years old. I also haven't found any specific motive to threaten Martha, unless there is some inheritance concern within the family. But, that will require more digging."

Jeanie displayed the Israeli side of Martha's family tree. Then she posted some photographs.

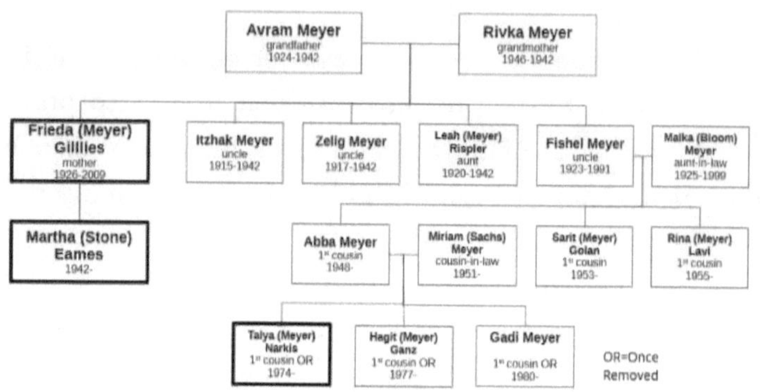

"This is a picture of Fishel Meyer, Frieda's brother and, therefore, Martha's uncle," said Jeanie. "Fishel Meyer was one of the pioneers who helped establish Kibbutz Nevo in Israel's southern desert, as we were told. This picture shows Talya Narkis with her sister Leah Ganz and their brother Zelig Meyer, who is called Ziggy. They're with their mother Miriam. Talya and Leah work on the kibbutz. Both of them served for two years in the Israeli Defense Forces. Ziggy is currently a highly ranked officer in the Israeli Air Force."

"The strange thing is, Talya's father is listed as Abba Meyer in her family tree, but I couldn't find anything at all about an Abba Meyer," said Jeanie. "When I did some more digging, I found out that Abba just means father in Hebrew, so the chart is showing 'Father' Meyer. I'm guessing that he's probably not a priest."

"Possibly Talya's father's name is unstated because he was in the Mossad, Israel's equivalent of the CIA," said Mayet. "I found out that his name is actually Shmuel Meyer and he's seventy-five years old, so probably no longer active in Mossad activities. But you never know."

"Okay, that makes sense," said Jeanie. "I found something else about their family that should interest you." Jeanie posted a news article on the video screen. "This article is from a newspaper in Berlin from last year that mentions Avram and Talya Meyer, who were Martha's grandparents. Apparently, they were quite wealthy and lived in a big house in Berlin. Avram and his ancestors were very successful merchants. They bought and sold all kinds of goods. A large collection of art was recently discovered in a Swiss bank that was stolen by the Nazis from the Meyers. The bank is in negotiations to return the art to the Meyer heirs."

"Mayet perked up excitedly and said, "Please send me that article right away. Does it say how much the collection is worth?"

"It says at least twenty-eight million euros, and possibly more. Valuation was in progress."

"So, what if Shmuel Meyer doesn't want to split his massive inheritance with his cousin, the despicable daughter of a Nazi?" asked Lili. "That could be motive for murder."

"Yes, that definitely could be a motive for murder," said Mayet. "Through his experience and connections, someone like Shmuel Meyer would be more than capable of deploying assassins to go after Martha. But let's not jump to conclusions."

"Think of it, though. All of the assassins so far have bungled the hit," said Lili. "Not up to Mossad's standards, I would think."

"One correction though," said Jeanie. "Martha isn't Shmuel's only living cousin. According to the family tree, Martha has two half-siblings, who are also Frieda's children. Sarah Duncan and Laith Gillies. They aren't tainted by Nazi blood, but they do have non-Jewish blood. They also have families."

"So, if the art collection is the motive, then Gemma Wells, Sarah Duncan, and Laith Gillies, and their families could also be in danger," said Lili.

"Leave this with me," said Mayet. "I'll make sure that MI-5 is notified that Frieda's other children and their families could be in danger. Also, I'll get an investigation going regarding Shmuel Meyer."

"How do you spell Shmuel?" asked Jeanie.

FIFTY-ONE

Gil led Miles Weston, an archaeologist working for the State of Massachusetts, and Trudy Finan, a state historian, to the spot where he had discovered the gold artifacts. Only a depression in the ground remained. The surrounding area looked undisturbed. "This is where I dug up the artifacts. There is flowing water under the topsoil."

"Your write-up said you used ground-penetrating radar and a metal detector?" asked Miles.

"Yes, I rigged up a GPR system on a remotely-controlled robot that I had previously used to search for evidence in the mole-people case. According to the powder horn inscription, there was a small stream with turtle stones at its mouth. A sack of artifacts was buried in the streambed, twenty paces from the mouth. The mouth of the stream had shifted because of the culverts under the road, so I had to search for the stream which, as you can see, is now completely underground."

"Turtle stones?" asked Trudy.

Gil pulled a sample out of his pocket. "It took me a while, but I figured out that what Samuel Stagg called turtle stones are actually gemstones called prehnite. Under flowing water they look kind of like very small turtles."

· · · ·

GIL BROUGHT MILES AND Trudy back to the police station. He showed them into an interview room where Karen had set up coffee and doughnuts from Adams Donut Shop. Karen brought in the gold artifacts and set them on the table. Trudy said, "I sent the pictures of these figurines to the Smithsonian for evaluation. They think these are probably Tairano from about 500 AD. The Tairano people were from around the area of Colombia, South America. Hands-on examination would be required to be more specific. The true value, though, is this whole intriguing story about what the gold may have been for, how it was stolen during the Battle of the Great Falls, and the way it was discovered from a powder-horn inscription at Fort William Henry. In our archives, we have a letter of correspondence dated 1676 from the Massachusetts Bay Colony Governor's office that talked about King Philip offering a gold tribute in order to solidify the ever-expanding border declared by the colony. The colonists were relentlessly encroaching on Indian villages and hunting grounds. There is no evidence of the tribute actually being exchanged."

"Wow, these artifacts could really be what that letter is talking about. But, back to the present, I suggested that the artifacts be returned to the Indians. What do you intend to do with them?" asked Gil.

"I'm concerned about the security of these priceless artifacts," said Trudy. "My plan is to have an expert examine them here, if possible. I've proposed a generous grant to an ongoing Native American project which is aimed at preserving the history of the Indians who lived in this area. The local Native Americans are gaining traction to obtain their own space, perhaps a museum. A grant to ensure security of these artifacts would help them to buy a place for a starter museum."

"That sounds like a great idea," said Gil.

"Gil, could you show me your GPR robot?" asked Miles. "Maybe I could use one of those. Our GPR units are very cumbersome."

· · · ·

LILI WAS IN THE AUDIENCE at the Greenfield High School auditorium. Gil was sitting on stage, dressed casually, along with members of local area Native American tribes, the US Department of Indian Affairs, the Commonwealth of Massachusetts, and the City of Greenfield. John Fontaine and Shawn Delaney were there, representing Fort William Henry. Paul Gabriel, a member of the Nipmuc tribe, was the main speaker. He was also dressed casually. "On behalf of the Indigenous Americans from this area, I am honored to accept the return of these artifacts from King Philip's War and the massacre at Peskeompskut. I want to thank the United States Government and the State of Massachusetts for their generous grant that will assure security for these and other precious items that belonged to our ancestors."

"To my people, King Philip's War was the beginning of the end of the traditional Indian way of life in New England. The massacre at Peskeompskut remains a deeply painful episode in our history. We are working to preserve knowledge of the rich and complex Indian cultures that existed in this region before European colonization, and to document the regretful events that occurred to end it."

"I would also like to honor the memory of Kevin Clarion, a young college student of New England history. During his summer job as a curator at Fort William Henry in New York, Kevin researched the powder horn of Samuel Stagg. Stagg had documented his participation in the massacre at Peskeompskut, and his theft of these artifacts from the Indians there. I'd also like to acknowledge the efforts of Gil Novak, a police consultant who was investigating the mysterious tunnels that Kevin Clarion and his friends created to search for these artifacts. With much effort and determination, Gil finally found these lost artifacts. I'd also like to thank Gil for recommending that the artifacts be returned to the Native American community."

"Gil Novak told me that, when he was a student in Greenfield, the history of colonization was told almost exclusively from the colonists' point of view. He'd learned very little about the culture of the Indigenous Americans in this area. I'm very pleased to note that this situation has improved somewhat over the years. I'm especially pleased to see a lot of local students here today, attending this ceremony."

• • • •

A REAL ESTATE AGENT had just finished showing Lili and Gil an attractive, moderately-sized house on the outskirts of Greenfield. "So, what do you think?" she asked.

"We'd like to talk in private for a few minutes," said Gil.

"Of course."

Gil and Lili went out onto the back deck where they could look at the pool and nice yard that led up to a forested hill. "So, should we make an offer?" he asked.

Lili hesitated. This wasn't only about buying a house. This was about living together, permanently. "Yes, I think so. What do you think?"

"I'm in."

• • • •

ON A HOT DAY IN EARLY-September, Gil, his son-in-law Mike, and Karen's husband Jeff, were dripping with sweat as they unloaded the last of Lili's furniture from the U-Haul truck. Jazz, Ziggy, and Dez were laughing and splashing in the pool, along with Karen's kids. Lili, Karen, and Julia were sorting dishes to see which of Gil's and Lili's would be kept, and which would be donated to charity. Lili got a text message and she turned the television onto MSNBC. "Gil, come quick!" she yelled.

"This is Deborah Penney from MSNBC News in Washington, DC. A congressional investigation has been convened concerning a country-wide militia network being formed over the past several years by a coalition of ultra-conservative members of congress led by Representative Borden Ritchie from Idaho. It's alleged that, in a series

of unrelated bills, land transfers have been made from sixteen states to federal government control under false pretenses. Land-leases and funding were provided to privately-run militia groups in order for them to create fortresses. In a public statement, Representative Ritchie said that the Constitution was written to ensure that the people of this country have sufficient means to defend themselves from a corrupt government."

"This boggles my mind," said Karen. "Worse than the militia threat, this whole thing shows that Congress probably doesn't even know what's in the bills that they approve."

"It's unbelievable that you guys blew the lid on this whole thing," said Julia. "Wow."

"We still haven't caught up with Keith Wyman. I wonder if he's even still alive," said Karen. "Our theory is that he was trying to kill anyone who knew details of his underground fortress. There have been similar cases in Tennessee and Illinois."

Lili had just pried opened a can of very light gray wall paint when her phone rang. She fumbled with it for a moment because she rarely received calls. People usually texted. It was Mayet calling. "Hi Mayet."

"Hi Lili. I'm calling with good news. Several months ago, our State Department initiated an investigative query with Israel's Ministry of Foreign Affairs about the possibility of Shmuel Meyer being the one behind attempts to assassinate Martha Eames, as well as your kidnapping. This week, I received an official notice through the State Department that we should consider the matter closed and there would be no more threats to Martha's life."

"Did they arrest Shmuel?"

"They did not provide any details or any admission of guilt in the matter. I don't think we'll ever find out what they did. You might get some hints if you and Martha talk to Talya Narkis again."

"Is this credible? It's really hard to believe."

"I was told only that we should believe it and accept it. There are no more threats to Martha's life, or yours."

"Or Gemma's. Wow. I'll have to get a message to Martha to tell her she can finally come home. This is big news!"

"MI-5 has been notified, so they will inform Gemma Wells. The only thing we found out was how Martha was compromised while she was in witness protection. I can't tell you any details, but it's being resolved."

• • • •

LILI, GIL, AND JEANIE drove up to Martha's house in Portsmouth, New Hampshire. When Martha opened the door, she and Lili yelped and hugged a long hug. Then she gave Gil a big hug. "Martha, this is Jeanie Peridot, our forensic genealogist," said Lili.

Martha served a pot of coffee and even remembered to serve a cup of decaf for Gil. She also brought out a plate with freshly-baked slices of coffee cake.

"How are you, Martha?" asked Gil.

"Oh, I'm fine. Really. Living underground, as they say, was a real hoot. It was kind of like going to Florida for the winter. I met lots of really nice people who I'll probably never see again. But who knows?"

"Well, get ready, because Jeanie has an amazing story to tell you," said Lili.

Jeanie unrolled a large colorful poster. "Martha, this is your family tree."

Martha looked at the poster, then at Lili, Gil, and Jeanie. "Oh my God! I've lived my entire life believing that I didn't have any family, at all. I don't even know how to make sense of this."

"I'll take you through it," said Jeanie. "One step at a time. You are part of a large family, and your family story is fascinating! But first, let me explain why your life was in danger. This was your biological mother, right here. Her name was Frieda Meyer."

Martha whispered her mother's name and tears filled her eyes.

"When you were born, she was just seventeen years old. She was from Berlin, Germany, and she was Jewish." Jeanie handed Martha several black and white pictures of Frieda at different points in her life. Martha's hands were shaking as she scrutinized each picture.

Jeanie opened a world atlas that she'd brought and showed Martha where Berlin was located. Turning back to the family tree, Jeanie pointed and said, "As a teenager, Frieda was the nanny for the children of this guy here, Horst Konig, and his wife, Helga. He was a logistics officer in the German army during World War II, stationed in Paris, France. A logistics officer is in charge of getting equipment, people, food, and fuel to wherever they are needed to fight the war. Horst's wife and children, along with their nanny Frieda, lived in Paris with him." Using the atlas, Jeanie showed Martha where Paris was in relation to Berlin.

"When it became apparent that France was going to be invaded by the allied forces, he sent Helga and their children back to Berlin, where it was safer. He couldn't send Frieda back because she was Jewish and she would have been sent to a concentration camp. Almost all of the family that Frieda left behind, members of your family, died at the hands of the Nazis, probably before you were born." Martha looked at Lili and tears were rolling down her face. Gil found her a box of tissues. They took a few minutes to drink some coffee while Martha regained her composure.

"Please go on," said Martha.

"Anyway, one thing led to another, and you were born. Horst Konig was your biological father. Your birth name was Rebecca but, due to the circumstances, your birth was never officially recorded. At the time, things were heating up with the war, so Horst somehow smuggled you and Frieda to Bilbao, Portugal." Jeanie showed Martha where Bilbao was. "Horst bought her a ticket on a ship to Rio de Janeiro, Brazil. But, for whatever reason, Frieda boarded a different boat and sailed to Bristol, England with you, her baby daughter." Jeanie pointed out the sea route from Bilbao to Bristol. "Soon after Frieda arrived in England, she gave you up for adoption, probably anonymously."

"I've never had a birth certificate, only an adoption certificate from the United Kingdom. I've always just assumed I was British. So, I was born in Paris, during World War II? I'm French? And German, and Jewish, and English? The Florida girls will never believe this."

Jeanie went back to the family tree. "Frieda ended up living in Glasgow, Scotland and where she married a man named Stephen

Gillies. Frieda and Stephen went on to have children and grandchildren. You are related to all of them. More on that later."

"Over here is the Meyer family. Your grandparents Avram and Talya Meyer, Frieda's parents, along with three of their adult children and their families, died in the Holocaust, in concentration camps." Hearing this, Martha broke down and wept. "I know this is very hard to take in, so we'll give you a few minutes." They all stood up and took another break, leaving Martha to herself. Gil helped himself to a second piece of cake. Lili made more coffee for everyone.

"I'm ready," said Martha. Let's keep going. I'm sorry."

"Martha, you have absolutely nothing to be sorry about," said Gil. "Some of your story is very tragic and sad, but a lot of it is very happy. You'll see."

Jeanie continued. "It turns out that only one of Frieda's siblings survived the war. He was your uncle Fishel Meyer. He eventually made his way to Palestine, where he fought for Israel's independence in 1948, when the country was first formed. When that war was over, he became one of the founders of a kibbutz named Nevo in their southern desert, called the Negev desert. Fishel Meyer and his wife Malka had three children, Shmuel, Sarit, and Rina, who are your first cousins." Jeanie showed Martha where they were located on the family tree. "We actually spoke to some of Fishel's grandchildren, your cousins' children, and they all seem very nice. They are anxious to meet you."

"Your biological father, Horst Konig, deserted from the German army during the war. He smuggled himself, his wife Helga, and their children to Rio de Janeiro. He changed their surname to Weber, which was his mother's maiden name. According to his grandson, Jonas Mauk, with whom we spoke, Horst searched many times for Frieda and Rebecca in Rio, but never found them."

"Now, it turns out that the Meyer family were very successful merchants in Berlin before the war," said Lili. "Recently, a cache of artwork belonging to the Meyer family was found in a bank in Switzerland. It had been stolen by the Nazis. It's worth millions of dollars. We suspect that Shmuel Meyer, your cousin, was trying to have you killed so that he and his sisters wouldn't have to share the valuable artwork with the child of a Nazi and his disgraced aunt. Shmuel was a former spy in Israel's Mossad and is apparently a very dangerous guy. Our State Department contacted Israel's Ministry of Foreign Affairs about him. After a while we were told that the matter had all been dealt with, and that your life is no longer in danger. We don't know how it was taken care of or what happened to your cousin Shmuel."

"This is crazy!" cried Martha. "It sounds like an old spy novel where everybody is trying to kill each other."

"That's exactly what it's like," said Gil. "But your story is fascinating and involves people from all over the world."

Jeanie pointed to several highlighted areas on Martha's family tree. "We've spoken with Talya Narkis and Leah Ganz in Israel," said Jeanie. "They are Shmuel Meyer's daughters. We've spoken with Jonas Mauk and his mother Liesl from Brazil. Liesl is your half-sister on Horst's side of the family. They are also very nice people. In England, Lili and Gil met a woman named Morag Wilson. She is your half-sister's daughter, from Frieda's Scottish side of the family, the Gillies. Lili, why don't you tell the rest."

"Martha, we also met a woman named Gemma Wells in England," said Lili. "Gemma is your daughter."

Martha looked at Lili, shaking her head. "I don't have a daughter," she said quietly.

"Martha, your baby was not stillborn. Your daughter is alive. I'm afraid she was stolen from you and your husband."

Martha slammed her hands down on the table and shrieked, "No!" as tears poured down her face. Gil found a bottle of peach schnapps in the kitchen and poured her a shot. Martha drank the sweet liquor and slumped in her chair.

"I, I don't know what to say. I don't know what to do."

. . . .

AFTER LEAVING MARTHA to rest, Lili, Gil, and Jeanie went to Portsmouth's quaint downtown area." Oh my God, this is like a shopping wonderland!" exclaimed Jeanie.

"Great," grumbled Gil. "It does feel a little like the market squares in English villages. There are a lot of shoppers out."

Once Lili and Jeanie tired of shopping, Lili found Gil on a park bench and asked, "How about dinner?"

Gil searched on his phone and said, "Over that way, there are some restaurants by the water."

They enjoyed fresh seafood at the Old Ferry Landing, overlooking the harbor. "This is the Piscataqua River," said Gil, as he looked at his phone. "I don't know how to pronounce it. I'll ask the server."

"I'm worried about Martha," said Lili. "We left her alone with all of those revelations about her family. Her daughter. I can't imagine what she's feeling about that."

"I think we should go with her to England and Israel to meet her family," said Lili. "Maybe even Brazil!"

"I'd love to do that," said Gil.

FIFTY-THREE

Lili, Gil, and Martha climbed out of the black London taxi and walked up the stone stairs to the large wooden door of a greystone row house. Gil clunked the brass door-knocker three times. The door was opened by a giggly young girl. She looked up at Martha and said, "Are you Mum's new Nan?"

"Why yes, dear. I guess I am your Mum's new Nan. My name's Martha. What's your name?"

"My name's Olivia. Please come in."

"As they entered the house, several adults and more children stood, quietly watching them. A smiling middle-aged woman walked over and said, "Martha, I'm your daughter, Gemma." She gave Martha a big hug and both of them cried, unable to let go of each other.

After regaining her composure, Martha asked, "Well, who are these other beautiful people?"

"These are your great-grandchildren Max and Kirsty. You have more great-grandchildren, too, but they haven't yet arrived. This is your granddaughter, Vera."

Vera gave her a hug. "And this is my husband, Daniel."

"Please meet my friends Lili D'Amico and Gil Novak," said Martha. "They saved my life, and helped me to find you."

"Come, let's go into the sitting room," said Gemma.

They had tea, coffee, and cakes to eat while they got to know each other. Rather than talking about the past, they spoke mainly about their current lives. Every few minutes, more people arrived. "Martha, these are your other grandchildren, Clara and Michael. I'll let them introduce their families in a minute. But first, I'd like to introduce you to my other mother, Emma. Emma Ableford."

Emma gave Martha a big hug. "I'm so, so sorry for what you've gone through in your life. I'll be more than happy to share Gemma with you."

"Thank you for giving Gemma such a wonderful life."

More introductions were made and, after much conversation, lunch was served in a large dining room. Before dessert was served, Lili stood and made an announcement. "Tomorrow morning at ten o'clock at our hotel, we'll be holding a reception for Martha's Scottish half-siblings and some of their children. So, Gemma, their children are your half-cousins. You are welcome to join us, if you'd like to meet them. Any of you who would like to attend, you're all invited."

· · · ·

THE NEXT DAY, MARTHA met her half siblings, Sarah Duncan and Laith Gillies. They introduced their spouses, children, and grandchildren. Morag Wilson, who had previously met with Lili and Gil in Torquay, was there. Gemma Wells was thrilled to meet her new cousins.

Gil asked everyone to get a drink and a snack, and to take a seat for a presentation. He projected Martha's family tree on a large video-screen for all to see.

Martha Eames Family Tree

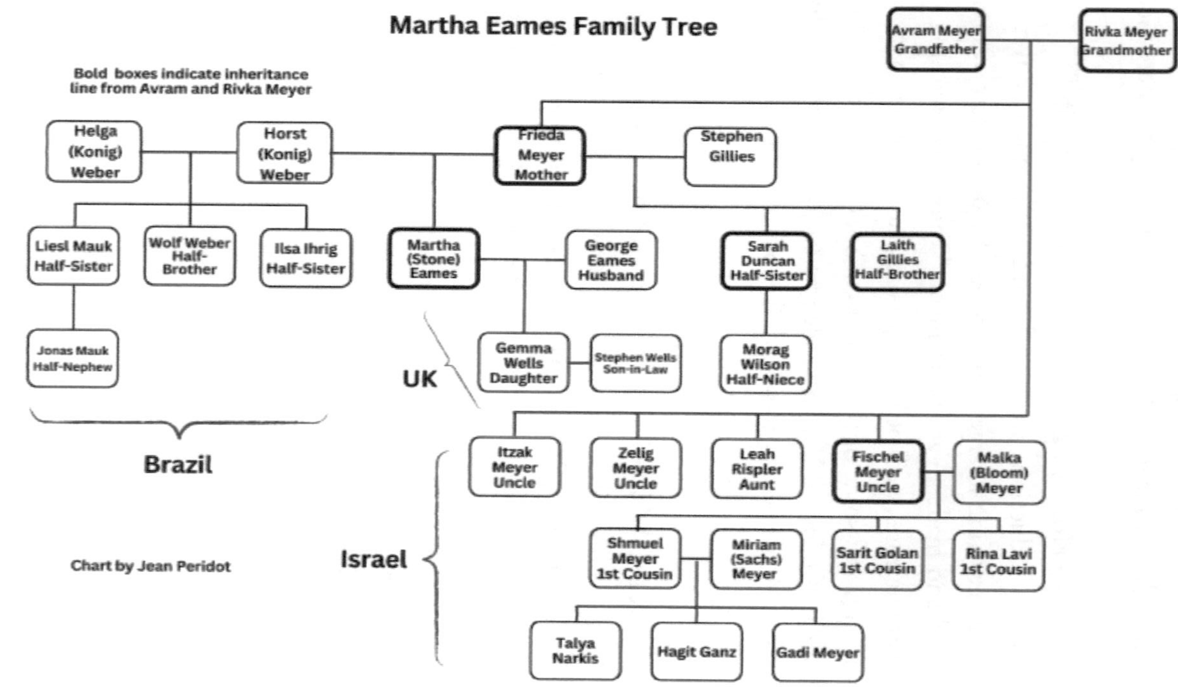

GIL EXPLAINED HOW EACH of the people in the room were related to each other. He explained how Martha had also found new relatives as far away as Israel and Brazil. There were many questions about that. Based on the chart, the Scottish relatives were only related to the English and Israeli relatives. Gemma was related to the Israeli and Brazilian relatives. It was all very complicated.

"So," asked Archie Gillies, "if I have the same amount of Jewish DNA as my cousins, Morag and Emily, why are they Jewish but I am not?" "We all have the same Nan, don't we?"

"The reason you are not Jewish is because your mother isn't Jewish. This aspect of Jewish lineage originates in Jewish laws that have been in place for thousands of years. To the Jewish people, you are considered a Gentile," said Gil. "These laws have been followed for millennia before anyone was aware of DNA. I don't claim to be an expert on this."

Lili spoke up. "One thing that's interesting is that, beside the fact that you and your cousins have approximately the same amount of so-called Jewish DNA, the female lineage also passes down a complete set of mitochondrial DNA. Mitochondria are cell-like organelles that are like the batteries inside each of the cells in your body. These organelles have their own DNA, in addition to the primary DNA in each of your cells. Morag and Emily have essentially the same mitochondrial DNA as their grandmother and many grandmothers before. Archie, you do not. Your mitochondrial DNA is from your own mother's lineage."

"Well, who are these people, our cousins that live in Israel?" asked Laith Gillies, Martha's half-brother. "What kind of people are they?"

"So far, all we've done is meet with them by video-conference," said Gil "The ones we've talked to seem to be very nice people. They speak fluent English. In a few days, we're going to meet them in person. So far, our main discussion was about Martha's history and how this all came about. We haven't really had a chance to get to know them, who they are and what their lives are like. Perhaps some of you will want to visit them, too."

"Gil, let's not sugar-coat all of my Israeli cousins," said Martha. "One of our cousins is an old retired spy who tried to have me killed. Gil, could you put up the stolen art slide and explain it to them?"

"I was hoping that this would have been a private discussion, but it's your show, Martha. This is a BBC news item about a cache of art, worth over forty million euros, stolen by the Nazis during the Second World War. It was recently discovered in a vault at a Swiss bank. The art was stolen from the house of Avram and Talya Meyer in Berlin. They were Frieda's parents, killed by the Nazis during the Holocaust, in a concentration camp. The art is going to be returned to the Meyer's heirs, who are Martha, Sarah, Laith, and your three Israeli cousins, Shmuel, Sarit, and Rina. Until Martha did her DNA search, your Israeli cousins didn't know there were any other heirs. Once Shmuel found out about Martha and her history, he tried to have Martha and Gemma assassinated to prevent them from inheriting. Martha had to go into hiding. Shmuel even had Lili kidnapped to Eastern Europe from America to use her to find Martha. Luckily, Lili escaped."

The room had gone completely silent except for some children playing tag. Gil took a sip of water and continued. "The American State Department contacted the Israeli Ministry of Foreign Affairs about this. A few months later, we were told that the problem was resolved, and that there would be no more trouble for Martha. But they wouldn't reveal to us what was done about it."

Martha said, "Part of the reason I'm going to Israel is to give this Shmuel a slap upside his head!" Everyone burst out in laughter. "He thinks that, since my father was a German officer, I'm some kind of Nazi girl. That's a bunch of crap! That's really how the Nazis thought, that anyone with Jewish blood should be put to death."

"Does this Swiss bank know that we are also heirs?" asked Laith.

"The American State Department has already notified the Swiss Department of Foreign Affairs that Martha, Laith, and Sarah are heirs to the Meyer estate," said Gil. "I recommend that you get some legal representation for this. What I understand is that all of the heirs must come to an agreement on how to disposition this art. Will it be sold, kept, or donated?"

• • • •

GIL, AND LILI SPENT the next few days touring London. Gemma spent most of her time getting to know Martha. Martha's half sister, Sarah Duncan, also seemed to develop a close relationship with both Martha and Gemma. When Martha, Gil, and Lili were on their way to the airport, Martha said, "I finally feel like I have a family! Gemma and Sarah are coming to visit me next summer. Oh, and you know what? They told me that Scotland Yard has started an investigation on how Gemma was stolen from me."

Talya Narkis and her brother, Ziggy Meyer, picked up Martha, Lili and Gil in a small white van. It was a little over an hour's drive, south along the Mediterranean Coast, to Kibbutz Nevo. The late-September weather was still very hot and dry. It would be another month or so until the cooler rainy season arrived. "I was surprised to be questioned so aggressively by Israeli security at Heathrow," said Gil. "We all were. I got the feeling that they didn't trust me because I'm not Jewish."

"They don't trust anyone, even if they are Jewish," said Ziggy. "That's their job."

"Your father tried to have me killed," said Martha. "Are we safe with you?"

"Our father is a very difficult man," said Talya. "He has always lived in the world of spies and counter-spies, threats and counter-threats. He was taken away from his house a few weeks ago. Maybe it's related to that, but he was often away all of our lives. We were not told anything. He doesn't really know how to live his life since he was forced to retire a few years ago. He doesn't know how to accept happiness."

"Well, I hope he comes back, said Martha. "I want to give him a piece of my mind!"

"What is this?" asked Ziggy. "A piece of your mind?"

Martha laughed. "I want to yell some wisdom at his face." They all laughed.

They pulled off the highway onto a dirt road and drove through the kibbutz gate. Ziggy and Talya helped them with their bags. Martha would stay with Talya and Lili and Gil would stay with Ziggy. Lili looked around. This is a tropical paradise!" There were flowering shrubs of all colors, palm trees, and twittering birds.

A strange-looking bird pecked at the ground. "That's a hoopoe," said Ziggy. "It's named from the sound it makes."

There was a very loud squawk and Martha jumped. "What the hell was that?" A deep-blue peacock strutted into view.

"This was originally all desert here," said Talya. "Our grandfather Fishel, Frieda's brother, helped build this kibbutz from nothing. We'll give you a little tour after you get settled."

After Lili and Gil put their luggage into Ziggy's house, they walked over to Talya's house. "This is my mother Miriam, and this is my sister Leah." They had a light lunch and got to know each other a little bit. Miriam had a sad look and didn't say a word.

As they started their tour, they walked by an elementary school. They could see many children engaged in their lessons. "I see that the windows have metal shutters," said Gil.

"The school is a bomb shelter," said Ziggy. "If the siren goes off, we only have fifteen seconds to get into a bomb shelter. The bedrooms where you will be staying are our bomb shelters."

"How safe are we here?" asked Lili.

"We're pretty safe," said Ziggy. Things have been very calm now for over a year. But we are ready, just in case."

"Our kibbutz is really just a very big farm," said Talya. "This building here is processing carrots that we grow here." Machines were washing and packing hundreds of very large carrots. People were packing them into crates for shipment. "Over there are avocado trees and over there are date palms." The farm fields and groves were vast. "This building is a greenhouse for growing amaryllis flowers. In this field, we are raising ostriches." A flock of ostriches was milling about, kicking up some dust. "Over that way is a dairy farm. We won't go there because it is very smelly."

· · · ·

THAT EVENING, THERE was a reception for them in the communal dining hall. Martha met more of her relatives, including her cousins Sarit and Rina and their children and grandchildren. Some of them came in from other parts of Israel; a few wore military uniforms. After dinner, Gil did his genealogy presentation, as he did in London. During the talk, a man asked, "So, how should we consider Martha, our cousin, if she is the daughter of a Nazi and a Jew who had a child with this Nazi?"

Rabbi Ari Landsman stood up and said, "I'll speak about this." He looked around the room for a few seconds. He spoke very loudly. "For all the Jews in Europe, the holocaust was a fight to survive, not only for our people as a group, but for every single individual. Two out of every three Jews in Europe were murdered! Every person ended up in a situation where they had to decide what they must do for themselves and for their families to survive. Most could not survive. Here was a sixteen year-old girl, stranded as a nanny in Paris, living in a city where she knew nobody and didn't know the language. Her whole family in Berlin was taken away to the death camps. Jews in Paris were dragged from hiding and shot in the street or taken away. What should she do to survive?" You could hear a pin drop. Even the children were silent. The older children knew English.

"Frieda decided to stay hiding in the German officer's apartment doing as he said. He wasn't an evil man. He was a logistics officer who later deserted his army. This, she thought was her best chance for survival. There was nobody to help this girl decide what to do. She had a child with this officer, but she survived. The officer tried to send her to Brazil so he could meet up with her later. He cared for her. She decided instead that her best chance to live her life was to go to England. Can you imagine yourself making a decision like this as a teenager? She did this in Lisbon, a port full of Gestapo spies and people speaking Portuguese."

"But, she did survive! Against great odds, she survived. Her innocent child survived. When she got to England, a country where she knew nobody and didn't know the language, she still had to survive. She was seventeen years old. She decided that the best chance of survival for her and her baby was to give the baby up for adoption. They both survived!" The audience was still silent.

"So here we have Martha Eames, Frieda Meyer's baby. Frieda was Jewish, so Martha is Jewish. That is our law. Martha didn't know any of this until a few weeks ago! Is Martha a Nazi? No, Martha is as far from being a Nazi as any of us here. What's for dessert?"

FIFTY-FIVE

Lili and Gil were travel weary when they returned from Israel. They walked into their new home in Greenfield, and were greeted by piles of boxes. They hadn't had time to unpack much before leaving on their trip. Over the next week, they made good progress. They had many duplicate household items, so they made quite a lot of trips to charity shops to donate what they didn't need. It helped that the early October weather was still mild.

Their houses in Saratoga and Northampton sold quickly. When each sale was about to close, they had to quickly empty them of the furnishings they'd left for staging. They gave some away, sold some, and brought the rest to use in their Greenfield home. While taking a break one day, Lili looked through an old photo album of hers. She started laughing and Gil sat down to see what was so funny. There were several pictures from the eighties showing Lili with a very big hair style. They looked through some more of her pictures while Lili described each of them to Gil. Until now, the couple really hadn't shared much detail about their earlier lives.

Lili's phone rang and she saw that it was Martha. "Hi Martha! What's up?"

Martha's voice was shaky. "Have you seen the news?"

"No, not yet. We've been unpacking. What's wrong?"

"Turn on the TV. Terrorists from Gaza attacked Israel! They attacked the kibbutzes there. Talya has been texting me. She told me that a lot of the people on her kibbutz were murdered, and some were taken hostage. One of her sons-in-law was killed! We met him. And also one of her cousins was taken hostage, along with her cousin's grandson. We met them, too!"

Lili whispered to Gil to turn on the news. "Oh my God. Are they still under attack?"

"All of the people from the kibbutzes near Gaza are being evacuated to safer parts of the country," said Martha. "The news said that over a thousand people were killed and hundreds taken hostage. It's a catastrophe!"

"Do you need me to come for a visit?"

"No, I don't think so. I just thought I should tell you since you and Gil met these people, too."

"Maybe you should call your daughter and your cousins in Scotland. They should know, too."

"Yes, that's a good idea."

"Don't forget the time difference. It's five hours later in England. Seven hours later in Israel."

Lili and Gil were glued to the news channels for the next few days as a new war erupted in Israel and Gaza. It was a horrible tragedy that shocked the whole world. Lili and Martha spoke frequently, and Martha relayed updates from Talya. Several weeks later, Talya's cousin and her grandson were released from captivity, but some of their family members were killed or wounded while serving in the military.

* * * *

BY EARLY DECEMBER, Lili and Gil had finally emptied and removed all of the cardboard boxes from their new house. Gil arranged to give the empty boxes to someone else in town who was moving. "Do you think we can cook at home tonight?" he asked. "I'm tired of going out to eat."

"Sure! What are you going to cook for me?"

Gil smiled. "Let me look." He sat down at his laptop and searched the recipe file that he and his late wife Cynthia had compiled. It made him think of her and gave him a fleeting twinge of sadness. "How about apple-cider beef stew?"

"Sounds great! Let's go to Stop & Shop."

• • • •

WHEN THEY RETURNED from the supermarket, Lili saw that the mail truck had just gone by. After they brought in the groceries, Lili retrieved the mail from the mailbox. She separated the mail forwarded from Gil's old address from hers. She noticed that they'd each received a letter from Israel. She opened hers and saw that it had the official letterhead of the Israeli Ministry of Foreign Affairs. "To the attention of Ms. Lili D'Amico. Enclosed is a cheque to reimburse you for Israel's failure to protect you from being kidnapped, and for the inexcusable danger you faced. The source of your reimbursement is undistributed funds from the sale of artwork previously stolen by the Nazis from the estate of Avram and Talya Meyer. The Government of Israel apologizes for your troubles and wishes you all the best." Lili gasped. "Gil!" She showed him the letter and check. She received a hundred thousand euros. You got one of these, too."

He opened his letter and said, "Hey, I only got ten thousand. Totally unfair. Actually, I don't know why I would get anything. This is really unexpected."

"They must be penalizing Shmuel Meyer for his evil ways," said Lili.

• • • •

THE HUGE METAL DOOR creaked a bit when Gil cracked it open. He listened to hear if anyone was coming, but he only heard voices further inside. Lili followed him into the inner sanctum of the empty weapons magazine at the defunct Fort Dearborn near Portsmouth, New Hampshire. As they moved deeper into the underground cavern, they could hear a man giving a fiery speech, punctuated by the stomping of feet from what sounded like a large audience.

Gil signaled for Lili to stop as they approached the entrance into the makeshift auditorium. There were about fifty people in the room, all dressed in olive-colored uniforms and standing in rows. Large red banners with black swastikas hung on either side of the temporary stage. A man with a blond crew cut and steel-gray eyes was giving the speech behind a swastika-adorned podium. Behind him were six older people seated in folding chairs, wearing black leather uniforms. One of them was Martha Eames.

Gil tried to listen to the speech, but couldn't quite make out what was being said. He crept further into the room, but suddenly he tripped on the uneven floor and grabbed a stanchion, which made a rattling noise. He held his breath, but the speaker stopped and everybody in the room looked toward him. Martha slowly stood up and pointed. "Gil Novak!"

Gil snorted and woke up out of a deep slumber. "I knew we shouldn't have kept that recliner," said Lili. "Help me carry these bags out to the car before it gets dark. We really have to finish loading the car and put the bikes on the rack. I want to get on the road first thing in the morning so we can beat the rush hour traffic at Springfield and Hartford."

"Coming." Gil felt embarrassed that he had fallen asleep and that he had dreamed such a silly dream.

FIFTY-SIX

"Four crak!" declared Martha, laying down her mahjong tile. "Seven bam," said Lili.

"Six dot," said Francine.

"Call!" said Ellen. Ellen picked up Francine's discarded tile and placed it with two other six-dot tiles on her rack.

"Flower," said Martha.

"South," said Lili.

"Mahjong!" said Francine.

"For crying out loud!" said Martha. "That's three in a row."

Lili paid Francine fifty cents and the other two players each paid Francine a quarter. They then dumped their tiles into the middle of the table and began turning them face down for the next round. The microwave timer beeped and Lili got up. She set out some Buffalo chicken dip with pita crackers.

"I can't believe how cold it is here," complained Martha. "I should've stayed in Portsmouth. Has anyone heard from Beryl?"

"I talked to her daughter, Charlene," said Ellen. "She said that Beryl still can't speak very well since the stroke. But she's in therapy and making good progress."

"The poor thing," said Francine. "So Martha, what are you doing with all of your money?"

"I got a lawyer who's helping me give it away. Shmuel Meyer was the guy who tried to have me killed. The Israeli government gave me half of his share, which came to about three million dollars. They gave a big portion of it to the family of my friend Barbara LeClerc who was murdered by Shmuel's assassin. I'm giving most of Shmuel's share to his kids and grand-kids. I don't believe that children should be punished for the sins of their father. That's what this whole damn thing was about!"

"What about your share?" asked Ellen.

"I'm working on it. I gave some to the families of the victims of the Hamas massacre in Israel. I also gave some to the organizations that are helping Palestinian families to survive the war, and some to the Ukrainians, too. I gave a lot to the underground railroad group that hid me away. With some of the money, I bought my new condo here. I definitely did not want to stay in the unit where I was attacked. Oh, and besides the money, the Israeli government sent me a funny little painting. The artists name was Mark somebody. Mark Chaygle, or something like that."

"Marc Chagall?" asked Lili, wide-eyed.

"Maybe."

"He was a very famous artist!" said Lili. "That little painting might be worth hundreds of thousands of dollars. Where are you keeping it?"

"Oh dear. I just stuck it in a drawer, back home."

"You know, many collectors loan their expensive works of art to museums so they can be kept secure, and the public can enjoy them," said Lili. "Maybe you could find a museum in Boston or something."

Gil came into the condo, clumsily fiddling with his fishing gear.

"Hi Gil," said Francine.

"Hi girls. It's starting to rain again."

"So, did you catch dinner?" asked Lili.

"All I caught were hardhead catfish, so I threw them back. What a pain. I hate 'em. They're always trying to sting me with their spines. They have just enough poison in them to make it really hurt. I guess we'll have to order pizza."

"Now we're talking!" said Martha. "We can work on planning our trip to Rio. Ha cha cha!"

Acknowledgments

I'd like to thank my editors, Anne and Sarah. My wife Anne has a keen eye for things that are out of place or just don't make sense. She frequently enlightens me about these sorts of things. My sister Sarah spent a lot of time and effort on line editing, providing a wealth of feedback. It was brutal. My family also helped me choose the book title and cover design. The cover design was created using the process provided by the company 99Designs. This was fun! The cover design was created by the designer semnitz™.

This story is completely fictional. However, there are some aspects that are based on fact. There is a network of brooks under the small city of Greenfield, Massachusetts, my home town. Information on these brooks was obtained from a book called *Early Maps of Greenfield*, compiled by a company called Old Maps for the town's 250th anniversary. One part of this network, called Graves Brook, took its name from the graves of three colonists who were killed by Indigenous Americans and buried next to the brook in 1724.

The horrifying massacre of Indigenous Americans at the Great Falls on the Connecticut River in 1676 was factual. I learned a lot of the background on this event from a fascinating YouTube video by David Brule entitled *The History of King Philip's War*. The involvement of a girl named Sequankoon and a boy named Nish N'keke is fictional. The characters Samuel Stagg and William Cass are fictional. The story about gold artifacts is fictional. The Indigenous American leaders in the story, Metacomet (King Philip), the woman Sachem Weetamoo, Sachem Sagamore John, warrior leaders Tuspaquin and Mawtemps were real people, but their words and activities in this story are fictional. I learned a bit about the wars between the English settlers and the Indigenous Americans during my childhood education in Greenfield public schools. My recollection is that the information being taught to me in the 1960s and 1970s was largely from the point of view of the English settlers. I did not know that the Battle of the Great Falls was fought on my old stomping grounds in Greenfield. I was pleased to learn about the Nolumbeka Project that is working to preserve the knowledge and cultures of the Indigenous American people in Western Massachusetts.

Information on performing family tree research aided by DNA analyses was largely obtained from the book *The Family Tree Guide to DNA Testing and Genetic Genealogy by* Blaine T. Bettinger.

Martha Eames and all of the characters in her family tree are fictional. The plot line of artworks stolen from Jewish families by the Nazis during the Second World War is based on factual occurrences that still crop up in the news from time to time. Of course, the portrayal of whole families being taken from their homes and shipped to death camps or slave labor is based on fact. It is the story of my family.

The author picture was provided by Mercy Street Studio in Eliot, Maine.

This book was written by a human.

Don't miss out!

Visit the website below and you can sign up to receive emails whenever Hy Shaw publishes a new book. There's no charge and no obligation.

https://books2read.com/r/B-A-LWEY-DWHND

BOOKS 2 READ

Connecting independent readers to independent writers.

www.ingramcontent.com/pod-product-compliance
Lightning Source LLC
Chambersburg PA
CBHW021344150726
47989CB00005B/2100

* 9 7 9 8 2 2 7 5 0 0 6 1 8 *